What if he'd married not only a virgin bride, but an *ignorant* virgin bride?

"Jennifer?" He spoke her name softly, trying his best to reassure her. "Didn't your mother tell you anything about marriage?"

She tilted her chin up and slowly shook her head, her eyes wide with what looked suspiciously like fright. And well they might. She was pinned beneath a man almost twice her size. Yet she did not flinch from him, her body forming to his, softening against him, even as tears blinded her vision.

"Hell and damnation," he blurted out, rolling from the bed. "I can't find it in me to force myself on a woman, no matter how horny I am. Even if that woman is my legal wife."

"Do you mean that?" Jennifer asked hopefully, wiping at the moisture on her cheeks.

"I told you before, I don't say anything I don't mean…!"

Reading, writing and research: **Carolyn Davidson**'s life in three simple words. At least, that area of her life having to do with her career as a Harlequin Historical author. The rest of her time is divided among husband, family and travel—her husband, of course, holding top priority in her busy schedule. Then there is their church, and the church choir in which they participate. Their sons and daughters, along with assorted spouses, are spread across the eastern half of the country, together with numerous grandchildren.

Last, but certainly not least, is the group of women who share Carolyn's love of writing: the Lowcountry Romance Writers of America. She is a charter member and holds her fellow members, due to their encouragement, partly responsible for whatever success she has achieved in the pursuit of her career.

Carolyn welcomes mail at P.O. Box 2757, Goose Creek, SC 29445.

BIG SKY RANCHER

CAROLYN DAVIDSON

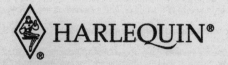

TORONTO • NEW YORK • LONDON
AMSTERDAM • PARIS • SYDNEY • HAMBURG
STOCKHOLM • ATHENS • TOKYO • MILAN • MADRID
PRAGUE • WARSAW • BUDAPEST • AUCKLAND

Special thanks and acknowledgment are given
to Carolyn Davidson for her contribution
to the MONTANA MAVERICKS series.

ISBN 0-373-81119-5

BIG SKY RANCHER

To the world's best agent,
Pattie Steele-Perkins

and

Mr. Ed, who loves me.

PROLOGUE

January 1868

HE NEEDED A WOMAN. Not just any woman, he realized, but one who knew how to sew on buttons and mend ripped seams. In fact, he'd welcome just about any female of *any* description, so long as she came complete with a stash of recipes for edible food.

The thought that such a female might be persuaded to share his bed was a plus he couldn't ignore, given the current state of affairs—but in order to gain that benefit, he suspected a wedding ring would be required. And he would be hog-tied to a female, forever responsible for her, unable to do as he pleased, go where he wanted and act as he liked.

And that was the rub. He'd spent his life doing as he chose even though some of his decisions had not panned out well. In fact, his latest endeavor, fighting the great war on the side of the North, had gained him nothing but a gimpy leg and a sour disposition.

Traveling alone to the gold rush in Montana had earned him a starvation diet and the dubious distinction of involving himself deeply in the small community he'd landed in, ultimately becoming its mayor. The salary the town was willing to pay him was quite an incentive. For being a figurehead and keeping an eye on the town's growth, he received enough cold, hard cash to feed himself, not to mention the respect of the townsfolk. Staking a claim had provided him with gold enough to build a house and gotten him a partner. All in all, he considered himself pretty well off for a wandering fella with no prospects.

Now, a woman was on the agenda. Not only was he desperate for decent meals, but his long suppressed, carnal needs were dominating his thoughts. No amount of cold stream water did the trick and it seemed that the only thing that would work was a wife. A warm woman would do much to blunt the harsh winds and the constant blowing of snow. And his house was ready and waiting for a female to lend her touch to his life. Between working his claim and tending his house, he was being split into too many directions.

A woman was *definitely* on the agenda.

The women available in Thunder Canyon were well-used and not interested in making their way in the world doing anything more strenuous than lying on their backs.

So he'd taken matters by the scruff of the neck and attempted to solve his problem. The letter he'd sent East had borne fruit, and the bride chosen by mail, from a list provided by the agency, seemed to fit his needs. Twenty-three years old, a homebody, skilled in the arts of keeping house and cooking.

Sounded like a done deal to Lucas. The money for her passage on train and stagecoach would be well spent, even if she turned out to be not as well qualified as her qualifications promised—even if her cooking left a bit to be desired.

Being a woman, she would surely come with all the feminine equipment necessary to keep him satisfied and to eventually provide him with a clutch of sons to carry on his name. His father, Toby O'Reilly, had placed great emphasis on passing on the family reputation, such as it was since Toby had gained his own status by being the toughest saloon fighter in Ireland. And that fact didn't seem worth bragging about—as least as far as Luc was concerned.

His own fighting had been done reluctantly. In fact, the faces of the men he'd killed in the name of his country haunted his dreams. The people freed from oppression in the South didn't seem to be much better off than before—some of them starving because they had no money, land or future. Others had gone back to their former owners and formed alliances that allowed them to work for pay. Those were the smart ones, Luc decided.

But his own days of working for someone else were over. From now on, he was forging a life that included a home and family, in a place where he could settle down and look to the future.

And for that, he needed a woman.

CHAPTER ONE

May 1868

MARRYING THE FOUNDER of a town in Montana had seemed like a fine idea back in New York. Such a man would surely have an air of gentility and a position of authority in the area, and be both wealthy and ambitious. Not to mention intelligent.

Lucas O'Reilly. The name itself was solid and seemed fit for such a man. Too bad he hadn't chosen somewhere else to locate his town. Maybe somewhere on the East Coast, very close to a big city, where civilization had a grip on things.

Thunder Canyon had sounded like an interesting spot—a scenic location, perhaps—in a huge area of the West. The reality was somewhat different, Jennifer Alston decided. A dusty thoroughfare met her eye as she stepped down from the stagecoach. The weather was warm for late May, but the road showed evidence of long-gone spring rains. The resultant ruts caused her to stumble as she took her first step on Montana soil. Not an auspicious beginning. She resolved to work more carefully, lest she break an ankle during her jaunt from coach to hotel door.

The odd assortment of men who watched from the wooden sidewalk were possessed of whiskers and unkempt hair, along with wrinkled and faded clothing. Their avid gazes remained fixed on her as she made her way up the single step to the porch of the hotel, as if the men had gone months without catching sight of a female.

And perhaps they had, for not one decent appearing woman had made her presence known to Jennifer's discerning eye. Either they'd all stayed at home today or there was a definite dearth of female companionship. And she'd bet on the latter, if the looks directed at her were anything to go by.

The stagecoach driver plunked her single bag beside her and grunted a message of farewell in her direction as he turned back to his post. She began to understand his lifted eyebrows and skeptical look when she'd given him the name of her destination upon climbing into his vehicle.

Thunder Canyon. Sounding like a cross between a deluge making its way through two towering cliffs and a green way station where spring rains fell in abundance—it was neither. Instead she had come to a town wherein dwelt dusty, nondescript men and a few females of dubious distinction, even now leaning over the low balcony above the town saloon across the street. A sign hung over the door, announcing that Pete Jackson owned the place and that the establishment was now under new ownership. The caliber of women Pete hired could have been improved on, Jennifer decided, but at least their presence on the balcony gave her an idea of the quality of the female population.

She turned back from her survey of the opposite side of the road and reached for the doorknob in front of her. The hotel door opened easily, apparently well cared for by its proprietor, and she stepped into the small, barren lobby. Her valise bumping into her knee with every step, she approached the desk, smiling gamely at the gentleman there. At least she held hopes of him being a gentleman.

"What can I do for you?" he asked, and Jennifer smothered a laugh. *Not much, I suspect.* The thought was frivolous but immediate and she swallowed her moment of panic as she found a smile for the desk clerk.

"I need a room," she said. "For a couple of days, I suspect."

"Is someone expecting you?" the man asked. "Is there anyone I can contact to announce your arrival?"

"I don't doubt but what the man in question will show up soon," Jennifer said. "He knows I'm to arrive today."

"Well, perhaps we'd best rent to you on a day-by-day basis then," he told her, turning to pick out a key from one of the cubby holes behind him. "Room 203 is just beyond the head of the stairs, ma'am. If you'll sign the register, I'll carry your bag up for you."

He turned the book around and handed her a pen, watching closely as she formed her name in clearly legible script.

"Jennifer Alston." He spoke her name in a whisper and his gaze swept over her, as if he took a quick survey of her visible parts. "Are you one of those gals coming here to marry up with one of our menfolk?" he asked. "Seems like I heard your name over in the barbershop last time I was in there." He grinned in remembrance. "Our Sally Jo sure does give a nice haircut and shave."

"Well, I won't be happy if my intended husband has bandied my name about town," she said. "I'm a woman of culture, with a background above reproach, and I deserve to be spoken of as a lady." Especially by a lady masquerading as a barber, and shaving men, to boot. Jennifer wondered if a bathtub stood in the back room of the woman's establishment, offering the chance for a man to bathe away his dirt and perhaps luxuriate in a shave even as he soaked.

"I'm tryin' to think who mentioned you," the clerk said,

rubbing his chin and looking afar, as if the answer might appear in front of him.

"I mentioned her name." A deep voice at her right elbow took Jennifer by surprise and she turned to face an angry man, dark hair ruffled by a strong wind or perhaps long fingers. It was definitely a job completed by a chronic gesture of impatience, she decided as his right hand lifted to shove a lengthy wave from his forehead. A strong nose, high cheekbones and *darkly* impatient eyes met her sight, and she winced as she considered the man, hoping against hope that he didn't answer to the name of Lucas O'Reilly.

It was not to be.

"Hey there, Luc," the desk clerk said. "It *was* you that mentioned the young lady, wasn't it?" He stuck out his hand and it was enveloped by a fist the size of a full-grown muskmelon, Jennifer noted. The two men shook hands and then eyed each other.

"Your young lady was just renting herself a room," the clerk said. He turned to Jennifer then. "My name's Harley Fedderson, ma'am. Sorry I didn't introduce myself earlier." Waving the room key by a short length of twine, he nodded toward the staircase. "I'll just carry your bag up now."

"Like hell you will," Lucas O'Reilly said. "She doesn't need a room here. She'll be living at my place, soon as I can get her over to the preacher's house. He said he'd be home today, and he's probably waiting for us now."

Harley shrugged and Jennifer sniffed as if she'd caught the scent of something sour and unpleasant. She lifted her chin, aware that her reaction right now to the haughty giant in front of her might forever set a precedent. And then the man smiled. More than a congenial gesture of welcome, it was a twisting of mobile lips that made her think of a cat about to pounce upon an unsuspecting prey.

"I may want to rethink this whole idea," she said. "I reserve the right to change my mind about marrying you, sir."

"I don't think so," he murmured, his mouth curling into a smile more suited to a man faced with a luscious bit of pastry.

Jennifer felt a giant fist clutch at her stomach as she faced Lucas O'Reilly. "You have no rights over me," she told him, even as she wondered at her own recklessness in challenging the man.

"Ah, but I have," Lucas said, his eyes roving over her navy-blue traveling suit and seeming to find it wanting. "I have in my possession a letter stating that you would arrive in Thunder Canyon today, prepared to marry me and move into my home."

She felt the buttons tugging across her bosom and recognized, not for the first time, that she should have allowed a bit more fabric in the bodice of the jacket. Sewing a wardrobe for this occasion had been a huge undertaking, one she'd shared with her lifelong friend, Sheila Burnham, and the suit she wore now had been the last item on the list of clothing she'd felt necessary for this trip.

Now she wondered why she'd ever thought traveling clear across the country to marry an unknown man seemed like a fine idea. She immediately squelched her regrets. She'd had no choice. Not really. Not with her brother-in-law hot on her trail, his grasping hands ready to snatch at her, his portly body set to crush her beneath himself.

Once Alma died, Kyle Carter had made it his business to plot a seduction of his dead wife's sister. And Jennifer had no intention of being involved with the unsavory man. Not only was he repulsive to look at, his breath was foul and he apparently had no concept of bathing on a regular basis.

Now the man beside her bent closer and she caught a whiff of peppermint as his warm breath touched her cheek. His hand gripped her elbow and she recognized the latent strength he held in check. Should she foolishly attempt to escape his grasp, he would no doubt exert whatever force was required to bend her to his will.

She would not give him the pleasure of watching her wince in pain, should those honed fingers tighten on her flesh.

"Ma'am?" Lucas said, pulling her a bit closer. "Shall we leave now?" He bent to pick up her valise and turned her toward the front door. Her feet tangled as she was thrown off balance and he caught her up against his side, the hand gripping her elbow snaking from there to settle around her middle, long fingers pressing into the curve of her waist.

"You won't be taking the room, I assume," Harley said, as if he saw money taking flight along with his erstwhile guest.

"You got that right, Harley," Lucas said. "She's got a nice feather tick waiting for her. A lot more comfort to offer than your skinny, miserable mattresses."

Harley looked taken aback, but only shrugged again, as if he would not stand up to the man in front of him. And that seemed a wise choice, Jennifer thought. Lucas O'Reilly looked to be a formidable opponent. She might be wise to take note of that fact herself.

The threshold she had crossed only ten minutes earlier awaited, Lucas's hand holding the door open for her as he ushered her from the hotel. They stepped out onto the sidewalk where a multitude of watching men appeared to know Lucas, heads nodding as they muttered words of greeting to the tall, dark-haired dolt by her side. A man who had possessed her as easily as he might have claimed a stray puppy.

A short, sharp nod of his head was the only reply Lucas seemed willing to offer, but the men watching their progress seemed to expect no more, only stepping back to make way for the man and woman to walk past them toward a waiting farm wagon.

"You don't have a buggy?" Jennifer asked, eyeing the sturdy wooden vehicle in front of her. A rough, splintered board seemed to be where she would sit, its surface just about even with her forehead, and she could see no step upon which to lift herself to a level placing her within reach of the rough seat.

She needn't have worried, for within the space of two seconds, she was lifted by two strong hands and plopped unceremoniously upon the wooden board. Looking down at the road was a new experience when a narrow, hard board beneath her bottom was her only support. She was dizzy, gripping the edge of her seat, watching as Lucas stalked around to untie his horses from the hitching rail.

He cast her one long glance as he lifted himself onto the makeshift seat beside her, and then the reins were snapped over the broad backs of the matching pair of horses. They set off in tandem, their big feet kicking up dust as they headed toward the end of town she had not seen previously.

The view from the stagecoach had been none too inviting, and the other end of the small community offered no more than the part she had traveled earlier. A motley collection of storefronts met her gaze on either side of the road. Just where the buildings began, the street split in two, curving around a green area where children played on the patch of grass and watched wide-eyed as the farm wagon passed by. A town square, she suspected, but certainly not of the caliber of the one in the midst of New York City.

Ahead of her, a series of buildings that might have been private homes stood side by side. Fences fronted the houses and gardens were sprouting between the road and the front stoop of many of the dwellings. Why the owners had chosen to forego grass for rows of radishes and beans was a question she set aside for now. The fact remained that vegetables were obviously of more importance than grass and flowers.

Thunder Canyon was definitely not New York City.

A small, white structure sat at the end of the row of dwellings, a church from all appearances. Beside it was another house, probably the parsonage, she thought, and was proved right when Lucas pulled the wagon to a halt in front of the white picket fence. At least some soul within these walls had a smidgen of culture, for grass fought with weeds for supremacy in two rectangles of green separated by a gravel path.

Jennifer braced herself as Lucas approached, lifting his arms to her. "I can get down alone," she muttered, fearful of his hands clutching at her middle once more.

"No doubt," he said. "But you're not going to. Now lean toward me, ma'am." Without giving her a choice, he gripped her waist, his fingers holding her fast as he lifted her from the seat. Caught off balance, she fell smack across his broad chest and felt her breasts flatten against him, then she slid the length of his body. He stood her on her feet, looking down at her with a new and different expression in those blue eyes.

She caught her breath, gazing around in desperation, as if there must be some haven she could claim, a bit of shelter from the storm invading her life. The presence of Lucas O'Reilly was one offering peril, she feared. Living with this arrogant man would be the epitome of disaster, for he would surely demand that she obey his rules, would certainly expect her to occupy his home and then supply all of his needs, beginning with the cooking and cleaning of said household and continuing on to satisfying his masculine desires.

Hopefully he would be willing to wait for the accomplishment of *those* details until she was able to get herself in order and above all, to get used to having a big, hulking man in her life. Hulking? Perhaps not, she decided. Big, certainly. Threatening, definitely. But in a primitive, graceful manner, more suited to a wild animal who prowled in search of a mate.

The idea of being a mate to this man was frightening beyond description. She'd envisioned a more sophisticated gentleman, such as might have founded Thunder Canyon from his place behind a desk in an office on Main Street. Lucas O'Reilly looked as if he were a stranger to such an amenity as a desk, let alone an office from which he did his business.

She'd warrant he'd formed part of the thunder that inspired the name of this town, that his bellowing voice had cut down all who might protest his superiority when it came to putting his seal upon the forming of this community. Thunder Canyon suited him, with its ramshackle street, storefronts claiming to be reputable places of business and ragtag assortment of men who seemed to have nothing more to do with their time than to sit on backless benches in front of the general store and the town barbershop.

Only the bank, a sturdy building situated next to the jailhouse, lacked a clutch of men holding up the front wall, its stalwart boards gleaming with white paint, as if daring anyone to soil its pristine surface. Even the small building in front of her now, the parsonage wherein she would lose her single status to gain the title of Mrs. Lucas O'Reilly, held its own porch-sitter.

A young boy stood as she gained the bottom step. "Ma'am? Are you lookin' for my pa?"

"Is he home?" Lucas asked. "He said he'd be here this morning."

"Yessir, he is," the boy answered. "I'll go get him."

Behind him, the screen door opened and a young man greeted them both. "Come on in, Luc. I'm assuming this young lady is the bride. Am I right?"

Lucas nodded, even as Jennifer shook her head.

"Well," the preacher said with a laugh, "I think you'll have to agree on this before we perform the ceremony."

"We'll agree," Lucas promised him, and once more gripped Jennifer's elbow, turning her to face him. "Go on inside, Preacher. We'll be right there."

The dark-clad man of the cloth smiled and stepped back inside the house, his son following close behind, probably at the urging of Lucas's threatening glare.

"Now, let's have no more foolishness," Luc snarled at Jennifer. "We're getting married, and that's that. You made a promise and you'll live up to it. I'll see to it, ma'am." His lower lip protruded a bit and his eyes narrowed as he spoke. No longer a deep blue color, they darkened beneath his lowered lids to a cast reminding Jennifer of midnight.

"You can't make me marry you," she sputtered, aware of his proximity, his muscular frame and the scowl he bent her way.

"Ah, but I can," he returned softly. "All I have to do is take you home and spend a few hours with you alone in my house. Maybe all night would be better, now that I think of it." His smile was feral as he bent closer. "By morning you'd be about as ruined as any young woman can get, and primed for a wedding ring." He pursed his lips and then grinned.

"We can do this the easy way and march in there to face the preacher, or we can do it *my* way. I'm not about to bicker over it. I'd just as soon bed you beforehand, but I'm giving you the choice."

"Some choice," Jennifer said. "Maybe we should see if the preacher is willing to marry a woman who's changed her mind."

"That settles it," Lucas said, turning her from the porch, hustling her back to the wagon. "We'll do it my way."

Jennifer skidded to a halt, her feet dragging against the gravel path. Dark brows lowered as Lucas looked down at her. "Changed your mind?" he asked. "Ready to say your vows right now?"

"Why don't you just take me back to the hotel and I'll stay there till the next stage comes through and I'll be out of your way?"

"Not a chance," he muttered. "I sent for a bride, paid the agency good money to get you here, invested a bundle in your fare and got my place all fixed up for you. You'll marry me, Jennifer Alston."

She wilted, her stamina fading, her staunch will daunted by his words. She'd promised, true enough. She'd accepted his money for travel, for her food and lodging on the journey and now was committed to fulfilling her part of the bargain. Besides, returning to New York and the dubious welcoming committee of one awaiting her there was no choice at all, really. Having to face Kyle again was reason enough to marry this man. Remembering the lustful expression of her pursuer made her shiver even now. And so she only nodded, her lips firm, her teeth clenched as she faced her choices.

"All right." As simply as that, she accepted her future,

faced the man she'd promised to wed and pledged herself to go through with that bargain.

If relief touched his gaze, she ignored it, unwilling to accept that he had ever doubted her response. He *knew,* without a shadow of a doubt, that she would fall in with his plans. He'd held the upper hand all along, and well she understood her position. For she actually had no position to hold. She would be his wife. But the man was in for a few surprises.

Jennifer Alston was a lady, born and bred, with no working knowledge of keeping a house or tending to a man's needs, in any way, shape or form. And that included cooking and mending, the two things Lucas had specified in his request for a wife.

SHE'D GIVEN IN almost too readily, Luc decided, a finger of disquiet running the length of his spine. But, he'd never looked a gift horse in the mouth before and he'd not do it now. With one hand at her waist, he ushered her up the steps and into the front hall of the parsonage. The preacher's pretty wife greeted him and opened the doorway into her husband's study, following them inside.

"I'm to be a witness," she explained to Luc. "Our neighbor, Ida Bronson, will serve as the second. Unless you've made other arrangements."

"No, that's fine with me," he said. "So long as it's official and legal, I don't care about the particulars."

A fussy little female, probably well past middle age if her white hair was any indication, slid through the doorway and waved her fingers at Jennifer. Her smile was broad, her short, squat figure matronly and her excitement apparent.

"I simply love weddings. Especially when the bride and

groom seem to be so well suited and pleased at the prospect of being married."

If Jennifer's sour look was anything to go by, she disputed the neighbor's assumptions, but he wasn't about to have a set-to in front of the rest of the wedding party. He nodded, smiled and looked to the preacher for guidance.

The words were short and to the point, the ceremony over with in minutes, and when the instruction was given to kiss his bride, Luc bent his head and sought the warmth of Jennifer Alston's mouth. Her lips were clamped shut but still lent a pleasurable glow to the whole event.

She was not willing to press her mouth against his, but he'd remedy that in short order, he decided, once he got her home and into his bed. He'd been told more than once that he had a way with women, and this one would be no different than the rest of the female sex.

They left the parsonage in a flurry of well-wishes and he lifted her to the wagon seat once more, tucking her skirts around her, even as she pushed at his hands in a futile gesture of denial of his right to do so. Delivering one last pat on her knee, he was the object of her anger as she scorned his smile and brushed away the traces of his touch.

He set off at a fast clip toward the big farmhouse outside of town, the place he'd bought with her in mind. Not that he'd known then who he would wed, only that there would be a woman in his home, a comfortable female to make his life pleasant and his bed more welcoming.

He'd sent for the remnants of his parents' belongings once he'd settled in, unwilling to admit, even to himself, the pleasure he gained from their presence in his home.

The gold he'd mined was safely deposited in the bank, and

the rich vein he'd uncovered seemed to be endless. The woman didn't know how well off she was, marrying the founder of Thunder Canyon, a man with a tidy bank account and the deed to a piece of prosperity known as a gold mine. The mine was shared with his partner, but there was plenty there for two men, and he had the utmost faith in the honesty and integrity of Alexander.

Probably more faith than he had in the woman he'd just committed himself to.

He glanced over at Jennifer now, caught a glimpse of her taut jaw and the frown she wore, and looked ahead once more. The backside of his team of horses was more welcoming than the woman he'd wed, and that thought didn't set well with him.

Getting married was a necessity. Having a wife was more of a needful thing than something he'd looked forward to as a pleasure. Yet beneath that god-awful blue thing she was wearing, he'd bet odds on Jennifer Alston O'Reilly having a round and luscious body, just made for loving.

He knew enough about women to recognize the curves and hollows of a lush, female form. Holding her against himself had given him good reason to venture an opinion. She was a female worth investigating, and she was his wife, two details that gave him hope that the distasteful issue of marriage might indeed prove to be worthwhile.

At least once he managed to lure her into his bed and make her his wife. For as it stood now, she was a bride, but that was a far cry from being a wife in every sense of the word. The sooner that was tended to, the better.

And that was a fact.

CHAPTER TWO

IF LUCAS THOUGHT for one minute that she would be willing to clean up the mess he'd made in this house, he was in for a big surprise. The floors were filthy and a layer of dust covered every available surface that could possibly hold dirt. And there were enough dirty dishes in the kitchen sink to feed a small army. An army of one, apparently. Lucas O'Reilly, by name.

Jennifer stood in the middle of the hallway, her vantage point allowing her to look into four rooms without stirring one step. In front of her was the parlor, an area of generous proportions, with a fireplace against the far wall, bookshelves reaching to the ceiling on one side and several pieces of comfortable-looking furniture scattered hither and yon.

To her left was a dining room, connected to the kitchen, which was behind her. The dining room held a massive table and ten chairs. A matching bureau, topped by a china cabinet of sorts, sat between the two windows. Filled to the edges of its shelves, half hidden by streaked glass, it was heavy with an odd assortment of dishes and glassware. Some of them matched, others were one of a kind, many of them obviously valuable. None of them appeared to be clean.

The other room visible to her eye was a bedroom of sorts, probably where Lucas slept. A narrow cot sat against one wall, a tall chest of drawers beside it, three drawers left open, bits and pieces of clothing hanging over the edges. From the bottom drawer, an assortment of stockings dangled onto the musty carpet.

The whole house smelled stale, and she wondered how Lucas managed to smell as clean as he did. For the man was indeed well-kept, even if he lived in a veritable pigpen.

Perhaps pigpen was too harsh a word to describe his habitat, but it came pretty close, Jennifer decided. She walked into the kitchen and met the man head-on. He was solid, firm and unmovable. Unwilling to reveal her revulsion at the condition of his house, she merely looked to one side, where the stove sat, its surface covered with pots and kettles. A huge coffeepot seemed to hold a position of honor, due to its placement on the front burner.

The stench of boiled, burned coffee polluted the air and she was tempted to immerse the pot in hot water and use a scrub rag on it, well doused with lye soap. In fact, everything in the kitchen, let alone the rest of the house, cried out for care—for the use of soap and water, a good application of beeswax or simply the business end of a broom.

She shuddered. It was a full-time job for a woman well versed in the art of keeping house, not an occupation for one such as she, a woman with not the slightest notion of how to run a place such as the one she'd been offered.

For indeed, he'd offered it to her. "Here's your house," he'd said blithely, ushering her through the back door, waving a negligent hand at the kitchen, where sagging curtains met her eye, barely disguising the dirt that streaked the windows they were intended to cover.

The kitchen dresser held a hodgepodge of dishes and the

table was barren of covering. She'd give much for the services of her mother's live-in cook and housekeeper right now. Even for just a couple of hours. Long enough to set the kitchen to rights and aim her in the right direction, arming her with instructions on how to make things livable.

"Here's your house," he'd said, and she feared he was right on target with those words. She was stuck with it, but if he wanted to live in this disaster, she'd let him. Only her own living space would show the touch of her hand, only her own food would be served on clean tableware and only her own bed would wear clean sheets.

"Our bedroom is upstairs."

She gawked at him. *Our bedroom.* Those were the words he'd said, but she found them unbelievable. Surely the man didn't expect her to crawl into a bed with him. Certainly not in broad daylight. She met his gaze and changed her mind. He had that same man-eyeing-a-bite-of-pastry look about him, his eyes blue once more, making a slow survey of her... her bosom, if she wasn't mistaken.

Although what he found so interesting about that assortment of curves was beyond her. Overabundant, her mother had said. Not in fashion, her best friend had told her. No woman of distinction had such a lush display attached to her chest, and for years Jennifer had lamented her overly endowed figure.

Now it seemed to be a point of interest to the man she'd married. He was making no bones about it, either. He stood in front of her and reached one hand to circle the back of her waist, the other idly working at the top button of her suit jacket.

"What do you think you're doing?" she asked, aware that

her voice held a certain breathlessness, her words faltering as she asked his intentions.

"What do you think?" he answered, which was really not an answer at all, merely a leading question that confused her. For indeed, she had no idea what he was up to.

"Leave my buttons alone," she told him, reaching to slap away the errant fingers that had managed to dislodge the first of a whole string of buttons holding her jacket together. His hand was like a chunk of wood, she decided, dead set on moving down the line of buttons, undoing each one in order.

Well, no need to be flustered, for beneath the jacket she wore a neat blouse, also bearing a line of fastenings. Fastenings he could no doubt undo with very little effort, she realized as her sense of comfort ebbed away.

In a moment her jacket had been pushed off her shoulders and left to fall on the floor. She bent to pick it up, heard his soft laughter as she lifted it and shook the dust from it. One big hand took it from her and he tossed it on the table, then pulled her into his embrace and held her tightly against himself.

Built like a tree trunk, not just a single chunk of wood, he was massive and sturdy against her own soft curves, and she winced. His whole body seemed to be made from some hitherto unknown mixture of muscle and bone, surely not the average, everyday ingredients most men were constructed with.

A wide chest formed above his narrow waist and his arms were well muscled and firm to the touch. *Her touch,* she realized.

She'd automatically held herself from him, pushing against his shoulders and then allowing her hands to fall to the tops of his arms. It did no good. He was not about to release her, if she was any judge. His mouth was a straight line, his jaw set.

"Are you going to hurt me?" she asked. If he was a wife beater, she wanted to know right now just what she could expect from him, and be prepared to defend herself. As if there were any defense against the inordinate strength of a man well over six feet tall and as wide in the shoulders as a normal door frame.

He blinked and his eyes fixed on her. For just a moment she thought she'd surprised him, and then he laughed. "I haven't hurt a woman in quite a while, honey. At least a month or so, I'd guess."

"Are you teasing me?"

He shook his head, a slow movement that was a threat in itself. "I don't tease, sweetheart. I might coax you, or seduce you, or even swat your sweet little behind, but I don't tease. If I tell you something, you'd better believe it, 'cause I don't tell lies and I don't say anything I don't mean."

She'd latched on to only a part of his soliloquy, that bit where he'd spoken of swatting her behind, which was neither sweet nor little as far as she was concerned.

"Swat me anyplace on my anatomy and you'll be sorry," she muttered. "I mean it, Mr. O'Reilly. I don't take kindly to threats against my person."

"I didn't think you would, ma'am, but believe me when I tell you that I'll keep you in line any way I have to, and if that involves treating you like a child, then just make sure you act like a grown woman and we won't have any problems."

"And how does a grown woman act, in your estimation?"

"In your case, like a grown, married woman. Like a woman who's come clear across the country to be a wife to a hardworking man, who's promised to love, honor and obey that man, and who is about to set to work, cleaning up this house and cooking a meal for that hardworking man, while he goes out to do the chores."

She stiffened her spine and jutted her chin forward. "You made the mess in here, mister. You can just clean it up yourself if you want it set to rights."

"You're telling me you won't keep house and take your place as a wife?" She noted that his jaw was rigid again and his shoulders squared as if he prepared to do battle.

"I'll cook something for myself to eat," she began, "and if there's any left over, you can have a bit. But don't expect to give me orders and have them followed."

"Well, don't expect access to the food supply unless you plan to include me in your plans," he said. "I'm not about to feed a wife if I'm to be left out of mealtimes."

Her glance around the kitchen left her with no clue as to where he hid the food. "I don't suppose you have any supplies on hand, do you?" she asked.

"Wouldn't you like to know?" He smirked. There was no other word for the gleam of enjoyment in his eyes as he laughed at her.

"I don't suppose I need to eat after all," she said. "I've managed to go without food for the past day or so. One more meal isn't going to make much of a difference, to my way of thinking."

He sobered swiftly. "What are you talking about? You haven't eaten? Since when? Yesterday? What happened to the money I provided for your meals?"

She shrugged. "A thug stole my purse two days ago on the train, just as I was getting off, in fact. I already had the ticket for the stage tucked into my—" She halted, unwilling to reveal the hiding place she'd used for the purpose.

"Tucked into—where?" he asked, his eyes making another slow survey of her person. Her shirtwaist seemed made of some transparent fabric, for she would have sworn he could see beneath it to the lacy vest and chemise she wore.

"None of your business," she retorted. "And as to my eating, I've been without food more than once in my life. Another day or two won't kill me."

"You'll eat," he said. "While you live in my house, you'll eat."

"You just got done telling me—"

"Never mind what I told you. I've changed my mind. You're entirely too skinny, and you need regular meals."

She looked down at herself in disbelief. "I'm not skinny. In fact, my mother once told me—" She halted again, taken aback by the expression he wore, as if he could see into her mind and knew her very thoughts.

"Yes? Your mother told you—what? That you were well-endowed?" He grinned. "She would have been right on that account. Your bosom is beyond reproach."

"Well, thank you very much, Mr. O'Reilly," she sputtered.

"As to the rest of you, I'll warrant I could trace every rib if I were so inclined, and I'd be willing to bet you haven't an extra pound of weight on your —" His pause was long, his words slow in coming. "On your sweet little behind," he finished softly, as if the words held some special import.

"Please," she whispered. "Don't say things like that."

He frowned down at her, and then in a swift movement that caught her off guard, he tugged her off balance and held her in a tight grip. "You'd better get used to it, sweetheart," he murmured. "I plan on saying a lot more such things in the future. You seem to forget that you are my wife. Maybe in name only for now, but legally, and that's what really counts. We're married, honey, like it or not."

"I don't," she said. "You weren't what I expected at all. I thought I'd marry a gentleman, someone with class, the founder of a town, a man with dignity."

He hooted, his laughter rebounding from the walls. "You want a man with dignity? You wouldn't know what to do with such a man. I could introduce you to the banker, Walter Powers. He's dignified. But then, he's also as ugly as the back end of a mule, so I can't see where you'd be any better off with him than with me."

"What makes you think you're so great to look at?" she asked, even as she considered the question to be most foolish. He was rough and uncouth, but with the dark hair and sparkling eyes and the smiles that caught her unaware, he was a handsome man. And the idiot knew it, she'd warrant.

"I've been told I cut quite a figure," he admitted. "Not that I care about what folks think of me."

"Only the feminine part of the population."

"Well, there is that," he conceded. And then he sobered. "I care mostly what you think of me, honey, and right now, I don't think your opinion of me is very high."

"I won't argue with that," she agreed. "I've seen rats in the city with more to offer than the one I found here in Thunder Canyon."

"Did any of them offer to marry you?" he asked "I not only paid your way here, but I married you without any hesitation. What more could you ask?"

"A little choice in the matter."

"You made up your mind when you got on that train. Hell,

even before that. When you accepted the money for your fare, you were committed to me."

"I didn't know you then," she said.

"You don't know me now. But, you will, sweetheart. Sooner than you think."

"I'm not sleeping in the same bed with you," she told him, anticipating his insistence on that issue. "You can stay right down here in the same bed you've been using and I'll go upstairs and find somewhere else to put my pillow."

"What pillow?" He grinned. "I have custody of all the pillows in the house. Not to mention the sheets and feather ticks."

"You'd deny me a bed to sleep in?"

"Now," he began, with a smile that threatened to become a full-blown chuckle, "you know better than that. I've got a nice, clean bed, soft as goose down, with clean sheets and nice, fluffy pillows. It's right at the top of the stairs, just waiting for you to set your dainty little feet inside the bedroom door and take possession."

"I don't think so." It was as firm a refusal as she could muster. Arguing didn't seem to be doing much good, so she clearly stated her case, denying his right to her presence in his bed.

"Shall we fight this out now or after dark?" he asked, his manner that of a man who knows he has the upper hand.

"I don't intend to fight with you," she told him. "If you'll tell me where the food is, I'll concede that I'm obligated to fix a meal for you. That's as far as I go."

"That'll do for now," he murmured, his arms tightening around her waist. "At least, that's almost enough for now."

She saw his head duck toward hers and felt her eyes open wide. Surely he wouldn't. But he did. His mouth met hers for the second time, this kiss a far cry from the sample of her mouth he'd taken in the parsonage. Now he nibbled and plucked at her lips, his teeth joining in the play as he explored the contours of her mouth and investigated the soft, vulnerable flesh just inside her lip line.

She tried to clamp her lips together, but it was no use, for his hand touched her chin and she felt the pressure of his strength against her jaw as he forced her to open to him. "That's a good girl," he whispered, and she wanted to laugh. She felt about as far from being a *good girl* as any woman ever had, what with this man's tongue touching hers, his mouth opening over hers, his laughter echoing in her ears as he took advantage of her lesser strength to invade her as might a man set on seduction.

For surely that was where he was headed, if she knew anything at all about it. And very little did she know, in actuality. Only that a good girl could get in the family way by allowing a young man to kiss her in a familiar manner. Oh, not that the kissing itself would turn the trick, but what came afterward could get her in trouble.

She'd heard her mother say, more than once, that a good girl never let a man touch her body without a wedding ring around her finger first. And that such goings-on led to perdition. As a growing child, Jennifer had heard much about that dreadful place, but never could figure out where it was.

She knew now. Directly due west of the town of Thunder Canyon, perdition was staring her in the face, if she knew anything about it. It wasn't a spot on the map, but a man…her husband, in fact. A man seeming to have no qualms about placing her in peril.

He looked down into her face and she was swept up in the dark glow of eyes filled with dangerous lights. A faintly wolfish expression lit his features and he towered over her, making her feel insignificant. Then he moved one big hand to the front of her shirtwaist again and his long fingers cupped her breast.

She shrieked, a noise fit to wake the dead, as her papa had told her more than once. He'd declared she had a voice that would carry a country mile and she remembered wondering if a country mile was longer than a city mile. No matter today, only that the volume of her cry had penetrated the absorbed expression of the man who held her. He blinked at her, his hand tightening in an automatic gesture, and then he smiled. That same, feral grin that told her he was set on hauling her up those stairs to his bed.

"No, Lucas," she said, her voice hushed.

"Lucas, is it? Are we done with Mr. O'Reilly now?"

"I don't know about you, but I'm done with this whole misunderstanding," she said, determined to escape his grasp, eager to move to the other side of the room, hopeful he would not follow her there.

"You're the one with the misunderstanding, sweetheart. I'm dead certain of what I'm doing here. As soon as you figure it out, we'll be in business."

"That's what I'm afraid of," she whispered. "I don't want to be in business, with you or any other man. I don't know what I was thinking of, to come here like this. But I've made a dreadful mistake. I see that now." She paused for breath and hastened on, hopeful of his cooperation.

"Please just put me on a stagecoach headed East. I'll pay you back as soon as I can."

"Where East?" he asked, his brow puckering as if he considered her request valid.

"Anywhere," she said. "Anywhere but here."

"I couldn't possibly allow my wife to run off before we've even begun our marriage," he announced after a moment's deliberation. "I promised to cherish you until death parts us, and I haven't even started with that part of the bargain."

"I don't want to be cherished," she blurted, only too aware of where this conversation was heading.

"You don't?" he asked. "I'd think being cherished would make a woman, or a man, for that matter, feel kinda special, sorta like a present waiting to be opened and enjoyed."

"I'm not a present. I'm a woman."

He grinned. "Yeah. I noticed."

Indeed, he could hardly help but notice, she thought. Her front was plastered up against him, and now that he'd moved his hand a bit, she felt the pressure of his chest against her tender breasts. Not to mention a strangely formed part of his anatomy that persisted in nudging her belly, as if offering a reminder of something she needed to know.

"Stop it," she said, responding to the pressure of his body against hers.

"Stop what?" he asked, one big hand against her lower back, the other on her chin again, as if he could not decide just where his lips would take hold. It seemed that her mouth was elected, and he suckled her bottom lip, then transferred his attention to her throat, where he nuzzled and murmured faint words she strained to hear.

None of them made any sense to her, her ears only catching a mishmash of sounds that seemed foreign to her. Something about her being sweet and soft, and smelling good. And wasn't that a bit of nonsense.

She'd never been called sweet, having been a sassy child,

forever in trouble because of her determination to have the last word in any dispute. And not by the greatest stretch of the imagination could she be described as smelling good. She wore no perfume or toilet water, and the only scent on her skin was that of soap and the powder puff she used after bathing, a vanity that seemed to getting her deeper into trouble by the minute.

She bent her head to one side, then the other, straining to remove herself from him, all to no avail. He was persistent, his hands roving over her hips and then to her waist, his long fingers almost circling her ribs. His thumbs were pushing at the bottom curve of her breasts, lifting them higher, pressing them together and causing her to shiver.

He leaned back a bit and looked down at his accomplishment. She was almost indecent, her bosom outlined by her shirtwaist, her flesh mounded over his hands as though her breasts might spill out of her clothing, given any encouragement at all. And Lucas seemed to be very good at encouraging illicit behavior in several parts of her body.

She tingled in places she'd rarely been aware of in her twenty-three years. Even as she looked down, the man ran his fingers over the prominent crests that puckered at his advance. She shivered again, feeling a slender thread of fire take hold in the depths of her belly.

"I think we've messed around long enough," Lucas said, his face taut, his eyes half hidden by long lashes as he watched her. A line of ruddy color touched his cheekbones and his breathing seemed erratic.

"Then let me go," she managed to whimper, fearful of his next move.

"I'm going to take you upstairs and show you your new

bedroom," he told her, and she caught her breath. The ways and means of how men and women came together in the act of marriage was a secret her mother had not seen fit to share with her.

Neither had her sister, Alma, but then, there hadn't seemed to be any love lost between that gentle soul and Kyle, the brute she'd married. Being a part of her sister's hours of labor, watching as the beloved link between the two of them was severed, she'd mourned not only the mother, but the child left behind with only Kyle as a champion.

Staying there had been an option she'd shrunk from, so she'd chosen the lesser of two evils, this trip to Montana, answering the letter from the agency she'd contacted about the matter of looking for a husband. Answering the mail-order bride ad had been a spur-of-the-moment thing. But upon contemplation, she'd decided that anything was better than facing life in the same house as Kyle.

She'd left the cemetary quickly, sad at abandoning her sister's newborn child, but too fearful of the infant's father to do otherwise. She rued her decision, watching from the sidelines as Kyle made a hash of being a father. There was nothing she could do but wait for news that would complete her journey to wedded bliss.

Now she stood in the arms of another man and searched her mind for any minute detail of married life she might have heard from Alma. She recalled nothing worth her attention, only a shuddering tale of shame on Alma's part, a painful using of her body by the man who'd promised to *cherish* her.

"I know about cherishing a woman," she said, recalling Luc's words. "I don't want any of it directed at me."

"How many men have directed anything at you?" he asked, his eyes on her, as if he thought she might be counting the number of masculine persons she'd allowed to touch her.

"I'm not interested in men or what they have to offer," she said.

"You're not?" he asked. "I'd have sworn you kinda liked me kissing you. And you didn't seem to take offense at my touching your—"

"Just stop right there," she blurted. "I don't welcome your advances, sir."

"I'm not a *sir* to you, sweetheart," he said. "I'm your husband, the man you're going to live the rest of your life with."

He turned sober then, his lips pressing together, and he bent to pick her up, holding her high against his chest. Her feet dangled, her arm hung limply over his back and she felt like a sack of oats hanging from his embrace.

"Put me down," she ordered him, aware that her position made her extremely vulnerable to whatever he had in mind. And what he had in mind was certainly not what she had planned for today.

He left her no choice, marching from the kitchen into the small, square hallway, then up the flight of stairs to the second floor of the farmhouse.

The hallway was apparently carpeted, for his footsteps were muffled as he walked. And then he halted in front of an open doorway and sidled into the room, taking care that he not bump her head on the door frame. From her position, she could see little of the room, aware that it held massive furniture, a large chifforobe and a matching chest of drawers.

Lucas lowered her to the floor, catching hold of her as if he feared she might try to escape. His grip was tight, but left her free to look around her, and she turned her head to view the big bed behind her. High posts adorned each corner. The headboard was tall, and resembled the one on her parents' bed at home.

The quilt covering the mattress reflected some woman's skill with a needle, for Jennifer caught sight of tiny stitches that bound the pieced patches together.

"This is my room?" she asked, already knowing the answer she would hear.

"I thought I made it clear that we would share this bed," Lucas told her, his voice patient, as though he spoke to a child who was extremely dense. "Now sit down, Jennifer."

"Where?" She looked up at him, dazed and frightened by the turn of events.

"Right here, sweetheart, on the mattress."

She looked down at the quilt, glanced at the pillows, fluffed and waiting for a weary head to be cushioned by their full-ness, and then looked back at the man who expected her to comply with his wishes.

"I'd prefer a chair," she said, her challenge obvious, even to a man as thick-headed as Lucas O'Reilly appeared to be.

"How about my lap?" he asked, and then turned to perch on the mattress, pulling her across his lap. It was a soft bed, a fluffy feather tick it seemed, and she felt Lucas sinking into its depths.

"Please, Lucas," she managed to whisper and then her throat went dry and she lost her ability to speak.

"You still think I'm going to hurt you?" he asked, and it seemed he was sincere in his concern. "I have no intention of causing you harm, honey. I was joking before when I told you I'd brought harm to another woman. Never have. Never will." He grinned at her, holding her upright on his muscled thighs.

They felt like two solid logs beneath her, with no give to cushion her bottom.

"I'm not afraid of you," she said, denying the panic that threatened to choke her.

"Yes, you are," he said, apparently more aware of her state of mind than she'd given him credit for. "But there's no need, Jennifer."

With a few easy moves, her placed her on her back, then lay beside her, his arms holding her, his legs trapping hers. "Comfortable now?" he asked, rising on one elbow, his free hand caressing her cheek.

He was going to kiss her again. As surely as she knew the sun would rise in the morning, she knew that look in his eyes. She turned her head away as he bent to her.

CHAPTER THREE

"SEE NOW, this isn't so bad, is it?" His drawl was more apparent when he lowered his voice.

"I don't want to be in your bed," she whispered. "And I lied. You frighten me, holding me down, making me a prisoner."

"Then just relax, honey, and cuddle up with me for a minute or two." He adjusted his position, sliding one arm beneath her head and lying down. She was pulled up tightly against him, her feet barely touching his shin bones, her head cushioned by his shoulder.

"I've never done this before," she protested. "I'm not accustomed to—"

"I surely hope you're new at this sort of thing, sweetheart. In fact, I'm counting on it. That way I can teach you how to be a wife, and you won't have any notions stuck in your head about being modest and ladylike."

"There's nothing wrong with being modest. And I *am* a lady."

"I don't doubt that for a minute, honey. And just to let you know, ladies are some of my favorite people."

Her mind swung back to the watching women who'd peopled the balcony above Pete's Saloon in town. "I'll just bet they are," she said, her vivid imagination able to envision him climbing a set of stairs to a room, wherein waited several of those lush beauties.

He frowned and changed his tack. "A little modesty goes a long way when it comes to two people in a bed," he told her. "Especially when those two people are married."

"I wouldn't know. I've never been married before."

"Well, you are now. And you're about to become a wife."

He'd waited long enough, given her enough time to get used to his touch, and his trousers were about to burst open on their own, given the pulsing erection he knew had to be pushing at her even now. Curved against him, surely she knew his problem. Certainly she had some glimmer as to what went on in bed between male and female.

And then a thought struck him. What if she didn't know? What if he'd married not only a virgin bride, but an *ignorant* virgin bride?

"Jennifer?" He spoke her name softly, trying his best to reassure her. "Didn't your mother tell you anything about marriage?"

She tilted her chin up and shook her head, her eyes wide with what looked like fright. And well they might. She was pinned beneath a man almost twice her size, lying in the depths of a feather tick in his bedroom, the sun going down outside the windows, and no notion of what he intended. Yet she did not flinch from him, her body forming to his, softening against him, even as tears blinded her vision.

"Hell and damnation," he blurted, rolling from the bed, watching as her head fell to the pillow as he rose to his feet. "I can't find it in me to force myself on a woman, no matter how horny I am. Even if that woman is my legal wife."

Jennifer sat up in the bed, which he knew was no easy task,

given the soft contours of the feather tick beneath her. "Do you mean that?" she asked, wiping at the moisture on her cheeks.

"I told you before, I don't say anything I don't mean," he pointed out, his barely concealed anger emphasizing each word.

"Well, in that case, I'll just go down to the kitchen and make you something to eat," she said, relief apparent in her voice as she pulled a handkerchief from her pocket and blew her nose. "Just tell me where you keep the food and you can go about your chores while I put something together for supper."

He nodded as she clambered out of bed. "Leave the jacket off," he said. "You're home now. You don't need to be formal here. In fact, there's an apron of my mother's you can put on over your clothes if you want to."

"Your mother's apron?" Her eyes were shiny with fresh tears as she faced him and he felt more than a twinge of guilt that he'd put so much pressure on her. She was young and inexperienced at any number of things, it seemed. Yet, her youthful body pled silently for his touch, for he'd felt her breasts firm up beneath his hands, had noted the way she'd curled against him on the bed.

"It was packed away in her things," he replied. "I'll get it for you and locate something for you to cook."

"I'm not very good at such things," she warned him. "Things like cooking and such, I mean. My mother had a lady who kept our house and made all the meals."

"Your mother didn't teach you to cook?" he asked, stunned by her revelation.

"I never needed to." Her eyes were frantic now, seeking the bedroom door, as if she might flee down the stairs and onto the back porch, given half a chance.

"Well, you're about to learn the hard way, ma'am."

He turned her around and escorted her from the room, then down the stairs to where he kept his food in a large pantry just off the kitchen. A curtain hung over the doorway, a limp bit of a rag. When he pushed it aside to allow them entry, it fell from the nails that held it in place, falling in a dusty heap on the floor.

"In here," he said, waving at the shelves, where cans and crocks held his supplies.

Jennifer lent a dubious look to the collection, then stepped inside the small room and peered beneath the plate that covered a crock of pickles. "I don't think you'll want these for supper," she murmured.

A can of beef caught her eye and she snatched it up, then peeked carefully into a wide crockery bowl that held his supply of eggs. "How about fried eggs and sliced beef?" she asked.

"Anything you fix will be just fine," he told her, hoping to encourage her efforts.

She caught sight of the calico apron then, hanging from a hook on the wall and lifted it from its resting place, placing the loop over her neck, allowing the apron to hang from her bosom to cover most of her dress.

Luc turned her around, tied the strings in a credible bow and backed from the pantry. He'd given her enough of a shock for one day, he decided. Hanging around while she found her way in his kitchen was too much to expect her to accept.

Jennifer gathered up the apron front, placed four eggs in the pocket formed there, and held it with one hand as she lifted the can of beef again and scanned the shelf for any more likely prospects.

Coffee. If she could figure out how to make a decent pot

of coffee, that might appease him. But first the pot must be washed, and then she'd find the supply of ground coffee.

The kitchen was a welcome sight after standing in the confines of his pantry, with him so close to hand. He lifted a hand to her, waved a farewell and headed out the back door.

"I'll be the better part of an hour, by the time I do the milking and feed the stock."

And what feeding the stock entailed, she had no idea. In fact, she had no notion of what *stock* meant. Unless it referred to his cow and team of horses. And somewhere he must have a flock of chickens, given the presence of eggs in the pantry.

She placed the four specimens she'd chosen on the table and sought out a clean pan. There didn't appear to be one without some residue of food clinging to its surface, so she chose the least grimy of the lot and took it to the sink. Some glimmer of her mother's cook wiping her iron skillets clean lingered in Jennifer's head and she decided to forego the soap and water she'd thought to employ, depending instead of the services of a handy rag, dampened with clean water from the pump.

The pan cleaned up nicely, much to her relief, and she replaced it on the stove. Only a faint warmth rose from the iron stovetop and she lifted one of the lids with a device stuck into it, bending to examine the coals within the black behemoth. There was an almost total lack of the blazing fire she'd hoped to find there. He'd left her with a cold stove and expected her to cook a meal.

However, a nearby box held wood cut into assorted lengths, and she gathered several pieces in her arms. Most fit neatly into the hole from which a modicum of heat warmed her hand.

She nudged three logs into place and watched with satisfaction as they settled down in the coals and took residence there.

The clean pan was placed on what she hoped would be the hottest spot on the stove, and she turned to the coffeepot, pumping water into it, then rinsing it thoroughly before she scrubbed at it with her rag. For this task, she added a bit of soap, found beneath the sink on a chipped saucer.

After a good washing she decided it was as clean as it was going to get, and filled it with water from the pump. At least the man had a good supply of what appeared to be clean water. That was a relief. She wouldn't have to carry buckets from a well into the house.

Back in the pantry, she found a metal can holding coffee grounds, from which she poured a generous portion into the coffeepot. And then, just for good measure, she filled the palm of her hand with more dark grounds and allowed the contents to float on the surface of the water. The pot would have to share the hot spot on the stove, she decided. She would wait for a few minutes before she cut the meat to put in the skillet, then cook the eggs last.

Recalling the cook's generous use of butter in her skillet, Jennifer searched for a covered dish on the kitchen cabinet and lifted the lid. To her relief, a full round of butter met her gaze. She found a knife in the dresser drawer and sliced off a hunk for her frying pan.

Within ten minutes the coffeepot was bubbling away and she opened the can of meat, slicing it into thick layers in the bottom of the skillet. Placing it on the stove, she watched as it sizzled and sent forth an appetizing scent.

Plying a utensil that appeared to be a pancake turner, she browned the meat on both sides and then watched in dismay as it flaked from neat slices to a mishmash of beef scraps.

This was definitely not what she had planned, but there was

no use in fretting about it, she thought. All she'd promised was food, not a gourmet feast, and food was exactly what he was going to get. Eggs and beef, mixed together, with perhaps a slice of bread alongside, if she could find a stray loaf in the kitchen.

A covered plate contained held a partial loaf and she sliced it into uneven wedges, hoping Lucas wouldn't care that his meal was not neat and tidy. The cook at home had always said that men were more interested in quantity than quality, and Jennifer was beginning to understand the basis of that statement.

She broke the four eggs into the skillet and watched as they mixed readily with the meat. Sort of like hash, she decided, turning them in a haphazard manner, three of the four yolks breaking as she plopped them atop the simmering meat.

She'd found two clean plates in the cabinet and searched out an assortment of knives and forks in a drawer. By the time Lucas arrived at the back door, a bucket of milk in one hand, a pan of eggs in the other, she was ready for him.

He placed the milk pail in a corner, the eggs in the pantry, and headed for the sink. Water cascaded over his hands from the pump and he used the soap, much to his credit.

She poured coffee from the pot into a cup for him, noting the dark grounds that floated on the surface but intent on ignoring them. Not so Lucas O'Reilly.

"Didn't you pour in a cup of cold water to settle the grounds?" he asked, pointing to the floating bits that emphasized her failings.

"I didn't know you were supposed to," she said stiffly, ladling out a portion of her meal onto his plate.

He looked down at it and frowned. "What's this supposed to be?"

"Supper," she told him, daring him with a stern look to make any more inappropriate remarks. "Eat it before you complain."

Spreading butter over his hunk of bread, he did not call her attention to the odd-shaped slice, only placing it on the side of his plate and then picking up his fork.

"Aren't you going to say grace first?" she asked, eyeing his laden fork as he aimed it toward his mouth.

"Grace," he muttered. "What are you? One of those missionary women, wanting me to mumble words over my food?"

"No, only a churchgoing wife, sir," she said. "And if you won't spare a moment to be thankful for your food, I'll do it for you." She bent her head and murmured words that somehow seemed insincere, even to her own ears.

"I haven't found much so far to be thankful for," he said, chewing as he spoke. Picking up his coffee cup, he sipped the thick brew and sputtered the contents of his mouth onto his plate. "What the hell did you do to the coffee?" he shouted. "It tastes like you used the whole damn crock of it for one pot."

"I put in a handful," she responded, holding her cupped palm to demonstrate her method.

"Your hand isn't big enough to hold the amount of coffee you used," he argued. Reaching for it, he uncurled her fingers and examined her palm, as if some hidden message might be there for his interpretation. "Are you sure you only used one handful?"

"I think so," she said, "but now that you mention it, I'm not entirely sure. I may have added a bit more." *May have?* She knew very well what she'd done and made a mental note to measure more accurately come morning.

"This isn't fit to drink," he said, frowning at her. "Pour some more water into the pot and let it simmer for a while."

"I told you I wasn't much of a cook," she said, even as she rose to do as he'd asked. Asked? *Ordered* might be more to the point, she thought, wondering if she should protest his high-handedness. She thought better of it as she looked over her shoulder at his grimace.

"I believe you now," he told her, lifting his fork again to his lips, valiant in his effort to eat her offering of food.

"It's not bad-tasting," she ventured, sitting again to finish her own meal.

"Well, it sure as hell isn't what I'd call a meal fit to eat," he said. "Surely you could have found something else to do with this meat. Maybe make some gravy and put it on a slice of bread?"

"Gravy?" she asked, frantically searching her mind for a vague memory of flour and water being stirred together and dumped into the drippings from a roast.

"You do know what gravy is, don't you?" he asked, his sarcasm unmistakable now.

She rose from the table and lifted her plate, carrying it to the sink, where she added it to the heaping stack of dishes he'd gathered up over the past days. "Actually," she said in a soft voice, "I was wondering if you had any inkling what clean dishes look like." She set aside the scrub rag she'd used on the skillet in favor of a clean dish towel she found in the kitchen drawer.

She sorted the dishes, rinsed them and then stacked them in the dishpan, drizzling a form of liquid soap she found in a quart jar beneath the sink over the whole mess. Using a fairly clean saucepan, she scooped warm water from the reservoir at the side of the cookstove and dumped it over the dishes, then returned for more.

"Why use a towel when a dish rag will do the job better?" he asked.

"If you want to wash these dishes, you may use anything you like to get the job done," she told him. "But if you'd like me to handle it, I'd suggest you leave well enough alone."

"That's exactly why I married you," he answered, obviously intent on getting her dander up.

It worked. She held the sopping wet towel in one hand and faced him, her heart pounding, her breath coming in short gasps. The towel flew across the kitchen to where he sat, water scattering hither and yon as it headed toward him. Her aim was accurate, he'd give her that much, for the towel hit him squarely in the face, the soap she'd poured into the dishpan burning his eyes, the warm water wetting the front of his shirt in seconds.

He stared at her in disbelief. Women were supposed to be well-mannered, biddable creatures; wives especially, he'd assumed. If Jennifer thought her actions came under the heading of obeying her husband, she was sadly mistaken. And, after all, the woman *had* promised to obey. He recalled her choking out the word, signifying her distaste for the vow she'd been forced to make.

And now, she'd insulted him. Ignored his needs as a husband and failed as a cook. Not to mention the fact that she made terrible coffee.

"Where on earth did you come from?" he asked. "You're not a normal woman, Jennifer."

"I'm as normal as they get," she answered, her eyes just a bit haunted, as if she rued the actions she'd indulged in.

"No, you're not," he said, disagreeing with her on all levels. "I sent for a wife, a woman who would cook and clean and mend my clothes. A woman to warm my bed and bear my children. Thus far, you've failed miserably to come up to my expectations."

"And what about *my* expectations?" she asked, tears filling her eyes, even as she lifted the front of his mother's apron to wipe them from his sight.

"Women aren't supposed to have any. Women are made to be wives and mothers, serving their families and doing all the womanly things that are assigned to them."

"You are an *idiot,* Lucas O'Reilly," she shrieked. "A full-fledged *jackass,* if ever I saw one." Her cheeks reddened as she spoke.

"Well, you're a spoiled, selfish child," he sputtered. "And you know what I told you about acting like a child."

"Don't lay one hand on me," she said, backing against the sink.

He rose and approached her, and she turned aside, primed to run from the kitchen. Losing her balance, she reached out and her hand touched the top of the stove. The odor of burning flesh rose from her fingers and she held her palm against her breasts, tears flowing down her cheeks.

"Let me see," Lucas said, ashamed now that he'd caused her to be hurt. "I never meant for you to burn yourself, Jen. Let me look at it."

She shook her head and he took charge, knowing that she was hurting, and her actions were those of a woman frightened by the pain that had almost brought her to her knees.

Seating her on a kitchen chair, he knelt in front of her and held her hand in his, blowing on the skin that was already blistered and puffy. "I'll get some cold water. It should help with the burning," he told her. "And then I'll get out my mother's home remedy kit. She had stuff in there for any sort of injury. I'm sure there's something for a burn."

"Butter," Jennifer croaked. "Spread butter on it."

"No, I don't think so," he told her. "I seem to remember Ma saying that you can get infection that way, no matter that it's an old remedy." He stood and found the clean saucepan she'd used to dip water and filled it half full from the pump. From deep in the ground, the water poured out in a stream that felt like ice to his hands.

To her damaged skin it would surely be almost intolerable, but it would take the burning away, stop the damage to her flesh before it went any deeper. He placed the pan on the table and lifted her hand, lowering it into the water. She stifled a sob and he knelt in front of her again.

"Leave it in the water, Jennifer. I know it hurts, but it'll ease the pain. Now, promise me," he coaxed, and was rewarded by a quick nod.

He brought the box holding his mother's salves and potions to the table and opened it wide, allowing Jennifer to look within. "I think this stuff is what she used," he muttered, lifting a jar from the neat collection. Writing on the label proclaimed it a "burn salve" and he opened it, revealing a thick, brown, pungent ointment that gave promise of being the proper cure.

He remembered having the stuff applied to his leg once when he'd tarried too long, burning the trash and playing with a stick that glowed with an intense heat. Heat he'd somehow transferred to his own leg by accident. His cries of pain had brought his mother running, and she'd calmly sat him on the porch and dressed his leg with this same potion, covering it with a thin layer of fabric torn from an old sheet.

Now he addressed the wound in front of him, smearing the ripe-smelling salve on Jennifer's hand carefully, mindful of the blisters, not wanting to break them. A neat roll of bandage from his mother's collection came into play as he tore off a strip and folded it, pressing it against her palm, then completed the task by tying strips of the white fabric carefully across her hand.

"Thank you," Jennifer told him, her voice shaking, her eyes still showing evidence of tears. "I didn't mean to be so clumsy. My father would have said it was because I don't think before I sail into action."

"You were angry," Luc told her. "And with good reason. I'm sorrier for that than you'll ever know. It was all my fault, sweetheart."

"Don't call me that," she whispered. "I'm not your sweetheart."

"Ah, but you will be," he said, correcting her assumption. "You'll be my sweetheart and my wife one day. Just not right now."

"You won't—" She waved her hand in the general direction of the hallway, where the wide staircase rose to the second floor.

"No, I won't," he told her, the words sour in his mouth. He'd just promised her that she was safe, that he'd leave her in her virgin state. And as he'd told her earlier, he always kept his word. "But I will help you get undressed and into bed. After I've done up these dishes."

So it was that Jennifer had what he was sure was the distinct pleasure of watching as her husband of less than a day washed a sinkful of dishes and stacked them to dry on the sink board. He caught her smug look with a quick glance in her direction and turned away, his grin hidden from her. The little fiend was enjoying this.

But then, so was he. The anticipation surging through him as he considered removing her clothing and tucking her beneath the sheet drove him to complete his task, so that she wouldn't have the chance to gloat over a panful of dirty dishes.

HE WAS GOING to undress her. It was her gut instinct that he'd drag it out, enjoy the blushes she was certain to wear, and no doubt inspect every inch of skin he revealed.

She was absolutely right, and for once in her life, she rued the fact that it was so. His fingers released buttons with ease and he slid her clothing from her in a ceremony of sorts. When she was garbed only in a petticoat and vest, plus the soft, thin chemise she wore next to her skin, he halted, his fingers slowing as he looked his fill.

"You're beautiful," he told her, his hands careful as he undid the strings of her petticoat and allowed it to fall to the floor around her feet. "Now sit down and I'll strip off your stockings."

"I can do that," she protested.

"No." He shook his head. "I may not get much loving from you tonight, but I intend to enjoy what little bit of satisfaction I'm being allowed during this process of taking off your clothing."

Kneeling in front of her, he lowered her garters and stockings, then placed them in her shoes. "Stand up," he told her, and if his voice sounded choked, she barely noticed, so intent was she on keeping her shift pulled down over her thighs.

He lifted her vest over her head, careful to slip her bandaged hand free without allowing the fabric to touch it.

"Get my nightgown," she whispered, hoping he would respond as should a gentleman, even though he had none of the characteristics of one. None but the fact that he'd dressed her hand and done the dishes, and now was doing his best to ready her for bed.

And why she should be thankful for that was a question she could not answer. Only that the man was showing a side of himself she'd thought not to have existed. Kindness came easily to him, it seemed, for he extracted her nightgown from the depths of her valise, careful not to disarrange her clothing, and then came back to her.

"Put it over my head, please," she said, holding up her arms.

"You're going to sleep with that thing on?" he asked, pointing at her chemise.

"Yes, I am. Now help me get my gown on."

"No." His single word of reply was harsh and he shook his head as if to emphasize his stand on this matter. "I'll close my eyes while we get that thing off of you and I won't look while you get your nightgown tucked in place, but that's as far as I go, sweetheart."

There was no choice, it seemed, for she'd found already that Lucas meant each word that passed his lips. "All right." Her acquiescence was reluctant, but it seemed he was satisfied with it.

His eyes closed and she settled her gaze there, lest he cheat and open them momentarily. His hands groped for her and he lifted the chemise over her head, once more careful to guard her hand against additional harm. How he could be so handy in the dark was beyond her, but she blest the fact that he seemed to have no trouble with putting the nightgown over her head and pulling it down into place.

"Thank you," she told him, relieved that the ordeal was behind her and she'd been unseen by those blue eyes.

"You're welcome," he intoned, and hid his smile. Peering through his lashes was not a satisfactory method, but he'd managed to catch more than a glimpse of pleasing curves. She was slender almost to the point of thinness, as he'd told her earlier, but her legs were rounded and well-formed, her hips narrow but shapely, and though he had only seen the front view, it was enough to keep him happy for the rest of the night.

Well, maybe not happy, but at least hopeful of a second viewing in the morning when he helped her put her clothing on. For now, he'd crawl in behind her and enjoy the proximity of a woman's warmth, with the pure satisfaction of knowing that this woman was his wife and would one day turn to him with passion lighting her gaze.

CHAPTER FOUR

SOMEHOW she'd managed to locate an all-enveloping robe and get herself into it by the time Luc awakened. He watched her as she reached thoughtlessly to turn the knob on the bedroom door, and heard her soft cry of pain.

"Stand still, Jennifer. I'll get the door," he said, swinging his feet to the floor.

"I can do it," she retorted, using her other hand to awkwardly twist the knob. The woman was not left-handed, he decided. And burning her right hand had damaged her independence, no matter how capable she might consider herself to be.

He'd stripped to his drawers last night and now they outlined, only too well, the shape of his early morning problem. So used to his inability to do anything about it, he ignored the pulsing of his erection and approached the door and the woman who stood in front of it, her gaze glued to his groin.

"Don't come any closer," she whispered. Had she not been trembling, he might have laughed and ignored her words. As it was, he felt a pang of regret that he'd so frightened her to this point and, after less than twenty-four hours, become a brute in her sight.

"I'm only going to open the door for you," he murmured, not halting his advance but slowing his steps, giving her time to move aside. Small, bare feet peeked from beneath the hemline of her robe, making her appear vulnerable and, somehow, almost naked.

"Thank you." It was a whisper, an automatic response from a well-brought-up young lady, and he smiled. The woman had little to be thankful for, as far as he could see.

Her independence had been shattered, her virtue violated—though not in the sense he'd have preferred—and she was in pain due to his impetuous behavior. He'd riled her to the point of total frustration, causing her to lose her balance and burn her hand, and now he loomed over her like her worst nightmare. And still she thanked him.

Guilt flooded him, even though he was still aching to clutch her against himself and spend his lust on her slender body. Jennifer was no more ready to be swept off her feet, and into his bed, than she was to fly from the barn roof. Her fear was palpable, her pain obvious and unless he missed his guess, she was about five seconds from dissolving into tears.

"I'm sorry," he muttered, standing in front of her, feeling like the worst sort of bully. "Just let me help you, sweetheart."

She blanched. There was no other word for it. A scattering of freckles stood out in bold relief, peppering her cheeks. He hadn't noticed them before, he mused, probably because she'd spent yesterday in a perpetual state of anger, her face flushed with emotion.

He turned the knob and opened the door wide, allowing her to slip across the threshold with haste, her sidelong glance telegraphing her fear that he might lay a hand on her. No chance of that. He'd already decided to tuck his lust away for another day and try to make amends for his blundering.

He couldn't follow her down the stairs until he was dressed, so he turned from her retreating back to where his clothing was scattered around the bedroom. A stifled yelp of pain from the staircase caught his attention and he bellowed out a question in her direction.

"Are you all right? What'd you do?" He danced on one foot, working at the toes that were caught inside the denim trouser leg. "Were you—tryin' to grab hold…" He punched the other leg into his trousers, buttoned them hastily as he headed for the hallway and then skidded to a stop. "You did, didn't you? You grabbed hold of the banister."

She was perched on the second step from the top, her upper body swaying from side to side as she nursed the pain of burning flesh.

"Damn." He uttered the word beneath his breath, but apparently loud enough for her to hear the single, angry syllable, for she turned to peer at him over her shoulder.

"I wish you wouldn't use vile language in my presence. You did the same thing yesterday, but I want you to know I won't stand for it, Lucas."

He made his way to where she sat, planting his behind on the step above her. With an easy movement, he picked her up and swung her into his lap. She stiffened and jerked from his touch. The movement seemed to throw her off balance, raising the very real possibility that she would fall down the stairs. He tightened his grip and she curled against him as though he were a shelter against harm.

He cuddled her close, his arms wrapped around her, his head bent over hers. "I'm sorry if my language upsets you," he said. "But I wasn't angry with you, sweetheart. Only myself."

She trembled and tears fell, dampening his shirt as she turned to press her face against his chest. "I don't usually cry so often," she managed to whisper between sobs. "In fact, I never cry. At least, I haven't for a long time—up until I met you, in fact." Her voice was accusing. "When I was a little girl, my mother told me I should practice self-control. She said tears would make my nose run and my eyes swell, and everyone would think I was ugly."

He squeezed her against himself and chuckled, unable to believe that anyone in his right mind would ever think this female ugly. She was blessed with fine features, dark, curling hair and blue eyes that stirred him to a fever pitch.

"I don't care if your nose runs," he said, leaning forward as he pulled a clean handkerchief from his back pocket. "And I think your eyes are beautiful, even when you cry."

She laughed, snatching the cloth from his hand and wiping the tears beneath her eyes. "I know better than that," she told him. "A woman is definitely at a disadvantage when she's blubbering and dripping all over the place."

He shook his head. "I fear your mother was wrong, for you have a distinct hold over me, sweetheart. In fact, you could pretty much have whatever you'd like. At least, whatever I'm capable of giving you."

"Does that include a ticket on the next eastbound stage?" she asked with a hopeful smile.

"Now, you know better than that," he said. "I told you to choose something I'm capable of giving you. And sending you away is beyond my ability. I'm just beginning to enjoy having you here."

"You're enjoying *this?*" she asked, including her position on his lap and the damage to her right hand in an all-encompassing gesture.

"I sure am, honey," he murmured. "Especially the part that

includes having my arms around you." He squeezed and then released her. "If you want to head downstairs, you can, but let me lend a hand, will you?"

She rose—a precarious maneuver, given her position—and nodded her acceptance of his terms. He gripped her arm with one hand, the other circling her, seeking out the narrowing of her waist.

They descended the stairs and she pulled from him, her footsteps taking her into the kitchen. At least it was neat and tidy, she thought with satisfaction. A far cry from the chaos she'd walked into yesterday. She reached for the handle protruding from a burner, her left hand awkward at the task, and then heard a muffled sound from Lucas.

"Let me do that," he said. "Don't try to manage the stove by yourself." She stepped back and he lifted the round, iron cover to expose the banked fire from the day before. Adding wood, he accomplished the feat of warming the kitchen in mere minutes.

Jennifer bent to lift the iron skillet from the oven and settled the heavy pan on the burner. "Do you want bacon?" she asked. "Or don't you have any?"

"Yeah, I've got bacon, but you can't slice it by yourself."

Anger welled in her anew, that her efforts to provide him with meals of a sort would be hampered for days to come by her injury.

"Probably just as well. I'm not a good cook, as you found out yesterday."

"Anyone can fry bacon," he said, apparently in an attempt to comfort her.

"Don't count on it," she muttered.

Ignoring her words, he went to the pantry and brought out

a large slab of bacon, wrapped in netting. Unwrapping it, he sliced it with quick slashes of a long knife.

Jennifer placed the slices in the skillet and watched as they began to sizzle and curl around the edges. Lucas placed a fork from the drawer in her hand and she nodded a silent thank-you in his direction as she pushed and prodded the meat, watching it brown.

"I've decided to get you some help," Lucas said.

"Whatever for?" she asked, unwilling that another woman should be privy to her carelessness, and her absolute ignorance of the basics of keeping house.

"I'd think that would be pretty obvious," he said, an air of arrogance spoiling his recent affability. "You're going to need some help getting settled in here, at least until your burns heal."

She thought about the idea of another woman within these walls, wondering for a moment if Lucas would be so persistent in his pursuit of her, should he have an audience. The notion that she might learn from a competent female just how to go about being a wife took root. That fact alone surprised her and she turned to Lucas, blurting out her thoughts before she considered what their import might be.

"If seems to me if you want me to be any sort of a wife, you'd better do something about my total ignorance, Lucas. Getting me a teacher of sorts might be the best idea. Not that I'm altogether pleased with the idea of cleaning up after you." She sucked her bottom lip between her teeth and considered her choices.

"I don't suppose you'll reconsider and ship me off, will you?" The plea in her voice riled her. She'd never in her life begged for anything, unwilling to make herself appear inadequate.

"You got that right," he said, emphasizing each word. "I

married you in good faith and I'm not about to look like a total failure at the marriage game in front of the whole da—" He hesitated and then continued. "In front of the whole *blamed* town. We're married, Jennifer, and we're gonna stay that way. No matter how little you know about cooking and cleaning and such, you're stuck with me."

"Well, isn't that a lovely way to start this marriage?" she asked. She didn't expect an answer, for she'd merely stated a fact.

"Don't be sassy with me," he warned her. "I'm about to do you a big favor and ride into town for a woman to lend a hand here."

She glared at him and then recoiled as the bacon sizzled and popped, spitting a bubble of grease against her cheek. She wiped at it with the back of her hand and Lucas took the fork from her.

"Don't you have chores to do?" she asked. "Give me back the fork."

"I'm frying bacon right now," he said. "Just bring a couple of plates from the dresser and find silverware in the drawer. I'll cook breakfast. This one time only," he said, his voice deepening as he spoke the warning.

This one time only. She cast him a dark glance at the words of warning. "I didn't ask you to cook," she reminded him. "Just give me back the fork and break some eggs into a bowl if you want to be useful."

He seemed to consider that idea for a moment and then handed her the utensil. He brushed the spot on her cheek that had received the drop of hot grease just moments before. "I could kiss it and make it better," he offered, an his expression softening as he bent to her.

"No, thanks. I'll be just fine."

He went to the pantry and returned with eggs clutched in his hand. How he could hold four eggs in one hand... The thought skipped through her mind and she watched as he found a bowl and cracked the eggs, one by one, into its depths. His hands were large, true, but not pudgy, as were some she'd seen. Long and lean were the words that came to her mind.

Long and lean all over, she decided, noting his stance, the narrow waist and hips, the frame that towered over her. He was taller than most men, wider through the shoulders than anyone else she'd ever seen, and yet there was about him a graceful but decidedly masculine aura. His hands were scarred but clean, the skin on his fingers calloused but well cared for. The memory of those hands touching her with care as he'd dressed her burns glowed in her mind like a well-tended fire, and she shivered as she recalled those same hands exploring her body, brushing over her breasts and then the warmth of him settling at her backside.

She felt a hot blush climb her cheeks as she thought of the previous day and the intimacies he'd taken with her. And yet, he was her husband and had a legal right to her, could claim her body as his own if he so pleased.

Having a stranger take up residence in the house wouldn't call a halt to his planned seduction of her. Lucas O'Reilly was too bold, too arrogant, to be deterred by the presence of another, should he decide the time was ripe to claim his bride.

"What's wrong?" he asked, his gaze intent on her face, the hot cheeks that gave away her doubts and fears.

"Nothing," she said, lying through her teeth. "I was just wondering if you'd slice some bread while you've got the knife out and handy."

He ran the back of his hand over her cheek. "You're all hot and bothered, sweetheart," he said. "What were you thinking?"

"Nothing," she repeated, desperate for him to look aside, to allow her a moment in which to rearrange her thoughts and drag her mind from its wanderings. She turned back to the bacon, relieved that it seemed to be uncurling a bit and turning crispy. "Get me a plate for this, would you?" she asked, and reached for the one he offered.

The eggs were at hand, the bowl easy to hold and tilt over the skillet. She stepped back as the hot grease spattered and the eggs began to cook.

"I'll dish those up," Lucas offered after a few moments, lifting a slotted spoon from the kitchen dresser and approaching. "Let me turn them over first."

In a deft movement he'd turned the eggs, one at a time, then after a few seconds he lifted them to the plate she held. "Scrape a couple onto the other plate for yourself," he told her. "And some of the bacon, too."

She did as he asked and sat. He shoved the skillet to the back of the stove, sliced off two thick pieces of bread and then sat across from her. After lifting the lid from the butter dish, he pushed it nearer her plate. "You want me to spread that for you?" he asked, motioning at her bread.

"No," she said. "I can do it." And then she closed her eyes and lowered her head, whispering a quick word of blessing on the food, feeling more thankful today than she had yesterday.

"Did you bless mine, too?" he asked, and she thought she detected more than a smidgen of mockery in his words.

"Yes, much as I was hoping you'd choke on it, I still asked for it to be consecrated on its way down your gullet."

He laughed, a genuine, rich, rolling sound that pleased her. She'd given him a moment of pleasure, and found that fact to be more palatable than the meal facing her.

"You're a real piece of work, Jennifer," he said as he settled back in his chair and gave her a thorough, unsettling glimpse of his interest in her person. His gaze skimmed her robe, seeming to peel away the fabric from her body, and she felt the heat of her own response.

Then he picked up his fork and set to with gusto, cleaning his plate in moments, wiping up the remnants of egg yolk with his bread. He'd done a credible job of slicing it, she noted, much better than she'd done yesterday.

He stood, gathered up his plate and utensils and placed them in the dishpan. "Don't bother trying to wash these," he told her. "I'm going to hitch the team. I'll be back in no time and maybe you'll have some help." He halted by the door. "If I can't talk Ida Bronson into coming back with me, I'll do the dishes myself."

"Mrs. Bronson?" she parroted. "The lady who served as witness?"

"Yeah," he said, stuffing his hat atop his head. "She's a widow lady who hires out to help sometimes when one of the ladies has a baby or needs a hand around the house."

And if anyone ever needed a hand around the house, it was the newly wed Mrs. Lucas O'Reilly. At least that was the message his eyes telegraphed in her direction before he headed out the back door.

CONTRARY TO HIS DOUBTS, he'd been successful in his quest. Mrs. Bronson was pleased, it seemed, to earn a bit of money for her efforts. She seemed shaken when Lucas told her of Jennifer's burns and without a moment's hesitation packed a small bag, tucking in a jar of some sort of salve, before she put herself at his disposal.

Now the lady stood in the middle of his kitchen and took a quick survey. "I'd say your poor little missus needs more than just a hand at this," she said, directing a dark look at Lucas. "I doubt those windows have been washed in a month of Sundays, nor the floor, either, come to think of it." She went to the sink, where Jennifer had obviously done her best to wash up the breakfast dishes and had left them to dry on the sink board.

"You've even made the poor girl do dishes, burned hand and all."

"I told her not to touch them," he said, his defenses up.

Her reply was a loud *humph* and Lucas was tempted to laugh out loud at the sound. The lady obviously didn't believe a word he said, but so long as she pitched in and gave Jennifer a hand, he didn't care one lick about her opinion of him. He'd thought on occasion that being the mayor of this town didn't guarantee a whole lot of respect from some of the folk here, and Ida Bronson seemed not to be any exception.

"Where's that little girl?" Mrs. Bronson asked, eyeing the pantry door as if he might have hidden his bride in the depths of that narrow space.

"Probably gone back upstairs," Lucas ventured. "I'll go take a look."

He left the widow lady in his kitchen and climbed the stairs. Jennifer was, indeed, in their bedroom, half-clothed, intent on donning her petticoat. Somehow she'd managed to put her vest and drawers in place, and even a blind man could make out the assortment of curves beneath those two pieces of apparel.

Lucas was not blind. Far from it, in fact, and he halted in the doorway, enjoying the view in front of his eyes.

Jennifer looked up at him, flushed and frustrated. "Come and tie this thing, will you?" she asked, holding the tapes in one hand as she attempted to hold her petticoat in place with the other. Her bandages hampered her and she was obviously ready to cry again, spurring him into action.

"Just hang on, sweetheart," he said. "Let me help." His big fingers felt awkward. Strange, he thought, that it was simpler to get a woman out of her clothes than it was to put her back into them. Setting that image aside as unworthy of him as a new husband, he lifted her dress over her head and buttoned her into it.

"Shoes and stockings?" he asked, and was given a look almost guaranteed to sear paint from the wall.

"I'll wear my slippers," she said, fumbling with one hand in her valise. The slippers appeared with little effort expended on her part and she dropped them to the floor, then slid her feet into them.

"Your help is waiting in the kitchen," Lucas told her. "Mrs. Bronson came back with me, and she's all set to put things to rights. Starting with my dirty windows and floors."

"It's not surprising," Jennifer said. "And from there, she'll no doubt locate a dust cloth and start on the furniture."

"Just don't let her forget to make dinner before she gets out of the kitchen," Lucas said, deciding to ignore Jennifer's remark about dust. The reason that women got all het up about a little fuzz on the furnishings was beyond his understanding. His mother had been the same way, back when he was a child and thought that writing his name on a steamy window was great fun.

She'd quickly disabused him of that notion and handed him a vinegar dampened cloth to clean the whole set of panes, and he'd learned his lesson: women had funny notions when it came to what went on in the house. Nothing had changed his mind on that subject since, even though his mother had tried.

He thought of the woman who'd borne him, recalling her soft voice, her rough hands that had spread warm turpentine on his chest when he had a cold, that had comforted him when he'd fallen and scraped a knee or cut a finger with his pocketknife.

She was dead and gone, leaving him only a few inanimate objects as a legacy—the apron he'd hung in silent reminder of the only woman who'd loved him, the box of home remedies he'd used for Jennifer's benefit only yesterday and the chest in the attic, holding mementoes of her past. Those long years when she'd worked hard at being a wife and mother had culminated with her dying on a spring morning, long after her only son had left home. He hadn't even made it back in time for her funeral.

"Are you all right?" This time Jennifer asked him the question and he blinked and nodded.

"Yes, I'm fine. Just thinking of something."

"It must not have been a happy memory," she ventured. "You looked almost…almost sad."

He cleared his throat. "I suppose I was, there, for a minute."

"Shall we go down and see Mrs. Bronson now?"

"You gonna do something with your hair first?" He wanted to know. "I like it that way, but it's not as neat as you had it when you got here."

"Maybe Mrs. Bronson will braid it for me," she said, lifting her left hand to brush loose strands from her face. It was a futile gesture, for the wave settled back into place in mere seconds. Snatching up a brush and a short length of ribbon from a small, metal box she'd taken from her valise, she faced him expectantly.

"I'm ready."

And she was, as bright-eyed as the bluebirds that sat on the fence posts and seemed to take over ownership of the yard. Or maybe she was more like the chickadees, he decided, small and sassy, yet neat as a pin, even with her hair down and bare feet stuck into her slippers.

"HELLO THERE, MISSY," Mrs. Bronson said as they found her sorting through the pantry shelves. The jars and cans seemed to be in a different order, Jennifer thought, and indeed they were. Lined up by content, they made the pantry look like a mirror image of the room just off her mother's kitchen. Although not as complete a store of food as her mother's cook kept on hand, Lucas's supplies were adequate for their use.

"I see you've got you a lard barrel," Mrs. Bronson said to her employer. Lucas stood in the kitchen, looking past Jennifer at the small, stout lady who had set about putting his kitchen in order.

"It's full of pork," he said. "From the last pig I butchered, in November." And then he corrected himself. "Well, not full exactly, but there's enough meat in there to feed us for some time to come."

"Meat in a barrel of lard?" Jennifer asked. "I've never heard of such a thing."

"Well, you have now," Lucas told her. "How do you suppose we manage to keep meat without it spoiling?"

"I suppose that's never been at the top of my list of things to worry about."

He frowned. "Well, you'd better start thinking a little more about such things. If you're planning on being a good wife, you'll need to take hold and work at it."

"Now, don't be giving the girl a hard time." Mrs. Bronson came to Jennifer's defense. "She's only gotten her feet wet, so to speak, and you're pouncing on her and expecting her to be up to snuff in one day. It doesn't work thataway, Lucas O'Reilly." She smiled at Jennifer. "Here, let me fix your hair," she said, reaching for the brush and bit of ribbon. Lucas's forehead creased in a frown and his lips tightened as he watched Ida Bronson set to work.

"I can see I'll be battling the pair of you," he said finally. "Well, just go ahead and do as you please while I take care of things out in the barn."

His blue eyes flashed as he settled his gaze on Jennifer, whose hair was now all braided and ribboned. "I suspect you will anyway," he said, and then he grinned, in a quick reversal that stunned her. "It's gonna be interesting," he said, "this living with two women, both of you ready to take my head off if I make a misstep."

"I already told him he was a jackass and I doubt I'll be changing my mind anytime soon," Jennifer said as the screen door slammed behind her husband. In the pantry, Mrs. Bronson only laughed beneath her breath and continued to sort out the shelves.

"What are planning on fixing for supper, girl?" she asked, scooping up two jars from the bottom shelf of canned good. "And where do you suppose that man got these vegetables, all nicely put in Mason jars. I'll warrant you he didn't can up the garden himself."

"Probably smiled at some pretty lady and persuaded her to feed him."

Ida sniffed and passed through into the kitchen. "Can't say that I've ever heard a word of gossip about the boy, now that

I think of it. 'Course, that doesn't mean he hadn't done any wandering around in someone's rose garden on a dark night."

She set the jars on the table and returning to the pantry. "How about some fried pork chops?" she asked. "Unless you have something else in mind?"

"How about ground glass?" Jennifer suggested, then regretted the words as Mrs. Bronson shook her head.

"Don't be nasty about the man, girl. He's just a man, don't forget. And that part of the population don't always use their heads. Except for a hatrack, my momma used to say."

"Well, pork chops sound fine to me," Jennifer told her. "I'd better let you in on a little secret, though. I don't know what to do with them, although I suspect I can put them in the skillet and cook them awhile."

"Never mind, child. I'll show you how to bread them and bake 'em in the oven. Makes a real tasty meal like that, and we can peel some potatoes and fix them up with milk and flour and such. Your man won't know what to say when he finds out what a good cook you turned out to be."

"I won't lie to him," Jennifer said. "He knows better, especially after yesterday. I broke three out of four yolks when I fried the eggs and the meat I cooked with them crumbled up into a mess and got mixed up with the eggs and—"

Mrs. Bronson held up her hand. "Hush, now. I don't want to hear it. All good cooks break a few eggs now and then, and sometimes canned beef does thataway." She looked askance at Jennifer. "It was preserved beef you used? In a Mason *jar?*"

"No, out of a can. It said it was corned, whatever that means."

"Hmm. I'll bet that tasted interesting anyway, didn't it? Next time, stick to bacon, honey. Goes better with eggs, any day of the week."

"Lucas managed to cook eggs for breakfast without breaking the yolks," Jennifer admitted.

"He's probably had more practice than you," the widow lady said, and then nodded at Jennifer. "You'll do just fine, girl."

"Well, I'll do whatever you tell me," Jennifer said with a lump in her throat. "But I don't even know where the potatoes might be, let alone how to fix them." And wasn't that the truth? She was feeling more helpless and worthless by the minute, and cooking seemed to be an occupation for someone a whole lot more intelligent than she'd ever hoped to be.

"If he hasn't got any stashed in the cellar, then he's probably got some canned up by that friendly woman you were talking about a while ago," Ida said with a grin. "Why don't you go down and scout around, see what you can find?"

"Where's the cellar?" Jennifer asked. "At home, we had a door off the kitchen and a set of stairs going down. I haven't noticed any such thing here."

"Well, land sakes, girl," her mentor said with a laugh. "I just thought you knew that any respectable farmhouse has a fruit cellar. You go out back and look for a door lyin' on the ground, kinda at a slant. Just lift on the handle and you'll find a set of stairs."

Jennifer was doubtful, but managed to swallow her discomfort and go outside. There, just to the right of the back porch, was the slanted door. With relief, she pulled it open with a mighty effort, then made her way down the rough steps into a room under the house. It was cool and damp within, and she felt a tingle of fear climb her spine as she considered whether there might be mice or even snakes there. But not both, she thought, her good sense kicking in. Snakes were fond of eating mice. It was a fact she'd learned somewhere, sometime.

A set of shelves sagged against the wall, filled with food-stuffs that might prove to be worth investigating, Jennifer thought. In one corner of the room, a pile of dark, dirty lumps lay in a heap, looking much like potatoes. She stepped across the earthen floor to where they lay, bending so as not to bump her head on rafters overhead. She'd barely loaded up five or six good-size specimens when she heard Lucas's voice from the yard.

"Who the hell left the cellar door open?" he roared. And then with a solid bang, the door was dropped into place and Jennifer heard the sound of a latch closing. She hadn't noticed one when she opened it herself, but now she stood in the darkness and searched her mind.

If it indeed was locked from the outside, she was trapped. Lucas would probably be tempted to leave her here with the spongy potatoes and the dilapidated shelves that held jar after jar of canned goods and piles of carrots and onions.

"Lucas?" Her voice sounded as though she'd just recovered from laryngitis. She tried again. But the only answer she heard was the slamming of the screen door. The man had gone into the house and left her to fend for herself. And it was dark. Darker than midnight, as a matter of fact, and suddenly she wasn't at all certain that snakes *always* ate mice. And what if the snakes down here were poisonous?

At least Lucas wouldn't have to worry about getting rid of her. She'd accomplish that little matter all by herself and he'd find her in a lump on the dirt floor, covered with snake bites.

She shivered as she wondered how long it would take to die from snake bites, and how many times such a critter might bite her before he gave up and went looking for a mouse.

The light from outside wasn't worth talking about, but it

managed to penetrate through a crack next to the door, revealing part of the stairs, She went to where she could see a clear spot on the least dirty step. Her hand brushed at the area for just a moment and then she lifted it in disgust. What difference would a little dirt make when she was probably going to die anyway? But surely Lucas would find her soon.

Her fanny fit nicely on the step and she looked into the darkness. Her potatoes were lost, dropped when the door slammed shut, and she decided to leave them where they were, unless the snakes decided to wait a while before their dinner and she got hungry in the meantime. A raw potato wasn't much to write home about, but anything was better than nothing at all. And nothing at all was what she'd had on the last leg of her journey to this god-forsaken part of the country.

In less than five minutes she'd worked up to a good cry and had only begun to search for a handkerchief in her pocket when she heard Lucas's voice calling her name.

Even as she looked upward, the door was lifted and he stood above her, the sunshine lending him a golden aura, as if he were a heavenly being. And then he ruined his image with a droll reminder.

"You told me you never cry," he murmured, his gaze seeming to count the tears that fell to stain her dress.

"I don't usually. Only since I met you."

He was looking more and more like an avenging angel. It was a wonder he didn't carry a two-edged sword, she thought, for surely she'd read somewhere in the Bible that the angels were armed for battle. At least those who fought the forces of evil.

And Lucas was sure to think by now that she was a prime exhibit of those who might anger the angels themselves.

CHAPTER FIVE

"WHAT THE HELL do you think you're doing?"

Lucas took one step into the cellar and reached down for her, hauled her outside by one arm, and then proceeded to shake her as he might a wet towel before he hung it to dry on the clothesline. Although the chances of him having ever had anything to do with laundry were pretty sparse.

Her teeth clattered together and her arms felt bruised as his big hands clamped around them. Her hair flew around her head, the ribbon holding her braid together flying off. She felt dizzy and disoriented, her hands reaching for him as if seeking a hold to keep her erect.

But there was no chance of her falling to the ground, or back into the cellar hole, for his grip was firm and she felt herself drawn into his embrace. Her shoulders shook as she fought the sobs that welled up in her throat, and she trembled from head to foot.

Her tears would not be held at bay any longer, and she felt like a watering can being dumped in one spot. In moments, the front of her dress was damp. And then, as his hand held her head against his chest, she proceeded to leave huge, dark spots all over his shirt.

"It's a wonder you weren't left down there all day," he said sharply, his voice muffled as he pressed his lips against her hair.

"Ida knew where I was," she muttered, "and I would have been just fine if you hadn't taken it upon yourself to shut the door on me." She hiccupped once, then again, and he chuckled.

"It's not funny," she managed to say. "I could have been bitten by snakes or mice or whatever else is down in that miserable hole."

"Mice don't bite," he said, tightening his arms around her. "And the snakes, if there are any down there, are harmless."

"Easy for you to say," she whispered, rubbing the back of her hand against her nose, wishing desperately for a handkerchief.

As if he sensed her need, he handed her his, neatly folded. Not ironed, but clean, and she wasn't in any mood to argue the point. She leaned back from him and blew her nose, and then rubbed her eyes with her fists.

"Stop it now," Lucas said. "You're getting your face all red and splotchy. Just calm down, sweetheart."

She reared back and aimed a scornful look at him. "How can you call me that when you've just shaken the stuffings out of me and treated me like an idiot? It certainly wasn't my fault I got stuck down there, and I resent you acting like it was."

She caught her breath and opened her mouth again, only to find his lips pressing against hers, silencing her tirade. He knew how to kiss—but then, he'd probably had a lot of practice. There was no doubt in her mind about that fact. And his hands were firm around her, holding her safely against himself.

"Did you find her?" Mrs. Bronson called her query from inside the kitchen.

"I found her," Lucas said. "I've got her, ma'am."

Mrs. Bronson said no more, apparently satisfied with his reply and in seconds Jennifer could hear her singing to herself.

"You can let me go now." Jennifer managed to work herself from his grip and regain her balance, stepping away from him.

He caught her elbow. "Now, don't be falling back down those steps," Lucas warned her, pulling her away from the gaping hole.

She allowed his touch, aware that it was comforting, that she had been in dire need of rescue, and Lucas had only been upset because he was fearful of what might have happened to her. His next words underlined that.

"I was afraid you'd fallen down the steps and gotten hurt," he said. "I wouldn't have shut the door if I'd known you were there."

"I thought maybe you were trying to get rid of me," she told him, tilting her head, the better to see his face.

He grinned. "Not a chance, sweetheart. After last night, I'm planning on keeping you around for a very long time."

"Last night?" She searched her mind for his reasoning. "What happened last night that persuaded you to continue this farce we've managed to create?"

"We slept together," he said, with satisfaction, as if his fondest dreams had come true.

"And that was all we did," she stated. "*Slept* is the right word. At least, you did. I was awake half the night, suffering with my burned hand."

"Well, for a suffering woman, you sure did snore up a storm."

"I don't snore," she said, certain of her ground.

"Haven't you ever slept with another person?"

"No. Except my sister when I was very small."

"Maybe you didn't snore then," he suggested. "And you really don't snore too badly now, just a little hissing and then puffing when you let out your breath."

"Well, thanks a whole lot, Mr. O'Reilly," she said, wondering how much hissing and puffing she'd done during the night.

"I didn't mind one bit. I was so pleased to be snuggling up behind you, your snoring was the least of my worries. I just wrapped my arms around you and hugged you tight and enjoyed the company."

"I think you took advantage of me," she said, feeling at a loss and just a bit abused. "You had no business sleeping with me."

"I don't know why not," he said. "We're married, sweetheart. And married folks sleep together. And some of them actually do more than that."

She felt a flush travel from her throat, the heat washing her cheeks and causing her an enormous amount of confusion. She stammered as she did her best to refute his words.

"Well, y-y-you can j-jus…just forget that idea," she managed to spout. "I have no intention of performing any such acts with you, sir."

"And you think that's going to stop me?" he asked, his smile reminding her of a bobcat on the prowl, with herself as the prey.

"I don't know," she said. "I suppose I was hoping to see some small grain of human kindness in you. I think that's a lost cause, though."

"I'll give you a little time. And that's about as much kindness as you're gonna get outta me, sweetheart." He looked beyond her into the cellar and changed his tone of voice. "Now, tell me what you were looking for down there. I'll go and get it."

"Potatoes. For your supper."

"And if I go down, will you slam the door on me?" he asked, tilting an eyebrow at her, a grin curving his lips.

"I'm above such shenanigans," she announced. "I'm going into the house to help with supper. You can bring in the potatoes. And I hope the snakes bite you."

"I've got on boots and long trousers," he said. "Not much chance of that."

"Well, good for you." She stomped up the steps and across the porch, allowing the screen door to slam behind her.

"What'd you do? Get lost down there?" Ida asked cheerily. "Luc came in here lookin' like a thundercloud, frettin' and stewin' over you."

"Ha!" The single syllable burst from Jennifer's lips. "He was a long way from being worried. He hollered at me and gave me what-for, and the whole thing was his fault. He closed the doggone door on me and left me in the dark."

"Well, you're out now and no worse for wear." Ida's eyes were sharp as they examined Jennifer. "Where's the potatoes you went after, girl?"

"Lucas is bringing them. I'll peel them as soon as he finds his way back upstairs."

"I'll do it. Probably do a faster job than you, young'un. I've been peelin' potatoes for more years than I can count. Just keep an eye open and watch how we put this meal together. Luc says you need a few lessons in the house."

"He would. I didn't tell him—" She halted and began again. "Well, I suppose I did, at that."

"You s'pose you did what?"

"Told him I knew how to keep house and cook and so forth. But it wasn't my idea. The man who took my application embellished my talents a little bit." She frowned and sat on a chair. "Actually, he embellished a lot, Ida. I told him I was a failure at housework and my mother had never let me cook at home. We had a lady who lived in and did all that."

"What *did* you do?"

"I made my bed and set the table most nights for supper. Oh, and there was schoolwork to do up until a few years ago, when I graduated."

"You graduated?" Mrs. Bronson's eyes widened as she asked the question.

"Of course. All young ladies need an education. Mine only went as far as secondary school, since going on to university was out of the question. I guess I was lucky my parents let me stay in school as long as they did. A lot of my friends had to go to work."

"What did they work at?"

"Belle was an upstairs maid and Sissy was a nanny for the minister's children. Some of the others worked at restaurants or dressmaker's shops." She smiled, remembering. "They thought I was lucky to be able to stay in school."

"You were. I sure wish my girls could've spent that long with book-learnin' and figurin' their sums and such." Ida seemed pretty sure of her ground, Jennifer decided. Apparently the young ladies here didn't have much of a chance for higher education.

"Well, if I'd been able to go to Normal school, I could have been a teacher in two years," she said. "It was what I'd liked to have done, but it costs a lot of money."

"You could teach here with a high school diploma," Ida said. "Our teacher now is just a little bit of a thing, not more than eighteen, I suspect."

Lucas stepped in the door and propped one shoulder

against the frame. "You got a diploma?" he asked Jennifer. "Then how come you were so hard up for a husband that you had to apply at an agency to get one? I'd think a man would snatch you up, with that piece of paper in your hand. You could make a good living with that sort of education, I'd think."

"I wasn't hard up for a husband," she said, wishing she'd never heard of Wives Incorporated, operated by Mr. Horace Bloom. "I just wanted to get away from New York City and see some of the country."

"You sure did that," Lucas told her. "This is about the largest part of the country there is."

"Well, I haven't seen too much so far to recommend it. Some scruffy miners and a rutted road that goes nowhere."

"Those scruffy miners have made this town into a thriving community," Lucas told her. "We put together a town charter and elected officials and hired a sheriff. In fact, you're looking at the mayor of Thunder Canyon, right here in front of you. What more could anyone want in a town?"

"You're the mayor? Yes, well, I guess I did know that, but somehow it lacks the prestige I'd attached to it." She looked at him with pity, and he glared back. He'd never seen such a little priss. What had she called them? *Scruffy miners.* And here he'd shaved just last night, all for her benefit. It would be the last time he snagged a razor across his beard with her comfort in mind. Of course, given the way she was behaving, he'd probably have to fight his way into his own bed come nightfall.

She tilted her head and pursed her lips. "What more could anyone want?" she asked, repeating his earlier question. "How about a decent ladies' store, where they sell clothing and shoes that are up to date? Or maybe even a bakery with bread and rolls and pies in the counter? And how about a furniture store?"

"You can find pretty much anything you want in the general store," he told her. "That is, if your needs aren't too highfalutin'. Around here, we're used to makin' do and baking our own bread and making our own clothes."

"How many shirts have you sewn lately?" she asked him. "And if you're so smart, why do you have two buttons missing on the one you're wearing?"

"Why do you suppose I sent for you?" he asked. "Besides needing a woman to warm my bed."

"Lucas O'Reilly." Mrs. Bronson's voice was sharp as she spoke his name, her meaning obvious. "You ought to be ashamed of yourself. What a way to talk to your new bride. If I were Jennifer, I'd find a bed for myself upstairs and keep you out of it."

"That sounds like a good idea," Jennifer said. She tossed her head, her hair flying, free from the braid that had held it immobile earlier.

"Sound like my worst nightmare," Lucas told her. "I didn't marry you to let you go settling down in one of the other bedrooms. You'll sleep with me."

"We'll see," she said. She waved at him. "Put those potatoes down here on the table. Ida is going to peel them."

"Why don't *you?*" Lucas asked. "Seems like you ought to be able to do something other than cause a fuss around here today."

Mrs. Bronson took the potatoes from Lucas, put them in the sink and washed them beneath the pitcher pump. "I'll take care of these," she said, ignoring the argument that seemed to be the order of the day.

"Who's in charge of this *town* you founded?" Jennifer asked, speaking the word as if it were something she'd just scraped off her shoe.

"I already told you. I am," Lucas answered. "I'm the official head of things around here, and I've got five men on my town council. Together we run the place. Along with the sheriff."

"Well, it didn't strike me as being too well run, from what I saw of it."

"You didn't see much. Just the lobby of the hotel, the church and the back end of my team of horses when we left town."

"You're right there. I was hoping for a city with a newspaper and—"

"We have a newspaper," he said, cutting off her tirade. "And a community hall where we hold dances and have parties. In fact, you might be surprised at what all goes on in this town."

"Like what? Drinking and dancing till all hours of the night, not to mention those old men passing gossip back and forth every morning."

"All of that, too," Lucas said. "And more. Like church socials and weddings and quilting bees and all that sort of woman stuff."

"How many weddings have you attended?" Jennifer asked. "And where on earth did they find enough brides to go around?"

"Well now, that does present a problem sometimes, I'll grant you that," Lucas drawled, sitting on a kitchen chair and stretching his long legs across the floor. "Most of the women coming into town are from back East, about like you. But, I'll have to say that most of them didn't cheat on their applications, lying about their accomplishments before they made the trip."

"And what is that supposed to mean?"

He tilted an eyebrow at her. "You said you could cook and clean and sew. You lied."

"I didn't lie," she told him quietly. "The man who filled out the paperwork lied, and I didn't realize it until I saw a copy of the letter. And that was after he'd already mailed it to you. You and half a dozen other men who were looking for a wife."

"But I was the lucky son of a pup who got you," Lucas said, his tone firm.

"Lucky? Are you being sarcastic again?"

"Me?" he asked, faking astonishment. "You think *I'd* be sarcastic?"

"Maybe not. Mean and nasty suit you better. And vindictive and hateful, now that I think of it."

"Mean and hateful wouldn't have left you alone last night, lady. You'd have been a real, bona fide wife this morning if I were mean and nasty. And if you don't watch your step, I can fix that in a hurry."

"Lucas O'Reilly." Mrs. Bronson waved a saucepan at him, her eyes wide with shock. "Don't you dare threaten this girl thataway. She's had a rough time of it today, and most of it is your fault. She didn't ask for—"

"She asked for exactly what she got," Lucas said. "She came here under false pretenses and married me with no intention of fulfilling her part of the bargain."

Jennifer stepped in front of him as he sprawled in his chair, glaring down into his face. "That's where you're wrong, mister. I'm willing to learn how to keep house and cook and even sew on your missing buttons. I thought that was why you brought Ida here. She's willing to help me learn and I'm willing to take lessons. What more do you want?"

He rose and she stepped back. Her retreat was halted by his hands on her waist. "I'll give you two weeks to make a dent in this mess," he told her, "and then I'll let you know how you stack up as a wife."

"Well, it's taken you a lot longer than two weeks to *make* this mess," she said, spouting venom with each word. "And I don't need even that long to make up my mind about you."

"You've already made that plain enough." He grinned down at her and she felt suddenly shorter and smaller than ever before in her life. For a moment she wondered at her own bravery at standing up to this man. He was a veritable giant among men, and he had the right to use her in any way he pleased.

And she was, giving him what-for as if she hadn't a qualm in the world as to her well-being.

His gaze softened for a moment and she could not look away from the midnight-blue eyes that seemed to see deep within her. Her voice was a whisper as she spoke his name. "Lucas. Please give me a chance. I've not been a success at much of anything in my life. I need to know if I can do this. Without any time limit, or high expectations on your part. I know I said I wanted to go back East, but if you'll give me a reasonable chance to be a wife to you, I'll try. And if I fail, you can ship me off."

He nodded and this time his smile was warm, almost admiring. In fact, a woman could lose herself in those blue eyes, could put up with almost anything if those lips curved in such a way with regularity. He looked almost like the man she'd hoped to wed, the tall stranger she'd dreamed about all the way from New York to the wilds of Montana.

A man of honor, dignity and even a bit of wealth. Forget the dignity. Her honest heart could not use that word, not in connection with Lucas O'Reilly. Maybe the honor part was possible, should he give her the chance she'd asked for. And then he spoke and she heard the words of her future, a sentence that would last for years to come.

"You're my wife, Jennifer. I don't take vows and then turn my back on them. I'm a fair man, and I'll give you what time you need. I expect you to learn what you need to know in order to run this house, and I don't want Mrs. Bronson doing all the work. I hope we've got that straight."

"Yes, of course," she muttered, looking down at the bandages that already showed signs of dirt from the cellar and dish water from the sink. His gaze followed hers.

"You need to have that bandage changed," he said. "Sit down here and I'll tend to it."

"I can look after her hand," Mrs. Bronson offered from her spot at the stove.

"No, I'll do it," Lucas said. "It was my fault she burned it, so I'll take care of it."

"Your fault?" The woman looked at him with scorn. "What did you do to her?"

Lucas managed to look penitent. "I was yapping at her and she stumbled and fell. Caught herself on the stove with one hand."

Mrs. Bronson shook her head, as if she could not imagine such a thing. "Go on then," she said. "I guess you owe it to the woman to mend your fences."

Jennifer watched them as they discussed her. Then, at Lucas's urging, she sat at the table. He brought out the box from the pantry again and opened it in front of her.

"Was your mother a healer?" she asked.

"They called her that," he told her, sorting through the jars and rolls of bandages to find what he wanted. Again the pungent salve was opened and Lucas bent over her hand to untie the bandage he'd put in place. His fingers were big, but gentle and Jennifer bit her lip as she anticipated the pain of the bandage being pulled from the burns.

"Give me a wet cloth," Lucas said to Mrs. Bronson. "Let's soak this a little."

The warm cloth was sopping with water, but Jennifer made no complaint. The bandage soaked for several minutes and then Lucas lifted it, edging it off with care. Beneath it, the wounds were seeping, the blisters leaking fluid and he frowned.

"Come take a look," he said to Mrs. Bronson. "Does this seem to be healing at all to you?"

"Kinda early to tell," she said after bending close to examine Jennifer's hand. "But I'd say it looks clean and a little more of that salve should do the trick." She bent lower. "Smells like the stuff I brought with me. My mama called it 'husk.'"

Lucas seemed satisfied with her opinion and fashioned another pad from the roll of bandages, spread salve on its surface and then applied it to Jennifer's hand. Tying it in place with a long strip of fabric, he made a knot on the back of her hand, careful not to put pressure on her palm.

"Let's make that three or four weeks," he murmured. "I reckon it'll take you that long to be able to use your hand."

"You'd be surprised what I can do with my left hand," she said. "You said two weeks to start with, and two weeks it is. I'm not asking for any favors, Mr. O'Reilly."

"Maybe not, Mrs. O'Reilly, but I may be asking a few of you, and I'd like to get things on a better footing between us."

His words were soft, carrying only to her ears, and Jennifer looked up at him warily.

"What does that mean?" she asked.

"I think you have a pretty good idea." His eyes softened as they swept over her. "And if you haven't, I'll fill you in later on."

THE SUPPER HOUR went well, with Jennifer serving the food, setting the table and following instructions from Mrs. Bronson. There wasn't nearly as much mystery cloaking the cooking and serving as she'd thought. Once the woman began explaining as she went, Jennifer's mind stored all the instructions for future reference. Timing was everything, she decided.

"You're not washing dishes," Mrs. Bronson told her after the meal was finished. "If you want to do something helpful, you can go and dust the parlor. Pick up all the knickknacks and dust them, one item at a time. Wipe them off good, and then run the cloth over the surface before you put things back in place."

That seemed simple enough, Jennifer decided, realizing that it was exactly what she and her mother's housekeeper used to do on Saturday mornings back at home. She peered beneath the sink for a handy cloth and Ida found one for her. "Let me dampen it a bit," she offered. "But just use the dry places on the rag for the wooden tabletops ans such. We'll use some beeswax on them later on. After you get done dusting, come back in here and I'll fix you up."

The parlor held a large assortment of items that required dusting, it seemed, from pictures in heavy frames to small bits of porcelain formed into statues and tiny baskets. Someone had had a collection at one time or another, Jennifer decided, holding one of the figurines in the palm of her hand and inspecting the minute details. Painted to resemble a picnic basket, it held a facsimile of a checkered cloth, lovingly formed and painted, looking so real, she bent closer to be certain it wasn't fabric instead of porcelain.

"What are you looking at?" From the parlor door, Lucas spoke and she jerked, turning to him and dropping the basket. She watched in horror as it broke into three pieces. The carpet covered only the area in the middle of the room and she'd been standing near the front window, where the bare floor was unforgiving of her blunder.

"Oh, Lucas." She was truly contrite, her voice trembling as she knelt to pick up the pieces. "I didn't mean to break it. I suspect it was important to you." She looked up at him, aware of his silence, and his measuring look as he approached.

He lifted her to her feet, careful not to touch her bandaged hand, and then took the three bits of porcelain from her. "I think it can be mended," he said. "I've got glue that should work."

"Don't be angry with me." She'd never thought to ask such a thing of anyone, instead taking the blame for her misdeeds without complaint.

"I'm not angry, Jennifer. I shouldn't have spoken from the doorway. I startled you."

"I should have just dusted it and put it back instead of being so nosy about every little thing you have in here."

"There's not much. Just some things of my mother's," he said. "I had them sent to me after I settled here." He looked around the room. "I kept some of the stuff she seemed to be fond of, and then put it in here. I guess I wanted it to seem like home to me."

"What happened to her?"

"She's gone." And that seemed to be all he would say on the subject.

"Can you really mend it?" Jennifer asked, reaching to touch the tiny fragments with her index finger.

"We'll sit down at the kitchen table and I'll see what I can do."

"I'll finish up in here first," she told him, picking up her cloth and approaching the big library table sitting in front of the window. "This just needs dusting off," she told him, moving books to one side and shifting the lamp out of the way as she cleared the spots she would dust.

"This is too much for you to do," he said after a moment of observing her. "You need two hands for this sort of a chore. I'll tell Mrs. Bronson."

"No." Her voice was firm. "Please don't. Just ask her for a cloth with beeswax on it for me. She doesn't want me to use this one on the wooden places." She watched as he turned to leave the room and then she spoke again, her words halting him in his tracks.

"I want to learn, and the only way I can manage that is to do it myself. What I can't do, I'll ask for help with."

He looked back at her. "Are you sure? I wasn't trying to be mean and hateful, you know."

The words she'd spoken, the traits she'd accused him of possessing, seemed harsh as they left his lips. Jennifer shook her head. "I know you weren't. I was angry with you, and I spoke out of turn."

"I'll get you the cloth from Ida and you can go on with your work, then," he said. "I'll go on out and do the chores and then we'll see about this." Looking down at the bits of porcelain he held, he waited until she nodded her acquiescence and then walked from the parlor, leaving her alone for a few moments while he talked to Ida.

Ida came into the parlor with a cloth in her hand. "I'll show you how to do it this time, girl. Next time you're on your own. All right?"

Jennifer nodded and watched as the furniture was polished, catching the scent of wax from the cloth, admiring the shining surfaces Mrs. Bronson left behind.

THE LIGHT over the kitchen table was bright, shedding a harsh glow on Lucas and Jennifer. Mrs. Bronson had already stated her view of tables barren of covering, declaring that oilcloth was cheap and right handy at the general store, Luc had agreed to purchase a length of it as soon as the opportunity to go into town arose.

The tiny basket was the object of their attention and Lucas carefully fit the pieces together, murmuring beneath his breath.

"I was afraid maybe we'd missed some tiny bits on the floor, but it doesn't look like it, does it?"

Jennifer leaned closer, shaking her head. "No, I think I picked up all of it."

His hands were deft as he glued and patched. She admired the length of his fingers, the clean, closely cut nails and the care he took to make whole the bit of froufrou she had damaged.

As he put the finished product on the table between them, he looked up at her with a grin. "Almost as good as new," he said, and she nodded.

"Ready for bed?" he asked quietly, and again she nodded.

"Mrs. Bronson went up almost a half hour ago," Lucas added, rising and circling the table to grasp Jennifer's elbow, helping her from her chair. As she reached for the porcelain basket, he halted her hand.

"Leave it, sweetheart. It'll dry by morning and you can put it back then."

She only nodded once more and followed his lead as he led her from the kitchen. Leaving her in the doorway, he retraced his steps and blew out the lamp, then found his way to her in the dark.

His hands felt warm against her, one on the small of her back, the other holding her arm as they approached the stairway. In the hall above them, a candle had apparently been lit for their benefit, the stairs were visible in front of them, shadows of the banister falling to the hallway below.

Jennifer walked beside him up the flight of stairs, not even considering a protest, lest Ida be disturbed from her slumber. What would be, would be, she decided, certain that Lucas would not harm her tonight, no matter that he'd been harsh in his threats earlier.

"You all right?" he asked in an undertone, and she nodded once more.

"Lost your tongue?"

She looked up at him, a considerable distance, and shook her head.

"Scared of me?"

Again she shook her head, and then nodded, indecisive and bewildered by her own hesitation.

"Good answer," he said, and chuckled. "Now you've really got me confused."

He opened the bedroom door and ushered her inside. "Get undressed, Jennifer," he told her. "I'll undo your dress for you." The buttons came from their buttonholes readily and he let the garment slide to the floor. "Now your petticoat," he muttered, bending to see the tapes that held it at her waist.

"Sit down on the bed," he instructed her, "so I can take off your slippers." She obeyed and he slipped them from her feet. "No stockings?" he asked, leaning back to glance up into her face, and then recalled watching her slide into the house-shoes earlier.

"My gown, please," she murmured, and he reached beneath her pillow to find it, holding it aloft, looking with disgust at the white folds that hung from his hands.

"Are you sure you want to wear this?" he asked. "I'd think you'd be more comfortable in your shift, or whatever you call that bit of stuff you're wearing."

"My gown, please," she repeated, and he sighed.

"I won't argue with you tonight, sweetheart. If you want to be all bundled up in this thing, that's your choice."

He pulled her vest off, untied the tapes for her drawers and purposely kept his eyes on the wall over her head as she slipped into the gown. "You didn't take off your shift thing," he said, looking down at her with a grin. "If I turn my back, will you do it?"

She nodded and he reached to lift her gown over her head again, and then turned with the garment in his hands, waiting until she whispered her readiness before he made his move. He faced her, his eyes moving over her, noting the fullness of her breasts, the narrow span of her waist and the length of her legs.

"Please," she whispered, holding up her arms, and he did not refuse her, lowering the gown over her head. "Thank you." Her voice was muffled as she bent her head, attempting to do up the line of buttons that centered her bodice.

"I'll do that," he offered, and brushed her hands aside, his own perhaps slower at the project than hers, hampered as they were by her soft curves. But in moments, he'd managed to sort out the buttons.

"Now, get into bed," he told her, bending to pull back the sheet so that she could slip beneath it. With one glance in his direction, she did as he asked.

Moonlight's faint glow illuminated the two people who watched each other, she from her position on the bed, he from his stance beside her. Lucas stripped without hesitation, his clothing falling to the floor. By the time he reached for the sheet, he was down to his drawers, and as he sat on the edge of the bed, he dropped them to the floor.

He pulled the sheet over himself and scooped her close beneath its sheltering folds. "Hush," he murmured. "I'm only going to hold you a little. I won't hurt you, Jennifer. You said you weren't frightened of me, remember?"

"I'm not," she told him. "At least, not very."

And at that he laughed, a full-bodied sound that no doubt should have frightened her, but apparently didn't, for she buried her face against his chest and lifted her arm to place it around his waist. Altogether a fine idea.

And that was his last thought as he drifted into slumber.

CHAPTER SIX

LUCAS CHANGED HER bandage again after breakfast, glowering at the greasy spot where bacon had splattered. "I don't want you to get dirt on this," he muttered, lifting the pad and peering beneath it with a satisfied look. "That burn looks better today than yesterday."

"I told her I'd do the cooking, but she doesn't listen well," Mrs. Bronson said.

"I know." Lucas shot Jennifer a look that made her smile. "She's got a mind of her own."

"We're going to do laundry today," she told him. "I can't use the scrub board yet, but I can hang clothes."

Lucas glanced at Mrs. Bronson for support and, at her nod, shook his head at his wife. "Not yet, you won't. You'll get that thing wet and I'll have to change it again. Why don't you just take it easy today and maybe by tomorrow you'll be able to fix a meal pretty much on your own?"

"I'm going to make dinner today. We've got leftover beef and cans of vegetables, and Ida will do the lifting and jar opening for me."

Her smile was radiant as she spoke of the simple chores she would accomplish. He didn't have the heart to deny her this small bit of independence, so he just nodded and then bent to kiss her lightly before he took his leave, only to turn back on an impulse.

"I've chores to do. You want to help?"

"Can I?" She glowed. There was no other word to describe the brightness of her eyes and the clarity of her skin—creamy, with an overlay like that of a pale pink rose.

"Think you can gather eggs? Or maybe give the horses their oats before we turn them out to pasture?"

"Of course, I can." Her tones were confident now. "So long as I'm back in the house in time to start dinner."

"You will be. I'm planning on being hungry along about noontime."

She accompanied him out the door and he grasped her elbow as they stepped down onto the grass from the porch. She didn't pull away, and he slid his arm around her waist, holding her against his side. She carried her bandaged hand against her breast, protecting it, and he felt a pang of guilt as he remembered his part in the injury she'd suffered.

Inside the barn, he leaned against the wall and pulled her closer, turning her to face him, his arms around her waist, then dropping a bit lower to press her body against his. She felt soft yet firm, her youthful form womanly yet strong, and he gloried in the scent of her as it rose to his nostrils. She was fresh, smelling of the sachets she had tucked in her valise. He'd caught the aroma when he hauled her nightgown from its depths the first night.

Now he inhaled it, recognizing it as typical of Jennifer. Soft yet invasive, filling him with an urgency he could barely contain. He wanted her, needed to feel the lush lines of her body pressed against his, without the barrier of clothing between. And yet he knew it was too soon. She was not yet ready to match his desire with needs of her own. And he would not force her into the choice. She must come to him, show him in some way that she was willing for their marriage to become a reality.

Yet she lifted her face to him now and he could not resist the promise of lips that curved as she met his gaze. He lowered his head and touched her mouth with his, felt the lush lips open beneath his teasing touch, and he accepted the kiss she offered. His tongue skimmed hers with an easy gesture, not trying to invade, only offering a caress that would tempt her into a closer union of their lips. Perhaps not now, he thought, but in the future.

He held her closer, fitting her breasts against his chest, her belly against his, aware that his arousal was prominent, his need for completion too obvious to be hidden from her. And yet, she did not pull back, only leaned against him and offered her lips. Her arms circled his neck and he rejoiced, aware of the unspoken message she sent.

I'm yours. When the time is right, I'll be your wife.

"Jen, I have to stop this," he said, his voice rasping as he bent his head farther to cradle his face in the curve of neck and shoulder. He found warm skin just beneath her ear and suckled there, pacing himself, lest he lower her into the empty stall and push her dress upward. She deserved better than that, at least the first time.

Another day he might take her here in the barn, where such a primitive act might well be accomplished, where passion and desire might meet in a collision of need between two people. But for today, he satisfied himself with the taste of her skin, the feel of her breasts, the knowledge that she was soft and giving, the curves of her hips filling his hands.

"Lucas?" She sounded bewildered, and with good reason. She was a virgin, untouched by a man, and his intent was no doubt more than obvious to her.

"I won't hurt you, Jen," he murmured. "I've promised that already and I don't break my word." He held her away and smiled at her, recognizing the effort of halting his seduction so swiftly.

"Use that can in the feed barrel and put one measure in each horse's feed bucket. Can you do that? Are you afraid of animals?"

She met his query with a look of scorn. "Afraid? Of course not. Animals like me, at least the ones we had at home did."

"Can you ride?" he asked, his thoughts surging ahead to a day when they might travel together the boundary lines of his property.

"I've never used a saddle. Only bareback." She grinned at him as if they shared a secret. "I have a pair of britches in my valise, you know. I wore them at home when I rode."

"Astride?"

"Of course. Is there any other way?"

He swept her into his embrace again, his delight almost a visible thing between them. "Ah, Jennifer. You're going to make my life interesting. I can tell already."

DINNER WENT WELL, Jennifer decided. The soup was simple, the meat being cut into chunks by Ida, who watched closely as if her prize pupil might try to do too much. She lent a hand with the chopping of an onion, but let Jennifer mix the corn pone with her left hand. The savory aroma filled the room by noon, and when Lucas came in the back door, he halted and sniffed.

"Smells good," he told both women.

"She catches on right quick," Mrs. Bronson said. "Next time we do this, we'll put dumplings on top. Would have today, but I thought of it too late."

"I'll settle for this." Lucas washed at the sink and touched Jennifer's shoulder as he passed her in front of the stove. She glanced up at him and he smiled.

"Maybe there's hope for me yet," she said, sitting at the table and lifting her spoon. Mrs. Bronson carried full bowls of soup from the stove, deeming Jennifer too unhandy with her left hand to do so. They ate silently, Lucas waiting and watching as Jennifer bowed her head, Mrs. Bronson following suit without hesitation.

"You could do that out loud, if you wanted to," he said. "I guess my food could use a blessing, too."

"It had one." Picking up her spoon, Jennifer stirred the soup in front of her. It was thick, the vegetables and meat swimming in gravy, and she felt a pang of hunger. "Looks more like stew, doesn't it?"

"Almost." Ida nodded and pushed the plate of corn pone across the table. "You did well."

"She gathered the eggs, too," Lucas said, as if proud of his wife's accomplishment.

"Once we get that bandage off her, she'll be tip-top." Her mentor beamed at Jennifer, clearly sharing Lucas's pride.

BUT IT SEEMED the bandage would not be discarded for several days. Lucas changed it daily, inspecting the burn with care, slathering salve over it and binding it again. Careful not to brush against it unwittingly, he took care at night to cushion it on his chest. If she turned to face the wall, he placed a small pillow beneath it.

"You're good to me, Lucas," she said, long after he thought she'd gone to sleep. They'd been husband and wife for more than three weeks now, and his need for her was uppermost in his mind.

"Am I?" His words were hoarse and he cleared his throat, aware that he sounded angry, or maybe just frustrated.

"Better than I'd expected," she admitted. "In fact, I was afraid of you at first."

"You said you weren't," he reminded her.

She laughed. "I lied. To tell the truth, I don't like to admit fear of anything. A matter of pride, I suppose."

"We're all allowed moments of pride. Especially a woman like you, with so much working against her. And yet, you persevere, as if to show all of us what you're capable of."

She turned to face him. "I want to prove myself. To you and Ida both. I want to learn all I can."

"She tells me you're doing well, and I've seen evidence of it myself."

"I want you to leave the bandage off tomorrow morning. I want to see if I can work with my hand uncovered."

"Not a good idea," he said, disputing her theory. "I don't want you to get infection in it. It'll take longer than ever to heal if you're not careful."

"It's my hand, Lucas. And I want to use it. It needs exercise."

He bowed to her opinion, bending his head to hers, his mouth touching her forehead. "All right. But, understand one thing. If you're well enough to use that hand, then you're in good enough shape for me to—"

"Not yet. Please, not yet," she whispered.

His hand settled over her breast and she caught her breath, holding it as if to make herself smaller, perhaps hide from his touch. "I won't hurt you." Once more he repeated the words, the vow he'd made over and over in the past weeks.

"I know. But no one has ever done that to me before."

"I know. That's what makes this…" His hand curved beneath her breast and his fingers clasped it. "It makes this something beyond the ordinary to me. To know that you're untouched, that you come to me with a purity I hadn't thought possible in a woman."

She uttered a soft cry, a sound of yearning that pleased him, and he bent his head, brushing his mouth against the curve of her breast, only the fabric of her gown keeping him from the texture of her skin.

It wasn't enough. He fought the urge to peel the gown from her, the need to possess her as his wife, and came close to succumbing to the desire that pounded through him, bringing him to a peak of passion that threatened to rule this moment.

"*Damn.*" The single word dropped from his lips and she stiffened against his touch. His fingers tightened and he felt her cringe, knew a moment of guilt as he released her from his hold. "I'm sorry, Jennifer. I thought I could hold you, touch you just a bit more, without being tempted beyond my control." He breathed deeply, bowing his head against her shoulder.

"I was wrong. If I don't leave you alone in this bed tonight, there'll be hell to pay. I fear you won't forgive me in the morning." He laughed, a sad sound with no trace of mirth to soften it. "You won't forgive me now, I suspect, and I haven't even done anything."

"You haven't?" She smoothed the bodice of her gown and her words were muffled, as if she might be shedding tears.

"No, I haven't." Cupping her breast in his hand certainly

didn't qualify as lovemaking, as far as he was concerned. Now, if he'd managed to get his hand on her skin, if the gown had been stripped off and her body exposed to him... Now that might qualify as lovemaking...almost.

He muffled his chuckle against her throat. Almost was just not good enough. He'd been too long alone, too many months without a woman's warmth to comfort him, and having a wife, yet not possessing her, was more than any man had the patience to cope with.

He was not a patient man. Not by a long shot.

He rolled from her, releasing her, then sat on the edge of the bed.

"Lucas?" She sat up behind him and his reaction was instantaneous. His snarl of warning was harsh and cutting.

"Don't touch me, Jennifer. Don't say another word, just lie down and let me be. Unless you want to find yourself stretched out beneath me, just leave me the hell alone."

He felt her movements as she moved as far from him as she was able, given the width of the bed, and then he rose, grabbed his pillow and stalked to the door.

"Lucas?" She sounded frightened now and he was glad. Better that she be frightened than angry. Better that she be confused than violated, and that was a dire possibility right now.

"I'll be in the other bedroom." He opened the door and stepped into the hallway, aware that he was naked, hopeful that Mrs. Bronson would not peer out her door, awakened by their voices.

The extra bedroom was dark and uninviting, the bed unmade, but he cared little for comfort. A quilt lay on the chair beside the bed and he wrapped it around himself, then lay down, his pillow doubled over beneath his head. It was a fitting end to a miserable day. Alone in a bed, his bride just a foot or so away on the other side of the wall. If ever there had been a moment in his life when Lucas O'Reilly felt sorry for himself, it was right now. He snarled a single curse word, recalled the ones he'd so recently uttered in Jennifer's hearing, and growled beneath his breath.

He wouldn't apologize this time, nor feel remorse for using what she termed *vile language.* The woman could sleep alone, and right now, he hoped she was miserable, all by herself in that big bed.

And then he heard her muffled sobs through the wall. He'd warrant she had the pillow over her head, but the sound carried through to him.

"Don't cry, Jen," he murmured, knowing she could not hear but unable to listen to her misery in silence. The sound of her sorrow ceased, and he wondered if she'd heard him. Surely not. The walls weren't *that* thin.

The headboard of the bed she slept in thudded against the wall then, and he knew she had turned from one side to the other, perhaps making herself comfortable before going to sleep. She'd been more than satisfied to lie in his arms, he remembered.

All too well, in fact. The memory of her soft curving form pressed against him might very well keep him from slumber tonight.

"Well, hell's bells," he muttered, swinging his legs over the side of the bed, his temper constrained. He strode to the door, and threw it open, uncaring now about his nakedness. Four steps took him to the doorway of his own bedroom and he turned the knob, closing the door behind himself, and making his way to where Jennifer lay.

The moon cast her in ivory and she looked up at him, her

face a glowing oval, her eyes huge and wary. "What's wrong, Lucas?"

"Nothing." He tossed back the sheets and threw himself down beside her. "Everything." Feeling more than a little foolish, he grinned, laughing silently at his own masculine ineptness. "This is a dandy way of showing you I don't want to sleep alone, isn't it?"

"You don't have to. I didn't leave you in here alone. You left me."

"And you cried." He lifted himself up on one arm and faced her, this woman who had him in a quandary.

She didn't bother to deny his charge, only nodded her head, looking up at him as he bent over her. And then she moved, one hand reaching upward to touch his cheek, the other held inert beside her, lest she crush it beneath his chest as he bent lower to kiss her. Her fingers were soft, her hand small and he rued the harsh treatment he'd leveled in her direction over the past weeks.

She seemed to hold no grudge, only smiled at him. "Please don't leave me again, Lucas. This bed is too big for me by myself."

"Don't expect me to always be a gentleman, Jen. For tonight, I'll behave myself, but I won't make any promises about tomorrow."

"That's good enough for me." She slid her fingers into his hair and breathed deeply of his scent, a wonderful, musky, masculine aroma that surrounded her. She wondered why she hesitated at the mating that would come, the act of marriage he would surely perform in this bed, and wished for just a moment that he would ignore her qualms and do as his body dictated.

For she felt the urgent pressure against her thigh, the outline of his arousal as it made itself known. But if Lucas was intent on being a *gentleman,* as he called it, even if only for this one night, she would not argue. He would give her another day in which to grow accustomed to him, another few hours to learn his ways, to seek his company. It wasn't that much to ask for, and he'd offered without any coaxing on her part.

He seemed to understand her willingness to lie with him, her need for his warmth. For although the night breezes were temperate, she felt bereft without his body next to hers, his long legs behind her, his breathing a silent rhythm against her back.

She turned from him, waiting till he should curl behind her, his arm circling her waist, his hand flat against her belly. She sighed. It was good, this part of marriage, this silent pairing with a husband, a time of peace, a comfort in the night.

And tomorrow she would face her duties, try to forget the urge to go East once more, to all that was familiar and known. It was time to take up her life here with full acceptance of all it entailed. And to that end she would strive to do her best.

THE MORNING BROUGHT about Lucas's departure to the mine. "I've been hanging around here too long. Sandy's due for a break. I need to be minding my business a little better," he said, explaining his actions as he readied himself for the day.

Jennifer sat on the edge of the bed watching as he buttoned his shirt. "Will you be gone all day?"

"Probably. Maybe even overnight. My partner, Sandy, has done his share and more. I need to work pretty steadily for a few days and give him a break. We've come across a good vein, and it isn't even safe for him to work alone, not when he's carrying gold into town by himself."

"I suppose I wasn't aware of the danger involved," Jennifer mused, frowning as she thought of Lucas being prey to those who might steal his gold, perhaps even harm the man for what could be gained. "I was going to ask if I could go along with you, but I don't suppose that's a good idea."

He was shaking his head before she completed the words. "Not a chance, lady. I'm not risking your life, taking you out to the mines."

"You're risking yours." She bent to pick up the clothing she'd worn yesterday, and deemed it ready for the wash basket. Her valise was almost empty, her undergarments having been stored in the dresser drawer after the last wash day, and she turned to the tall chest to seek out clean clothing.

"It's my mine," he reminded her, sitting to pull on his stocking and tug his boots over them. "Mining is always a dangerous occupation, and even though most of the men out there are honest, there are always a few willing to risk all for a big strike. And some of them aren't particular where they find it."

"You mean, out of another man's pack, instead of the ground, don't you?" She sat again on the edge of the bed, stricken suddenly as she thought of Lucas being borne home on a wagon, his life snuffed out by such a thief.

"Don't worry, sweetheart," he said, approaching her, lifting her to her feet and holding her in an embrace that was pleasantly familiar. "I'm going to go grab a bite to eat and I'll be on my way."

"I'll be dressed in a minute, and eat breakfast with you. Don't go without…"

"Without what? Kissing you goodbye?" He grinned. "Not a chance, sweet. Not a chance. I grab every opportunity, in case you haven't noticed."

She met his gaze, stunned to see the dark gleam of desire there. "I've noticed." Her heart beat a little faster as he stood in front of her and looked his fill. She felt the swelling of her breasts, free of constraint beneath her nightgown, knew a rush of heat that pounded through her veins, to center in the depths of her belly. With only a look, he could melt her resistance, and she wondered again why she hesitated to take that final step that would make her his. For surely she was ready for this link to be formed.

"I like the look in your eyes," he said, his mouth brushing against hers, a tender, gentle blessing, as if he would leave her with a memory of whispering desire.

"My eyes?" What hidden message had he seen there? A softening perhaps? A need she had only just acknowledged even to herself?

"I like just about everything about you." Grinning, he released her and went to the door, opening it and tossing one more glance her way. "I'll expect you downstairs in five minutes."

She watched him leave, too stunned by his final remark to move and aware for the first time that he had a decided limp. And then she moved, catching up her clothing and shedding her nightgown, a swift exchange of garments. She gave her hair a quick brushing and left it to hang down her back, a dark mass of curls and waves she was sorely pressed to contain in a braid most days. Unable to separate and plait it, she would ignore the propriety of a proper hairdo and he could just take her as she was.

From the look in Lucas's eye when she walked into the kitchen, he was more than willing to accept her presence, unbound hair and all. In fact, his hand reached for her, tangling in the length that tumbled down her back, and he uttered words beneath his breath that she could not decipher. And then he was away from her side, leaving her to sit on the far side of the square, wooden table.

"Are you ready to eat?" She nodded at the question and sat as Ida brought coffee to her, then dished up two plates of fried potatoes and eggs.

"This looks good." The fork felt awkward in her left hand and Jennifer shot a pleading look at Lucas. "Don't forget, you're going to take off my bandage and let my hand air today." She yearned for a few minutes alone with him and the chance to find out why he limped—whether he'd hurt himself and not told her, or whether the limp was a reminder of an old injury.

"I'll look at your hand and decide," Lucas said. It seemed he would not give way on that point, and she was silent.

"That's probably a good idea, Jennifer," Ida said. "But I can take care of it later, Luc. I know you're in a hurry to leave."

"I'll do it." His tone left no room for argument and so it was that he finished his meal in short order and moved to Jennifer's side of the table. His box and a roll of bandages torn from an old sheet accompanied him, and she watched as he removed the bandage. Beneath it, her skin looked red, but to her untrained eye it seemed much as it would have been, had she not been blistered to a fare-thee-well by the iron cookstove.

"I think it's doing all right, don't you?" she asked, seeking his gaze, trying to read his response before he spoke.

"For today, we'll leave the bandage off. If you promise to be careful and not use your hand too much. Wiggle your fingers and exercise it off and on. If it gets too sore, Ida will put more salve on it and a fresh bandage." He waited for her acquiescence, and she nodded.

His smile told her he saw through her ready agreement, and he bent to kiss her, an impulsive move, she was sure. "Don't forget, Jen. You promised."

"I won't forget. And I'm sure my watchdog won't let me, anyway."

"I've been called worse," Mrs. Bronson said. "And you can mark it down in your book, girl. I'll be keeping an eye on you."

Lucas went to the door. "I'll see the pair of you tonight or maybe tomorrow night. If I don't show up by dark, don't worry." His gait had improved, she noted, as he walked toward the barn. Probably just a hitch.

IF I DON'T SHOW UP by dark, don't worry. "Easy for him to say," Jennifer muttered, watching as twilight turned the brightness of day into a starlit canopy overhead.

Beside her, Ida murmured futile words of comfort. Jennifer was not consoled by them and she spoke her mind out loud.

"How can I miss a man who aggravates me so?"

"He's your husband. We always miss them when they're gone, even though they aggravate us to death when they're hanging around, acting like men."

Now *those* words seemed more able to fill her need, Jennifer thought, than a trite statement meant to pacify her concern.

"He won't be back tonight." Jennifer's pronouncement accepted his warning. "But we'll have all day to plan a good supper for him tomorrow."

"If I didn't know better, I'd think you were batty over the man." Ida laughed as she spoke.

"I don't want anything to happen to him. I'd be as concerned over anyone who might be in danger."

"Really." Not a question, but rather a droll remark meant to make Jennifer smile, and it served its purpose.

Her nod was resolute. "I'm going to bed. Morning will come early. The sun is coming up before the rooster crows these days."

"Not quite. Blasted bird woke me today when it was still dark." Ida was a grumbler when it came to her sleep being disturbed, it seemed, and Jennifer wondered for a moment if her shenanigans last night with Lucas had deterred the woman from nodding off.

She smiled. No matter. The result had been to her good, for she'd slept in his arms and had reveled in the comfort he offered. And one day she would know him in a different way, as a wife.

He was being patient, and she knew it was difficult for him. Hard for him to wait. And that was the word, all right, she thought with a soft chuckle. *Hard*. It described Lucas in more ways than one.

"Private joke?" Mrs. Bronson shot her a curious look.

Jennifer smiled and then relented. "Kind of. Yes, I guess you could say that."

She made her way to bed and hugged Lucas's pillow. It wasn't the man, but it carried his scent, and that was certainly better than nothing.

CHAPTER SEVEN

THE MAN got off the train and sauntered up Main Street, almost as if he owned the town. Jennifer was stunned. There was no other word to explain the sudden stillness that swept over her very spirit. What Kyle Carter was doing here in Thunder Canyon was a question without an answer, so far as she was concerned.

That her former brother-in-law had followed her here seemed to be a stretch of the imagination, for surely he wouldn't toss his money away on a train ticket merely to seek her out. Or would he?

It seemed her answer would not be long in coming, for he caught sight of her, his sharp gaze pinning her where she stood in front of the general store, her arms loaded with her purchases. Ahead of her, the wagon awaited her, Ida having harnessed the horses after Jennifer had assured her she was more than capable of driving the big vehicle into town. Ida was lingering behind in the Emporium, having a good gossip with friends from church, and so Jennifer was alone as she faced the man who had made her life miserable in New York.

"Well, sister dear, it's good to see you," Kyle said, as if honey coated every word, turning his message into a sickening address. He bent forward, as if he would kiss her cheek, and Jennifer lifted her bundles higher, placing herself just beyond his reach.

His eyes narrowed at that and he grasped her arms, without a doubt leaving bruises in his wake, so hard was his grip on her. And he then bent lower again. His lips were wet and she flinched as they brushed against her mouth. He smiled, a particularly evil grin, she thought, as if he was pleased with her reaction to his caress.

"I can't say I'm delighted to see you, Kyle," she managed to blurt, wishing she dared speak the words that welled in her throat. Language such as she'd never allowed to pass her lips begged to be uttered. She had the urge to call him names—harsh, vile descriptions of his character—but the audience of men on the bench behind her would not allow her to vent her anger out loud.

"How can you say such a thing, sister dear?"

"I'm not your sister." The word were sharp, but he seemed to ignore her message.

"Perhaps not, but you were once. My sister-in-law, at least. The aunt of my child." And then he paused as if waiting for a reaction to his words.

He received it immediately. "Where is she?"

"If you behave yourself and come with me, you'll find out," he told her. "If not, you'll never see her again." His threat was spoken in a casual manner, his voice pitched low enough so as not to carry to their audience.

"I wouldn't walk across the street to spit on your dead body."

"You don't love me anymore?" he asked sweetly, this time speaking a bit louder.

"I've never *loved* you. Only hated what you did to my sister."

"That's all in the past. Now there's just you and me."

His grin was evil, purely evil, she decided, making a mask of his features, seeming to turn him into a caricature of a demon.

"There'll never be a *you and me*." Her words were clear, and he winced.

"Don't make me angry, my dear." His warning fell on deaf ears, for Jennifer had had enough of his hateful mouth.

"I'm married, Kyle. I have a husband. You don't interest me in any way. Never have. Never will." She couldn't have made it any clearer, she thought, but he persisted.

"A husband? A dirty, scruffy miner? Is that supposed to impress me?"

"I have no intention of impressing you, but believe me, if he showed up here right now, you'll be impressed in a big way."

His laugh was taunting. "I can buy and sell any man in this town. Show me this husband of yours and I'll give him five thousand dollars for your hand."

"It isn't available. I'm well married, and besides, he doesn't need your money. He has enough of his own."

"Well married? Well then, you won't mind dishing out a few favors in my direction, will you?" His arms curved around her and only the presence of her packages kept her from his body.

"Drop that garbage, Jennifer, and let me feel your—"

"Don't touch me!" Her shriek was piercing and the men on the bench rose as one—even the gentleman on the end of the seat, the one she sensed was deaf as a post, given his inattention when his cohorts spoke.

"My husband will kill you for this," she shouted. "Lucas O'Reilly is twice the man you are. No, three times. More than that. I love him and I wouldn't look at another man, no matter what he offered."

The men watching broke into applause and gales of laughter. "That's tellin' him, missy," one called, and the others agreed.

Kyle backed off, clearly outnumbered, especially when Ida came out the door of the Emporium and approached. "Is this fella bothering you, Jennifer?"

She could only nod and Mrs. Bronson looked around, as if seeking a handy weapon. Snatching at a cane held by one of the watching men, she lifted it and then lowered it in a crushing blow, aiming obviously for Kyle's head, and only missing because he ducked. Instead the cane slashed across his chest and he shouted out his anger.

"Damn fool woman. You trying to kill me?"

"Sounds like a fine idea to me," the storekeeper said, opening his door and stepping out to the sidewalk.

"This is none of your business," Kyle told him. "Mind your manners, mister."

"Any time a man attacks a woman, I make it a point to call it my business." The storekeeper's jaw stuck out as he stepped closer to Kyle. "Now get out of here. Mrs. O'Reilly told you flat-out she's not interested in anything you have to say, and if you're a smart man you'll leave town before her husband finds out you've been molesting her."

Ida grasped Jennifer's arm and hustled her to the wagon, putting the bundles in the back. "I'll go in and get the rest. You just stay here." Her words were spoken in an undertone, but firmly and Jennifer nodded, only too happy to let the woman take charge.

"I'll get your things." The storekeeper held the door for Ida as Kyle moved off down the sidewalk, bent over as if his chest was giving him discomfort. Then, going ahead of Ida, the clerk retrieved her additional box of supplies. In short order, he'd put them in the back of the wagon and waved farewell to the two women.

Jennifer was still silent, and Ida scrutinized her. "You all right, girl? Did that fella hurt you any?"

"No, I'm all right. *That fella* is my dead sister's husband. A bas—" Jennifer bit her lip, holding the curse back, lest she offend her companion.

"Go ahead and say it. There's two kinds of bastards, girl, and I suspect he's the very worst sort. The other kind can't help their beginnings, but *that* one—" She waved her hand back at the stores behind them, "I'll warrant he's one to really show his colors, ain't he? I'd have called him even worse than that."

"I hope Lucas is coming home tonight." It was a statement of longing such as she'd never felt, and Jennifer hugged herself, a chill passing down her spine even as the hot summer sun beat down on her head.

"He'll be back as soon as he can. I suspect he's up there hiring someone to work for him. He don't want to leave you alone, girl. I figured that out already."

"I really shot off my mouth, didn't I?" Jennifer recalled her words, all too aware of the statements she'd made in front of what seemed to be half the town, at least the male half.

Lucas O'Reilly is twice the man you are.... I love him and I wouldn't look at another man no matter what he offered. Her face burned as she recalled her shouted words, and she spread her fingers wide over her cheeks, feeling hot tears stream down to fall in her lap.

"You only said what was true." Ida stated the words as a fact, then she turned to smile at Jennifer. "Don't be bawlin' now, girl. Saying you love a man is just fine in my book, especially when that man is your husband. And if he isn't already, Lucas O'Reilly will be soon."

"Of course he's my husband. I just told half the town, didn't I?" Wiping her tears, Jennifer swallowed, her hands groping in her pocket for a handkerchief. A large, white square met her fingertips and she tugged it forth so that she could mop her eyes.

"Yeah, you did." Ida smiled, her hands firm on the reins.

"Do you want me to do that?" Jennifer waved at the horses, willing to handle them herself.

"Nah. I've been driving a horse and wagon for more years than I can count. How'd you think I got so good at putting the harness on?"

"I don't know, but I watched you, you know. Next time, I'll try it myself."

"After your hand heals, and that's a fact. I think you made it sore, handling these reins and then carrying all those bundles out of the store. Lucas will have a fit if you've damaged it."

"Lucas doesn't need to know everything that goes on, does he?"

"He'll look at you, first thing when he gets home."

It was a prediction that bore fruit at sundown, when the familiar figure rode up on his dark gelding. He dismounted and she thought his limp was more pronounced, as if he were weary from riding.

"Jennifer." His call blared into the kitchen through the open door. "Come out here, will you?"

She cast one long look at Ida, who was stirring a pan of gravy and stepped out onto the porch. The man looked fit to be tied, she thought and perhaps with good reason. He was tired, his leg was probably hurting and something had obviously upset him.

"I had a visitor from town when I was cleaning up to come home," he said harshly. "I heard that some dude from back East was bothering you right out in front of the general store."

"Who told you that?" She tilted her chin, unwilling to seem cowed by him, just as she'd defied the man who'd attacked her in front of the townsfolk.

"Never mind, honey. I want to know who he was and what he meant by grabbing you and demanding that you go with him."

"It was Kyle, the man who was married to my sister. He wouldn't believe I was married."

Lucas smiled wolfishly. "Yeah, I heard. And I also heard what you told him."

"Did you now?" She folded her arms across her chest and glared at him. "Then you also know that Ida hit him with a cane and sent him off."

"She's pretty protective of her lone chick, isn't she?" His smile turned to a grin as he looked past Jennifer to where the widow stood in the doorway. "Thank you, ma'am," he said, his tone respectful, his words sounding most sincere.

"Not a problem. You left her with me, and I took care of her, just like I would have if she'd been my own daughter."

"I know that. And I appreciate it, more than you can—"

"That's enough, Lucas. I just did my job," Ida said, cutting his words of thanks short as she opened the screen door and motioned them both inside.

"Now, the pair of you come eat supper. This girl has cooked for three hours to make you a good meal, Luc, and you'd better appreciate it."

"I intend to, as soon as I put my horse in the barn. I'll be in in a few minutes. And then I expect to hear the whole story."

SHE DIDN'T LOOK any the worse for wear, he decided, feeling older than his years, limping as his bad leg cramped beneath him. He recalled Jennifer's erect stance, her quick replies. But if that man had left a mark on her, if she wore bruises, he'd hightail it into town and thrash him within an inch of his life.

Your wife didn't leave no doubt in anybody's mind, Luc, his informant had said. *She told the whole bunch of us that she loves you.* Harv Painter's face was red as he'd repeated the words Jennifer had said, and Lucas repeated them over again now as he unsaddled his horse and led the gelding into the barn.

She told the whole bunch of us that she loves you. He'd have given ten years of his life to hear her say it himself, he thought. Still would. But only if she meant it. If she'd said it to scare off the man named Kyle, if she had only used the man she'd married as a shield, that would be all right, too. He'd be dadblamed if he wouldn't hold her to it, though. She'd made a statement and she'd better back it up with actions.

Supper was tasty, but Jennifer ate little. Her sleeves were long, buttoned primly at her wrists, and he wondered for a moment why she'd chosen to wear so warm a dress this afternoon. For he knew she'd taken a bath and donned clean clothing before his arrival. The tub was still upside-down on the porch, two towels and a washcloth hanging from the line, and the woman's face was shiny, her hair lustrous and loose down her back.

He'd bet a bundle that she smelled fresh, like the apple-blossom-scented soap she used, and again he wondered at the dress she'd chosen to wear.

HE FOUND OUT AT BEDTIME what was hidden beneath her sleeves. "Take off your gown," he said, standing in front of her like an avenging angel. Although he didn't feel angelic right now, he knew his stance was that of a man ready to do battle.

"No. You know I'm not going to stand here in front of you and drop this gown on the floor. You're out of your mind, Lucas."

"Pretty sassy for a little girl, ain't you?" His grammar left a lot to be desired, but he had a need to stun her with actions and words.

"I'm not little, and I've been called worse than sassy in my life," she told him.

"Well, close your mouth and unbutton that nightgown." He left her no out, waiting till the count of five before he lifted his hands to her bodice, setting the first two buttons free before she could move.

"Don't do that." She jerked from his grasp and he turned her, his hands gentle but firm, as if he would not leave his mark on her. For indeed, he had no intention of hurting her. He feared she'd already felt pain at a man's hand today, and he would not add to it.

"I want to see your body, Jennifer. I want to see what he did to you."

"I only have a bruise on my arm. Just where he grabbed me."

"Let me see." He would not be swayed. If a simple bruise was all she had to offer him, he'd be thankful, but his better sense told him it was more than that.

She undid the front of her gown and slid one arm from the sleeve, baring her shoulder and the upper slope of her breast. She pulled the gown up to cover her as if she realized her degree of nudity. He smiled.

"I've seen that much and more already. You have no reason to be shy with me. I'm your husband." And then he caught sight of finger marks on her upper arm. In two separate places, as if the brute had grasped her and then released his hold only to grip her again, digging his fingertips into her soft flesh.

"The other arm, Jennifer." His tone was guttural and filled with a surging anger.

She obeyed, probably thinking there was no use in arguing. If she feared him, a man who intended her no harm, how much greater must have been her fright when faced with a man who cared little for the bruising he inflicted.

She held the gown against her breast, allowing him to inspect her skin, unflinching as he touched the purpling welts. His eyes darkened with the fury of a man helpless in the face of pain.

"I'm all right, Lucas. It doesn't hurt, and Ida put witch hazel on me. I won't have any marks left after a week or so."

"That's a week or so too long, as far as I'm concerned." He lifted her sleeves, making it convenient for her to shove her arms back into them. Then, as if it were a task he must do as penance, he buttoned her gown again and lifted his hands to frame her face. "I'm sorry, sorrier than you'll ever know. I gave that brute the chance to hurt you. I should have been with you, Jennifer. All the gold in that mine isn't worth one bruise on your body."

"You'd better watch your step, Mr. O'Reilly. I'll begin to think you like me." Her gaze was filled with him, the presence of the man, his mouth, eyes, the dark hair that lay in disarray on his head, the broad chest where she'd been comforted more than once. And she realized that her words might seem to him a demand for his caring. It wasn't what she wanted, and yet—perhaps it was. She *yearned* for his caring.

To know that he felt some degree of affection would sit well right now, she decided.

"I do like you." He spoke without hesitation, the words firm, as if he had no reason to search for a reply. "Probably more than is wise, Jennifer."

"And what is *that* supposed to mean?" The words were a puzzle and she felt unable to solve it.

"I hadn't thought to really *like* my wife, when I sent for a woman. I hadn't realized I could care for a female like you, an easterner, a woman who sought out a husband through an agency. I'd expected a different sort than the girl who arrived here."

"You were disappointed, I know. But I didn't set out to deceive you, Lucas. The man at the agency—"

He held up a hand to halt her. "I know. I know. He made up the description of your household skills out of whole cloth. The only thing he said that was the unvarnished truth was that you were a woman of quality, more attractive than most. I guess he figured that would make up for your faults."

She felt perplexed for a moment. "I don't remember that in the letter I saw."

"It was in mine. Would you like to see it?"

She shook her head. "No. I believe you." And then her mind seized on his words. "What do you mean, my faults? What faults?"

His brow twitched, a prelude to laughter, she'd learned. He did not disappoint her, for his chuckle was rich and bold. "You have a temper, Mrs. O'Reilly, and a sassy mouth. A mind of your own—" He stopped for a moment, counting his fingers as he enumerated the items he'd listed. His brow furrowed just a bit as his voice softened and his face turned sober, as if his joking were set aside.

And yet, how much of it was joking, she wasn't certain. He'd listed her faults accurately, so she added her own contributions to the list. "I can't cook, don't know how to make bread or milk a cow. And worst of all, I'm not much of a wife where it seems to count the most."

"You're *my* wife, and that's what counts," he told her. "I'll decide how inept you are when it comes to our private life together. And trust me, sweetheart, I have no complaints yet."

"You haven't? I thought—" Perhaps it was better if she didn't think too much about their *private life*. "I thought you were disappointed in me."

He threw his head back and laughed, not a chuckle, but a full-bodied snort of laughter that began in his belly and rose upward, erupting in a sound that could not be anything but pure enjoyment.

"You told half the town today that you love me, that you had no intention of looking at another man, no matter what he had to offer. Did I quote that right?" His hands rested on his hips now as he faced her and she felt foolish, as if she'd sealed her fate with the size of her mouth.

"Kind of," she said finally. "It's a pretty loose quotation, but you have the gist of it."

"You love me? Right?"

"That's what I said."

"Did you mean it?"

"Maybe comparatively speaking, when I thought about feeling anything for Kyle, and then considered you."

"Now what the *hell* is that supposed to mean?"

"Don't curse, please. I don't like to hear it."

"You'll hear worse than that if you compare me to that bastard again. I've damn well treated you nicely, and now you act like you had a hard time choosing between me and some dude from New York, who wasn't worth a minute of your attention."

She was stunned at his accusation. "I didn't say that. I never even thought it. Not for a minute." She felt battered by his words, insignificant in front of him, and stepped back lest he touch her again. The bed was directly behind her and she sat down on the feather tick.

"Jennifer." He reached for her, his frown intense, as if he feared she were hurt. With a total lack of finesse, he lifted her into his arms and held her. *Finesse* wasn't the most important thing in the world, she thought as she felt his solid, lean strength holding her against him. "I'm sorry," he murmured.

"I'm all right. I just lost my balance." She winced as her arms ached from his handling and he set her aside.

"Now what did I do? Hurt you again?" His eyes were sharp, focusing on her body first, then sweeping up to her arms. "I grabbed you, didn't I?"

She leaned on him again and, to his credit, he wrapped his arms around her, steering clear of her bruises. "Just hold me tight, will you, Lucas?" Aware that she hovered on the edge of tears, she inhaled, lest she dampen his shirt again. Crying seemed to be a habit of hers, one she refused to use to her advantage.

"I'll hold you all night." The words were solemn, almost a vow, and she accepted them as such.

"Thank you. I think I need to know you're here. I missed you while you were gone."

"I'm going into town in the morning to find that New Yorker, Jennifer. I hope you won't be angry if I mop the floor with him."

"He has the baby with him." Her remembrance of Kyle's words struck her. "Be careful he doesn't hurt her."

"The baby? Your neice?" He leaned past her to pull the

quilt and sheet back, then fluffed her pillow. "He won't hurt her. I'll see to it, sweetheart. Now, will you crawl into bed?"

She obeyed, not about to argue with him, unable to think of anything else but curling up in his arms. She watched as he undressed, turning her head aside as he reached his small-clothes, and then felt the bed sink beneath his weight. He pulled her into his arms and she went willingly. "Put your head on my shoulder," he said, coaxing her with soft tones. "I want to kiss you, Jennifer. Is that all right?"

"You've never asked before," she reminded him. "But I don't mind. Truly, I don't."

"I'm done with pouncing on you, honey. From now on I'm going to behave myself and bide my time. If you think enough of me to tell the whole town you love me, then I'm willing to wait till you're ready to be my wife."

"It wasn't the whole town, only that row of old gentlemen who sit on the benches in front of the stores, and half a dozen ladies who came out of the general store to listen to all the fuss."

"That row of old gentlemen are the biggest bunch of gossips you've ever laid eyes on, Jen. By now, everyone in town knows what you said, and the ladies are all aflutter with the story. And the men are envying me, every last one of them, except maybe the preacher, who seems pretty well smitten with his own wife."

She turned her face into his chest and giggled. There was no other word for it. And she hadn't giggled like a child for more years than she could remember. "I didn't say I was *smitten.*" The words apparently amused him, for he laughed again and then squeezed her.

"I know what you said, and I can't tell you how pleased I was to hear it."

She tilted her head back and looked up at him. "Really? You were pleased?"

"You have no idea. Now," he said, smothering a yawn, "tuck yourself right back here and snuggle up."

She did, willing to obey, not considering for a moment that his tone was overbearing, that his arms held her as if he took possession of her very self. For tonight she was willing to be his possession, his wife.

And the truth of the matter was, she *did* love him, more than she'd ever thought possible. It just might not be wise to repeat that again, though. He was arrogant enough as it was. No sense in giving him anything else to gloat over.

CHAPTER EIGHT

LUCAS HEADED FOR TOWN early in the morning, after breakfasting on a cup of coffee and a piece of bread. "I won't be long. Just want to look around to see if your brother-in-law had the good sense to leave on the morning train."

"If he did, he took the baby with him," Jennifer said sadly. "I'd hoped to see her."

"How old is she?" Mrs. Bronson apparently had an interest in the child, too.

"Almost a year old. She was the image of her mama, even when she was born. I'd like to know what kind of care she's getting from Kyle, given his slapdash methods of fathering during those first few months. I kept track of her as best I could, talking to his neighbors and such. Right up till I left to come here."

Lucas bent to kiss Jennifer's cheek. "I'll find out. One way or another."

He made good time, his horse fresh and ready for a run. The morning train was pulling in from the west as he reached the station and his quick scan of the platform gave no evidence of a stranger waiting to climb aboard.

"Damn fool must have stuck around." Lucas felt a surge of pleasure as he considered the confrontation that might occur in the next little while. The hotel was his next stop and the desk clerk waved a hand in welcome.

"You got a stranger here?" Lucas was tempted to turn the book around to look at the names written there, himself, but thought better of it.

"Man came in yesterday, totin' a young'un and causin' trouble in town, I hear. I suspect you're here to talk to him, Luc. But do your talkin' outside, if you please. I just paid a pretty penny to fix this lobby up. All new furniture and a nice new carpet. I'm not lookin' to have it bloodied up once you get your hands on that fella."

"Where is he?" His blood pumped through his veins as Lucas recalled the vivid bruising on Jennifer's arms. Anger was a harsh companion and he'd shared company with it all through the night. Now, just thinking of his wife and her fragile, feminine body being the target of some scallawag's cruelty made him shudder with anticipation.

He wanted nothing more than to satisfy his thirst for revenge by planting his fists in the culprit's face. "Where is he?" he repeated, his voice rough.

"In the dining room. Sitting all by himself. Don't know what he done with the little girl, but he's alone, eatin' his breakfast." The clerk's face held a degree of disgust. "I didn't hear her cryin' or makin' any fuss when I went up and listened at his door. Maybe she's sleepin'."

Lucas nodded and turned away, intent on gaining the threshold of the restaurant. Seated at a number of tables, hotel guests and townsfolk in search of a good breakfast, ate in an almost silent ritual. The sheriff sat alone near the window and Lucas wondered for a moment how that gentleman would respond to his plan of action.

And then it didn't matter, for he caught sight of the only stranger in the room, a dapper man with his hair carefully combed, his suit pressed and his shirt pristine. A sight to behold, Lucas thought sourly. He'd change that in a hurry.

With one hand he lifted the man from his seat, even as he spoke the hateful name out loud. "Your name Kyle?" Eyes bulging, the man nodded, and Lucas lifted him to his toes and headed for the door.

"Here now, Luc. What you up to?" The sheriff erupted from his chair and crossed the dining room, his hand on his gun.

"This son of a pup insulted my wife and left bruises on her." His words were an accusation in themselves and the sheriff paused, as if he considered the reason for Luc's actions.

"I can't let you go killing the man, Luc," he said. "No matter how mad you are. And bein' the mayor don't make a difference, either. That's cold-blooded murder. You came in here with criminal intent. And I can't allow mayhem in this town, no matter how much the fella deserves it."

"I didn't do anything," Kyle managed to squeak just before Lucas dragged him to the doorway and across the lobby. Lucas pushed the wide doors open and the man found himself on the sidewalk, Lucas hands holding him upright.

"You hurt my wife." The words were accusation enough, apparently, for Kyle blanched and shuddered.

"She belongs to me," he said in a confident tone that was likely false.

"Well, I've got news for you, fella. I'm the one who married her and it's my house she's living in, and my bed she's sleeping in, so I'd say you don't have any chance at her."

"She's from New York. She belongs in the city."

"She belongs right here. With me." And with that, Lucas

released Kyle from his grasp, only to swing his right arm in a wide sweep, catching Kyle's jaw with a crushing blow. The man hit the sidewalk and groaned.

Lucas gave him only a moment to catch his breath, then lifted him by the front of his not-so-pristine shirt and slammed his other fist into the man's nose. Blood spurted and Lucas stepped back out of the way, unwilling to wear mute evidence of his attack.

And yet he was not finished with him. His long fingers clenched the shirt collar, dislodging Kyle's tie and almost throttling the man. "Head back to New York if you know what's good for you," Luc said and, with a mighty blow that sent Kyle flying into the street, he finished his duty.

He turned to face the sheriff, that man having followed him out of the hotel. "You want to arrest me, Joshua, you just go right ahead. Remember one thing, though. If Jennifer was your wife, you'd have done the same thing."

Josh Tyler looked down pityingly at the man who lay in the street, his nose bleeding, his jaw already swollen and one eye turning purple. "Too bad that fella walked right into that door, ain't it?" He looked at Lucas with a grin. "Why don't you give me a hand with him and we'll let him sleep it off in a cell?"

"The pleasure's all mine." Luc held out his battered hand to the sheriff and the other man gripped it. "There's a baby girl somewhere in that hotel, Joshua. I'm gonna take her home with me."

"Who is she?"

"Jennifer's niece. We can look after her for a bit."

"If the baby belongs to this gentleman—" Joshua pointed at Kyle "—then you have no legal right to the child."

"It's a temporary measure." Lucas felt uncomfortable telling the lie, knowing that Jennifer would not be willing to give up the child once she had her hands on her.

"All right. I'll know where to find her when this bird is ready to leave town."

The baby girl was soft and feminine, and somehow felt as though she belonged in his arms. With an angelic smile she welcomed Lucas, snuggling against him.

She was dark-haired, petite and weighed less than a sack of groceries. Lucas carried her to his horse and settled her in the saddle, coaxing her to hold the saddle horn while he climbed on behind her. She fit on his lap and he reached for the small bundle the desk clerk handed him.

"It's all I found in the room that looked like baby clothes. If anything more turns up, I'll save it for you, Luc."

Tilting his hat down a bit to shade his eyes from the early morning sun, Lucas smiled his thanks and turned his gelding in the direction of home. He'd grown so used to thinking of the mine and the tent he'd lived in there as his home, that it was still a novelty to consider the farmhouse as his residence.

With Jennifer there, it had become home to him.

SHE'D MANAGED to make the bed with fresh sheets and to sweep the kitchen floor, using a pot holder to pad the broom handle lest her hand rub too hard against the wood. Now she was learning the fine art of churning butter.

"How will I know when it's done?"

Ida laughed, as if she were enjoying this series of lessons she'd undertaken to give. "You'll know. When it gets too stiff for the dasher to move, it's done. And it looks to me like you're about there."

Jennifer halted the motion of the dasher and lifted the lid. Sure enough, a firm pile of butter lay in the bottom of the wooden barrel, looking surprisingly like the pat still on the table from three days ago.

"Now we scrape it out into the wooden bowl and shape it with the wooden paddle. All the water has to be pressed out," Mrs. Bronson warned her. "That'll set it up real good and you can form half-pound rounds from it."

"How will I know if it's a half pound?" This whole procedure was more complicated than she'd thought it would be, and Jennifer doubted her ability to ever run a kitchen on her own.

"You'll know." With those confident words, Mrs. Bronson brought the wooden butter bowl to the table. Together they turned out the contents of the churn, Jennifer using the wooden paddle to squeeze and form the yellow substance. Fluid gathered, a watery byproduct of her churning, and she dumped it into a smaller dish.

"We'll mix that in with the food leftovers for the hog." Ida Bronson certainly knew her way around the place. Jennifer hadn't even known there was a hog.

She winced as her right hand cramped and she switched the paddle to the other. "Is this the way to do it?" The butter was firming up nicely, she thought, but a word of encouragement would not be amiss.

"You're doin' fine, girl. Luc's gonna be proud of you. Just don't make that hand sore or he'll be after me with the broom."

Jennifer laughed, which apparently was the purpose of the woman's gibe, and then set to work, scraping out a portion of butter and forming it in her palms into a credible imitation of Mrs. Bronson's work of just a few days ago.

She'd completed the task when she heard a horse, its

whinny loud outside the screen door. "Lucas." She jumped up and hastened to the doorway, looking out at the man who sat astride his gelding, a small bundle across his lap.

"I brought you something, Jen. Come take a look."

"Susan." The single word was a plea, a cry of triumph and the aching sound of a woman's heartbreak.

"Here you go, Jen." Lucas bent from the saddle and handed her the small form, a doll-like creature dressed in white batiste, dark hair curling, almost in imitation of the woman who held her. He watched as the child lifted a tiny hand to pat Jennifer's cheek, and then the small voice spoke a single word.

It was enough to wring tears from an old reprobate, and since Lucas had no aspirations to that position, his vision blurred, his throat tightening with emotion as he coughed, as if to belay the tears that begged to fall from his eyes.

Two small arms crept around Jennifer's neck and she laid her head atop that of the child she held. "Thank you, Lucas." It was a simple phrase, yet the import was enormous, holding a wealth of meaning, all of it directed at Lucas.

Jennifer turned, seeking a seat on the edge of the porch, and still the child clung. Jennifer stifled the cry of pain that tore at her heart. If only she could be mother to this child. If only Kyle would disappear from the face of the earth. She bit her lip, holding Susan close. And then she looked up at Lucas.

"Where is he?" There was no need to be more specific.

"Hopefully he'll be on the evening train back East. Right now he's resting in a cell in Joshua's jailhouse."

"The sheriff arrested him?"

"Not exactly." Lucas seemed uncomfortable with his own answer and Jennifer watched him as he dismounted in a graceful movement. He approached and she frowned, her sharp gaze taking note of his hands, both of them grazed and scuffed, with traces of dried blood marring the surface of his knuckles.

"What did you do to him?" Her heart beat rapidly, fearful that Lucas might have gotten into a fix because of her. "You didn't break the law, did you?"

Lucas shook his head and grinned. "I don't know of any law that says a man can't defend his wife's reputation and guarantee her personal safety. I just did both."

"You did?" And just what had he done? Her gaze flew again to his hands and she motioned him forward until he stood almost knee to knee with her dangling legs. She touched his right hand, then the left, running her fingertips over the scratches and traces of dried blood.

"You hit him, didn't you?" And more than once, it looked like.

"Yeah, I hit him, Jen. Off the sidewalk and into the street. He won't be messing with you again. I'll guarantee it, sweetheart."

"I don't see any bruises on you, Lucas." Her keen eyes scanned his face, seeking any trace of another man's fists.

"I don't have any. He didn't have a chance to throw a punch. And the sheriff watched the whole thing. Took Kyle off to a cell and sent me home. I went in to the hotel first and picked up the baby for you."

"Thank you." She repeated the phrase and again knew that it was not sufficient. Not for the overwhelming blessing he'd granted her, the safe delivery of her sister's child. *Susan.* A child she yearned to keep for her very own.

"Got any food in that kitchen?" Lucas asked. "I'm ready for something to eat, as soon as I do a few chores."

"Of course. Come back as soon as you're done." She

scooted from the edge of the porch and climbed the steps to the back door. "Ida, come see what Lucas brought home to us."

A smiling face greeted the newcomer as Ida took the child into her arms. "Aren't you just the cutest little chick to ever hatch from an egg?" The words were soft, whispered into a tiny, shell-like ear, and Susan cuddled closer to the ample bosom.

"I'm not so well equipped as you, I fear. She seems to like her resting place." Jennifer subdued a pang of envy as she watched Ida charm the child with a few phrases and a series of pats on her back and kisses on her forehead.

"She'll like you just fine," Ida said soothingly, and as if to prove her point, Susan reached for Jennifer, almost lunging as she sought the shelter of her aunt's arms. "See. What did I tell you? I don't know how you could leave her behind with that brute of a father, though." Ida frowned.

Jennifer sat and held the baby against her breast. "I didn't have a lot of choice then. I suppose I thought if Lucas were really well-to-do, I'd be able to send for Susan, and Kyle might be satisfied with sending her to me if I paid him well enough." She stood. "Now, where shall we put her? And how do we go about getting her cleaned up a little? Kyle must not have known what to do with a baby girl."

"Might as well stick her in the bedroom Lucas occupied for part of the night once. That'll keep *him* where he belongs. As to washing that little one, we can wash up her clothes, too. What there are of them. We'll get her clean in a jiffy and then keep her that way."

In the bedroom Lucas occupied for part of the night once. Jennifer felt a blush cover her cheeks as she picked a phrase from Ida's words, and she buried her face in Susan's dark hair. "In the room Lucas slept in? I didn't know you heard him."

"I don't miss much." Ida's eyes held a wealth of mirth as she took cheesecloth from a drawer and wrapped the rounds of butter in square pieces of the loosely woven fabric. "You want to sell some of this in town? They're always in the market for some at the general store. Using a churn is a thing of the past for those women in town. I think they forgot how to use a dasher, about the same time most of them lost their knack of milking a cow."

"You mean, I could actually get paid for working? For making butter and whatever else I can do to earn money?" Somehow the duties of cooking and cleaning assumed new meaning to her as Jennifer thought of using her newfound talents to her own advantage.

"Lots of ladies do pretty well with butter and egg money."

"And they get to keep it? For themselves?"

"Why not?" Ida asked. "They're the ones who've earned it. Just like Sally Jo at the barbershop. She runs a good business there, and does pretty well at it. Women are starting to fend for themselves more and more these days."

"Don't the people in town have farm animals of their own? Or isn't there room in the lots thereabouts for cows to be kept? I'd have thought some of those pieces of property are big enough for animals to be penned in."

"Lots of folks have chickens, and a few of them raise a young bullock every year for butchering, but most of the ladies buy their milk and butter at the store. A couple of farmers take big five gallon containers of milk to town every couple of days. Some of them even sell it from the backs of their wagons."

"Well, if I lived in town, I'd have a cow and chickens, too," Jennifer said. "It's too expensive to buy everything you need at the store. Makes sense to me to provide your own."

From the porch, she heard a hoot of laughter and then Lucas was in the door. "You'll make a farmer's wife yet, sweetheart. Next thing I know, you'll be doing all the chores."

"Not on your life, Lucas O'Reilly. If I ever do all the chores, it'll be for myself. Not for some man's benefit."

His hands went to his hips and he faced her with a frown. "What's that supposed to mean?"

"If I lived in town, I'd be sure I was still self-sufficient. I wouldn't be dependent on a man to provide for me."

"Like you are now?" His smile was taunting.

"You don't think I could do it?" Her hair flew as she tossed her head.

"I think you'd give it a good shot. But a woman on her own doesn't stand much of a chance." He sounded a bit arrogant, she thought, more than a little pompous, and anger began to seize her.

"We'll just see about that." Recalling her conversation with Ida, she stated a fact that was fast becoming foremost in her mind. "I happen to know that Sally Jo runs her own establishment and has made a success of it."

"She provides a service to the men of this area," Lucas said, as if explaining facts to a child. "Hers is the only barbershop around, and the men need a place to go where they can clean up and get presentable after a hard week of working their claims."

"And you don't think I'm capable of making a success of anything, do you?" She felt a pang of disappointment as he grinned at her.

"You're just beginning to make a success of being a wife, Jen. Don't push yourself beyond that."

She bent her head, the flare of anger growing instead of

abating. She'd thought to simmer down and call it a draw, but his words tugged at her, challenged her, and she began to ponder on an idea that had lain dormant for several weeks.

If she could run this house, then a larger establishment would not be beyond her capabilities. Maybe a boarding-house with paying tenants. And if she had help, someone like Mrs. Bronson to lend a hand and direct things, it might be a positive way to show Lucas that his wife was a capable woman, not a child to be scolded and talked down to.

They ate silently, Lucas apparently in a fit of pique, with Jennifer as its target. She was no better, having difficulty in keeping the pout from her lips, as she considered his high-handedness. The man needed taking down a bit. He was haughty, arrogant and several other things she couldn't put a name to right off.

The dishes were washed, dried and put away, Jennifer tending to the chore while Ida rocked Susan in a chair brought from the parlor for the purpose. She'd put it in front of the window and had been searching her memory for old hymns. Jennifer realized she'd missed being in church on Sundays, and vowed to rectify that situation forthwith.

Her hand was stinging from the hot dishwater, but she refused to pamper herself and so ignored the twinges of pain. Until Lucas came in the door, his chores finished, the animals brought in from pasture to the barn. He frowned, watching her as she stacked the plates in the kitchen dresser.

"What are you doing?" he asked.

"Taking my goldfish for a walk." Her lips pressed together as he glared at her. "What does it look like I'm doing?"

"Let me see your hand." As a request, it left a bit to be desired, she thought. And she was in no mood to take orders.

"My hand is fine. I'm busy right now, Lucas. Go tend to your horses, or something."

"My chores are finished. Now I want to see how your hand is healing."

"It's my hand. I'll see to it."

He looked at Mrs. Bronson and found no help there. The lady ignored him, singing beneath her breath to the child she held.

A large kettle of water boiled on the stove and he shifted his attention there. "What are you going to do with the hot water?"

"Wash diapers. Susan uses a lot of them."

"Tonight?"

"Actually, they should have been washed earlier, but since we didn't get to it, tonight will have to do, Lucas."

"You can't do that. You'll open the sores on your hand."

She narrowed her gaze as she looked daggers in his direction. "Don't tell me what I can or can't do, or you'll be in for a big surprise."

He laughed harshly. "Not much you can do would surprise me, Jennifer."

She dropped her eyes and placed the silverware in the drawer. "We'll see."

The simple statement seemed to wave a red flag in front of him, and Jennifer likened him to a bull, raging and ready to attack. She wasn't too far off.

He stood behind her and his fingers clutched her shoulders. Her hands ceased their movement, her breath seemed captured in her lungs and she felt a resurgence of the panic that had gripped her when Kyle had seized her in much the same way.

"Don't." The single word was whispered, the message clear, for it was accompanied by a shuddering chill that ran the length of her spine and then manifested itself in a series of shivers.

His hands fell to his sides and he inhaled. "I'm sorry, honey. I didn't mean to hurt you."

"You didn't. But not because there was no intent on your part," she said. "You meant to frighten me, intimidate me, perhaps. It won't work, Lucas." She went to Ida and took Susan from her. The baby's eyes were almost closed as she neared slumber.

The stairs were long as she climbed them, and the room she carried Susan into was barren of anything smacking of femininity, with no fripperies or frills to be seen.

"This will do for now," she whispered to the baby, settling her on the bed. She sat beside her, stripped off her clothing and sorted through the small bundle Lucas had brought from town. "I'll get you some clothes tomorrow," she said, soothing the child with soft tones and gentle touches as she changed a wet diaper and then bundled her up in a gown that hung well below her feet.

Padding the sheet so as not to allow a wet diaper to stain the mattress, she covered the little girl and lay down beside her. "Time to sleep, sweetie," she murmured, waiting till Susan turned on to her stomach and began to relax. With one hand Jennifer patted gently at the narrow back, and she sang a song of nonsense beneath her breath.

THE MAN AT THE DOOR watched silently, his mind focused on the woman in front of him. Would she stay the night with the baby or would she come to their bed later? Maybe she'd be going back downstairs to wash the diapers before bedtime, as she'd planned. Either way, she didn't stand a chance of getting out of his sight.

He retraced his steps to the kitchen, just in time to catch Ida lifting the heavy kettle of water from the stove. "I'll get that," he told her. "Where do you want it?"

"Pour about half into this tub," she instructed him. Using a saucepan, she added cold water from the pump and then gathered together the soiled diapers and clothing the child had worn throughout the day. Soap was added and Ida bent over the tub, sloshing the items in the hot water, and then lifting them, one piece at a time, to scrub them out on a small board she'd found in the pantry.

One by one she cleaned them, wrang them out and laid them aside. "Dump it please, Luc," she said simply, and waited till he carted the tub out the door and splashed the water over the flowers that bloomed at the end of the porch.

"You need this again?" He carried it back in and, at her nod, carried the kettle of hot water back to dump in a goodly amount.

"Thanks." It seemed she wasn't in a mood for small talk, and that was all right with him. He'd had all the talk he could handle for one night. If Jennifer didn't shape up and get the chip off her shoulder, he'd have to do something about it.

The sound of her footsteps coming down the stairs alerted him and he retrieved a length of clothesline from the pantry, wanting to appear busy. "You want this strung?" he asked Ida. She nodded and waved, her index finger pointing to three nails driven into the walls where he could hang the line. He did as she bade him, then sat to watch.

"Here, girl. Hang these while I finish rinsing, will you?" Her instructions to Jennifer were short and sweet, but the *girl* seemed to have no problem with taking orders from Ida. Apparently it was only her husband she defied with such an abundance of insolence. *Insolent.* That was a good word, he decided.

When the baby's laundry was done and the tub dumped once more, Jennifer murmured a good-night to Mrs. Bronson and headed up the stairs, Lucas fast on her heels. He followed her into their bedroom and watched as she withdrew her nightgown from beneath her pillow. She shook it out, apparently deemed it wearable for another night and headed for the door.

He stood in front of it. "Where do you think you're going?" As if he didn't know.

"To sleep with Susan."

"I don't think so." It was an ultimatum. The woman could take it or leave it. If she defied him, he'd keep her in their own bed any way he had to. The bed in the other room held a baby girl, and unless she was sick or fussing as babies sometimes did, she'd sleep alone.

"Don't try to stop me." Jennifer held the gown in front of herself as a shield and Lucas grinned.

"You're sleeping in my bed." Leaving her no room to bicker, he frowned.

"I don't want to sleep with you. Besides, Susan needs me."

"Susan is fine, sound asleep in fact. The one who needs you is me."

"I don't want you to touch me."

"Is that supposed to be something out of the ordinary?" he asked. "It seems you never change your tune, Jen. It's like you're a statue in a museum. Look but don't touch. And I'll tell you, lady, I'm tired of it."

"Too bad." She turned her back and unbuttoned her dress, then allowed it to drop to the floor, her petticoat fast behind it. The nightgown went over her head and he watched as she maneuvered beneath its folds, removing the rest of her clothing. After picking up the bits and pieces and folding them neatly, she went to the bed and pulled back the sheet and quilt.

"I'm sleeping here, Lucas, but only because I don't want to air my anger in front of Ida. I'll figure something else out tomorrow."

"I think maybe you ought to figure it out tonight," he said, tossing his shirt aside, then beginning on his shoes and stockings. In moments, he'd stripped and occupied his half of the bed.

Jennifer blew out the candle beside the bed and covered herself. "Are you threatening me?"

"If you want to call it that. I'm just telling you that I'm tired of being the bottom man on the totem pole around here."

"You're the *only* man around here." She smiled as she spoke and he rolled to lie half atop her. Her smile disappeared and she caught her breath.

"Don't push me." As a warning, it sounded pretty ominous, he thought. Anyone else would have taken heed. But not Jennifer.

She sat up, catching him off guard, and pushing him aside as she turned her head to face him. "I'd like to go to sleep, Lucas. I've had a long day and tomorrow isn't looking to be any better. Please just let me alone for now."

He relented, not because he felt sorry for her, but because he recognized the truth in her statement. Antagonizing Jennifer wouldn't do his cause any good. She was already fit to be tied and he didn't want to push her any further.

"All right. We'll talk about it tomorrow." It was the best he could do, torn between kissing her and turning her over his knee. And that was one thing he'd never do. He didn't have it in himself to hurt her. What he wanted to do was to strip that stupid gown from her and make her his wife.

And that was God's own truth.

CHAPTER NINE

SUSAN DEFINITELY NEEDED more clothing than Kyle had brought along for her, and the general store was the only place to find it. With the kitchen cleaned, Lucas on his way to the mine for the day and dinner simmering on the back of the stove, Jennifer made plans.

"I thought we'd go to the Emporium and then I've got a little side trip to make, if you'll keep the baby happy for a bit," she told Ida.

"I can do that. And don't forget we need a couple of good heavy pads for this child to sleep on. We can't have her soaking through to the mattress."

"I thought a piece of oilcloth might work." Jennifer halted in her list making to look up at Ida for confirmation.

"That might work. And she needs more dresses. Two just ain't gonna be enough. We can't be washing every day. Honestly, how do you suppose her father managed to keep her in one piece? With just a handful of things to do with."

"That's the problem. He didn't, at least not well," Jennifer reminded her. "But I need to keep remembering not to make long-term plans for her. After all, we may not have her forever. Once her father gets out of jail, he'll be hot to trot, all the way back to New York, and he'll take this baby with him, I'll bet. If the sheriff lets him."

"Not if he can't find her, he won't." Ida pulled a face, muttering a rebuttal. "Now, just forget I said that."

Jennifer brightened. "That might not be a bad idea. I wonder where we could hide her."

"We could move her into my place, and I could stay there with her till the fancy man is gone," Ida suggested. "It's a big barn of a house, far too big for me to handle by myself, but he'd never find her there. That house was all right when I had a houseful of young'uns running around, but after the mister died, I rattled around in it like a loose walnut in a bushel basket. We'll just keep our heads down and not make a stir in town. Folks don't have to know we're there."

"That might work," Jennifer said. "But I was thinking…" She paused and aimed a long look at the other woman. "This is just between you and me, you understand. But I've been mulling over an idea."

Ida was silent for a moment and then she nodded. "All right. I won't say a word. At least not to anyone else. But let me tell you, girl, you'd better watch your step with Lucas. He's been good to you, and more patient than most men would have been, waiting for you to put this marriage together. And don't look at me like that," she said. "I live in that house with you, and if ever a man was hard up for some comfort from his wife, it's Lucas O'Reilly. You need to play fair with him. He brought you out here in good faith and he's got the short end of the stick, in my opinion. 'Course, you haven't had an easy ride of it, either, but a woman can put up with stuff better than a man. It's ingrained." She paused for breath and went on.

"I don't want you mad at me, but I had to speak my piece,

girl. You could keep him happy with a little lovin' and he wouldn't be such a pain in the patoot. Now, I know you're champin' at the bit, thinking about making a move on your own, but think it over, long and hard before you make a decision. You're a woman, after all, and you need Lucas and the protection of marriage to keep you safe from that Kyle fella."

Jennifer nodded, not that she agreed with everything Ida said, but she had to admit the woman had a point. Several, in fact. Coaxing her into the plan Jennifer had dreamed up might not be as easy as she'd hoped after all.

With four hands, they harnessed the horses readily, then headed for town. Mrs. Bronson drove, Jennifer holding Susan beside her. The general store was busy, buggies and farm wagons lining the street out front, but they found an empty spot at the hitching rail and went inside.

The assortment of baby clothes was limited but adequate. "I don't dare get too much," she said in an aside to Ida. "I'm putting this on Lucas's bill, and I'll have to figure out how to pay for them myself."

"You sound like you've an idea up your sleeve." She spoke the words in an undertone and Jennifer nodded.

"Yes, but it all depends on you. Whether or not you're willing to go along with what I talked to you about and what I'd like to do."

"You said you wanted to chance earning a living, and I suspect it has to do with moving out of Lucas's house, but beyond that, I'm still not sure of your idea. Let's have the whole plan, girl. I'm willing to listen."

"After we leave here," Jennifer said, and Ida seemed to be satisfied with that.

By the time they climbed back into the wagon, Lucas had

amassed a tidy amount on his running account. The bundles were stacked in one corner of the wagon and when Ida picked up the reins, Jennifer pointed to the far end of town.

"That's down near my place," Ida said and, at Jennifer's nod, she grinned.

"Like I told you, I'm thinking about a business I can go into," Jennifer told her. "There are a bunch of men who are sleeping in tents, and who'd probably give an arm and a leg for a decent bed and decent meals. What do you think?"

"You need a boardinghouse to make that happen." And then as if she'd just caught a glimmer of where Jennifer's mind was going, she snapped the reins and the horses broke into a trot. "You want to use my house and set up business there." She did not ask a question but made a statement.

"That's right. And I want to stop and see Sally Jo at the barbershop, too. She's made a success of her business and I thought she might have some ideas to offer."

THE WOMAN did indeed have ideas and her obvious delight at Jennifer's notions sent both of them searching for pencil and paper as they wrote down plans as fast as their pencils would fly.

"A cook is the first thing you'll need."

"I hope to have one," Jennifer said. "If Ida Bronson is willing, and I think she will be."

"You can't ask for better than Mrs. Bronson," Sally Jo announced. "And how about girls to clean and do laundry?"

Jennifer grimaced. "That's me, Sally Jo. We can't afford to hire help right off. And I'm a good hand at cleaning these days. Ida has been tutoring me for weeks. I swing a dandy dust cloth, let me tell you. And putting together beds is a snap."

"I'd say you've got things pretty much under control,"

Sally Jo told her. "You need to go to the bank and open a business account. I can introduce you to the man in charge there. Mr. Walter Powers, by name. He gave me a loan, and I'll bet with Mrs. Bronson backing you and providing the house, he'd be willing to get you started in business." She paused and looked at Jennifer. "What about Lucas?"

"What about him?"

"He's gonna be madder than a wet hen, you know. Or is he kicking you out and leaving you on your own?"

"Lucas wouldn't do that. He's too honorable."

"And you? Will he think this is an honorable thing for you to be doing?"

Jennifer shook her head. "He's going to have a fit, but I can't help that. I guess I just need to prove myself capable of being a success at *something*. So far I've fallen short in everything he's expected of me. So I'll be not only trying to prove a point as far as Lucas is concerned, but to myself." She felt troubled suddenly by the things she'd set into motion, things involving Ida and leaving Lucas out of the picture. And then Sally Jo spoke again.

"Well, I'd say your plans sound solid thus far, and you're a smart lady. You should do well."

"You think so? Really?" It seemed almost too easy, Jennifer thought, but she'd never been one to cause problems where there were none and she wasn't about to start now.

Jennifer climbed back up onto the wagon seat and the two women moved on down the road, Mrs. Bronson intent on the lists she held, offering suggestions as they went. Arriving at the big house, Jennifer was almost stunned by its size.

"I don't remember seeing your house the day I got married, and we were right next door at the parsonage. I must have been in a daze. And you didn't tell me it had three floors. Will you look at that front porch? It's wrapped all the way around one side, and you've got two swings on it."

Ida preened a bit. "My mister wanted me to have the best. A good, solid place, he always said, and with the gold he mined, we could afford it. I've still got a nice nest egg in the bank, and Lucas has paid me well for the weeks I've been at the farm. We'll do just fine, whether Walter Powers wants to make you a loan or not. Women aren't considered a good risk. Just remember one thing, Jennifer. I'm not dead certain this is a good idea, and if Lucas puts his foot down, I won't blame him a bit. But it sure would be nice to come back home. And even have all these rooms."

"If he puts his foot down, it'll have to be a pretty heavy foot, Ida. I don't plan to give in to him on this. I want to try to do it on my own, so if I have to ask for a loan, I will, but if we can work it out without borrowing money, that's even better. For now, let's just see the house and go on from there. We'll have to stock up on food and get linens for the beds and then put up a sign and we'll be open for business."

"A sign?" Ida looked dubious.

"Sally Jo said we needed a sign on the porch with our prices spelled out clearly. Or even in the front hallway, so there's no room for discussion. She even offered to paint it for us. Did you know she'd painted her own? And the front of her shop, too?"

"Can't say that I knew that. But it doesn't surprise me any. She's a smart woman. There were those in town who said she'd never make a go of it, and some of them whispered about the bathtubs in her back room, but once some of the husbands went by and got haircuts and shaves and saw what really goes on there, things quieted down and folks pretty much left her alone."

"She *doesn't* bathe the men…does she?" The words were whispered and Jennifer looked around as if someone might be privy to this conversation that had suddenly tuned to private matters.

Mrs. Bronson hooted. "Of course not. Sally Jo has her hands full with the men who come courting every chance they get. She's the most popular woman in town. I suspect it's because some of these fellas like the idea of having their own personal barber."

The two women clambered from the wagon, Ida passing the baby down to Jennifer. Susan looked around and her eyes were wide, with so much to see—so many bright flowers blooming and, most exciting of all, a dog in the front yard.

She pointed her tiny index finger. "Goo." Plainly she had seen such a creature somewhere else, Jennifer decided, but hadn't yet figured out what they were called.

She laughed and Ida joined them, speaking to the mutt who had run to the gate to greet them. "Hey there, Buster," she said cheerfully. "Are you glad to see me?" She turned to Jennifer then. "I really missed the mutt. My old neighbor feeds him for me. I knew it wouldn't do for me to be trotting back and forth just to take care of a dog, so Mr. Thomas calls Buster to the fence every day and puts a bowl of food over here for him, then dumps a bucket of water into the big basin we keep filled for him."

"We're going to have a dog in our house?" Jennifer was delighted, the bonus of a pet cinching the bargain, so far as she was concerned.

"Well, I've never made much of a pet of him, but he sneaks indoors every chance he gets. It's nice to have him around, kinda fills the empty places. He kinda goes with place, if you don't mind."

"Of course not. I'm taking over your house and placing myself and Susan in the midst of your life, Ida. I'll do whatever you think is right. I can't tell you how happy I am that you're willing to be my friend and help me in this."

They walked together to the front porch and Jennifer climbed the steps slowly, wanting to make the excitement last. But the house awaited her and she was champing at the bit to make final plans for her new establishment.

"I've never been so excited over anything in my life," she said, opening the front door and stepping into the wide foyer. Three doors opened from the entryway and a staircase soared upward to the second floor. The first room on the right was a parlor, large and welcoming, the furniture looking plush and comfortable. The room was shadowed, with the draperies pulled closed.

"I didn't want the carpet to fade, so I shut everything up when I moved out to the farm." The filmy curtains beneath the heavy drapes were exposed as Ida pulled the layer of fabric back. Sunlight poured through the white lace and illuminated the flowered sofa and chairs that formed intimate groupings around the room.

"How beautiful." Jennifer was in the middle of the floor, holding Susan in her arms, turning in a slow circle, the better to inspect everything. "This will be a lovely place for folks to sit in the evening. We might even add a table for chess or checkers."

"Mr. Bronson had a chessboard. I think it's up in the attic. We can bring it down if you like." As if she were revisiting a site precious to her memory, Ida traveled the perimeter of the room, touching small ornaments, adjusting the antimacassars to lie neatly, and then moving on to the mantel, where a row of pictures gave Jennifer a view of the children born to this lady. They were portraits done in watercolors and oil, and someone had possessed an abundance of talent, for the faces seemed almost lit from behind, so sharply were the features drawn.

"Who did the paintings?" Jennifer suspected that an artist had been brought in for a family visit. Upon a closer look, she spotted the same assortment of faces in the large portrait that hung low over the fireplace. A younger version of Ida Bronson was the focal point of the painting, with a tall, handsome man by her side. Surrounding them were seven children, three of them almost grown, the others scattered in ages from a toddler to a gangly teen boy.

"Your family." Jennifer stepped closer, wanting to get a first-hand view of Ida's past. "Where are they all now?"

"Scattered. A couple of the boys live here in town, but the girls married and moved away. The oldest—" she pointed at a tall youth who looked much like Mr. Bronson "—Robert is a doctor in Philadelphia. I don't see much of him. But, Belle, my youngest girl, is just a few miles from here. She has four youngsters now. She married young. They all have their own lives now."

"No wonder you're so good with Susan," Jennifer said, feeling the warmth of a happy family in this house. "And I can understand why you didn't want to live here all alone. It would have been difficult with no one around, after you'd shared your home with so many."

"It was the final leaving that broke my heart, though," Ida said. "When my mister died, it was like the sun quit shining and there was no more left here for me. I'm thinking if we fill this place with people who need a good home and decent meals and comfortable beds, it'll be a happy house again."

IT SEEMED that the difficult part was in front of her, Jennifer thought after they arrived at home and it was time for her husband to show up for supper. For telling Lucas that their marriage was, in effect, null and void, over, as far as she was concerned, was going to create a real problem, one he would put all his energy into solving. One she was wishing with all her heart could be fixed with a simple solution. Lucas had found a place in her life and giving him up would not be easy, torn as she was between her independence and the fact that she had learned so quickly to love him. And for a moment she wavered.

And then she found that telling him wasn't going to be difficult at all, for Lucas came home from the mine with his eyes flashing fire.

"What the hell do you think you're doing?" he said, shouting at her from the doorway as he entered the kitchen.

"Cooking your supper." It was, it seemed, the wrong thing to say, for the kitchen chair standing in front of him hindered his progress and he threw it across the room.

"I don't need a smart answer, Jennifer. I want to know why you're intent on making me a laughingstock in town."

She turned to face him, suddenly aware of her precarious position. "I'm doing no such thing. I simply decided that if I'm going to be cleaning up and cooking for a man, I might as well get paid for it."

He seemed stunned for a moment, his eyes widening, as if he could not believe what he'd just heard. And then he stalked across the room and she was trapped by the cookstove behind her and the raging male in front of her.

"You get paid. Probably more than you're worth," he snarled. "You get free room and board and you've got a roof over your head. What more have you earned since you've been here?"

She closed her eyes. Her importance to him was obviously at its lowest level. The man considered her as almost worthless, it seemed. In fact, if she understood his words as well as she thought she had, he was not happy with her performance as a wife.

She attempted to answer his challenge. "Not much, apparently, Lucas. Obviously, I haven't done enough to even earn your respect."

His fist clenched at his sides and then opened, and he rested his wide palms against his hips. "Lady, let me tell you something. If I didn't respect you, you'd know it by now. I've respected your wishes, done whatever you wanted, ever since you got here. So don't go giving me that claptrap about not respecting you."

Ida got up from the rocking chair and headed for the kitchen door. "I think the baby and I will go take a walk while you finish putting supper together, Jennifer." She let the screen door slam behind her as she paraded across the porch and down the steps.

"I think I'd better tell you that I bought the baby some things at the general store today, and put the whole total on your account. If you want me to, I'll figure out some way to pay you for them later."

"You know better than that. I'll gladly pay for anything she needs." He inhaled sharply and his tone changed, becoming strident once more. "Now get away from that stove so I can talk to you."

"I'm cooking," Jennifer said. "I need to be in front of the stove to stir the beans and make the gravy."

"I don't want you falling back against the pots and burning yourself again." He backed away two steps. "Come over here."

"I'll talk to you after supper, Lucas. Now isn't the time or place for this discussion."

His mouth tightened as if held back words that begged to be spewed out, and then nodded. "All right. After supper."

JENNIFER CARRIED SUSAN upstairs and put her to bed, the routine almost an exact duplicate of the night before. She sat beside the baby, propping pillows on either side of the child, so that she couldn't roll off the bed, and then waited until Susan was sleeping, her fist in her mouth, her small body relaxed in the middle of the big bed.

Finding her way to her own bed took more strength than Jennifer possessed tonight. She dreaded the coming confrontation with Lucas, knowing that the man had a point, that his anger was not entirely unwarranted. It seemed even Ida was siding with him. But, Jennifer could not budge from her stand, no matter how upset he was. No matter how much Ida tried to impress on her the danger in what she'd planned.

"Now, let's have it." Lucas was waiting for her and the door was barely closed before he took his stand. "I'm sick of hearing secondhand from men in town that my wife is the topic of gossip."

"Gossip?" She was astounded that her activities could be construed as cause for gossip.

"Yeah. What else would you call it? Mrs. Lucas O'Reilly is about to open a boardinghouse for miners. She's gonna leave her happy home and set herself up in business."

"'My happy home.'" She repeated his statement and smiled. "Maybe that's the problem, Lucas. I'm not happy here. I've been a failure as your wife and I know it. I work hard, harder than I've ever worked in my life."

"That wouldn't be too difficult to accomplish, I'd think. From what I've seen, your life was a bed of roses before you got here. I doubt you did anything more strenuous than combing your hair in New York City."

"Well, thank you very much." Recoiling, she thought she caught sight of remorse in his eyes.

"I'm not trying to give you a hard time, Jen. I'm just trying to figure out what you want from me. What do you expect me to do? I've gotten you some help in the house, and Ida Bronson is the best there is. I've given you a free hand at the general store, within reason anyway, and I've been patient."

"Patient isn't a word I'd use in connection with you." Jennifer spoke quickly and then wished she had the words back, as Lucas's eyes narrowed.

"You don't think I've been patient? Well, let me tell you, lady, I'm about the most patient man you'll ever find. I've been sleeping with you for weeks, and I've yet to find any comfort in your body, except for a few kisses, and those weren't often freely given."

"That's not true. I've kissed you numerous times. And I've slept all curled up beside you every night."

But I haven't given you my body.

That thought sounded in her mind and she turned from him. She'd been wrong to deny him his rights, and yet it frightened her to think of a man's hands on her, to consider his strong fingers clasping her tender flesh. She was beyond the age of most brides, but perhaps this was part of the reason. She'd been pursued as a young girl, but never been tempted to allow a man's touch upon her person.

Now, Lucas, unless she was mistaken, seemed about to overcome her objections and do as he wanted with her.

His next move proved the point, for he picked her up in his arms, as easily as if she weighed less than nothing, and she knew for a fact that she was a bit plump in the hips and in no way could be called skinny, although Lucas had seemed to have that opinion of her. And now, he held her close, looking down into her face with an expression like that of a man set on pleasing himself.

She was dumped onto the bed and his hands were busy, undoing her buttons and tapes, pulling her clothing from her and tossing it hither and yon, with no care for the bits and pieces of undergarments and smallclothes she wore. In less time than she could have imagined, he'd reduced her to a shivering bundle of naked femininity, and the shivering was not due to a chill in the air.

But rather to the man who hovered over her with anger and lust in his gaze.

He took off his own clothing, and she did not protest his actions, knowing it would only cause a fuss that would be audible in Ida's bedroom across the hall. She held her fears close and watched him. He had the art of undressing down to a science, she decided, ripping his boots and stockings from his feet and tossing them aside, then shedding shirt, trousers and drawers in less than a minute.

"Now, who's supposed to pick up your mess in the morning?" she asked, pressing home her point. "I'm nothing but a maid here, and I can earn money cleaning up after men in a boardinghouse, Lucas. Men who will no doubt appreciate me."

"I'm about to appreciate you, ma'am," he muttered, falling to the bed beside her.

"I don't want you to do this." Her voice was thin, without inflection, and she felt a sense of hopelessness that made her almost immobile.

"I'm tired of doing what you want, Jen. This is going to be an example of what I want." He reached for her, pulling her closer, and she winced as his fingers touched the bruises left by Kyle so short a time ago.

"Are you going to be a wife beater? Or just a man who takes what is his, no matter who he hurts?"

He snarled at her, a word she flinched from, and then he smiled, a feral look of triumph lighting his features.

"I'm not apologizing for my language or my actions, lady. I'm not planning to beat you. I'm just going to be a husband tonight, and if you never speak to me again, at least I'll have known just once what you might have been to me."

"You mean a real wife?" It was a whisper of disbelief.

"Yeah. We might have had a good marriage, might have found pleasure in this bed, but you wouldn't have it, would you?"

"Pleasure? For whom? I've never heard of any pleasure for a woman in circumstances like these."

"You might be surprised at what occurs in a marriage bed when two people care for each other, when a woman is warm and willing."

"I'll never know, will I? I'm neither warm nor willing, Lucas. And tomorrow, you'll remember I said those words. I hope you regret this for all the days of your life." She laughed, a bitter sound as she considered her hope for his future. "Although, now that I think about it, I doubt you will."

"I don't plan on regretting anything that happens here tonight. I'm planning on celebrating my marriage, and if you find some small bit of joy in it, I hope it haunts you, knowing what you might have found here with me."

He bent lower over her and took her mouth in a kiss that seemed to have no ending. His lips were firm, his tongue a weapon as he invaded her mouth and ravaged where he willed. Even though she tried to evade his kiss, he held her chin with one hand. She was pinned beneath him, obviously providing him with some sort of satisfaction.

And then his mouth softened against hers, his tongue withdrew from the battle he'd instigated and his hands framed her face, holding her in front of him with a tenderness that made her want to weep. This was the Lucas she'd known, the gentle man who kissed her warmly and held her carefully, cherishing her.

And then he raised himself above her, even as his mouth traveled across her throat, tasting her skin, suckling the soft flesh beneath her chin. Her breasts were the focus of his attention next, and he held one cupped in his palm, then touched the crest with the tip of his tongue. She jerked, surprised by the strange heat that cascaded through her body.

"You like that, don't you?" His whisper was hoarse, guttural, as if he'd lost his breath, and then he suckled her, his mouth opening wide to enclose as much of her breast as he could hold. She stiffened beneath him, afraid of his passion.

But there was more, for his hands sought out all the secret places on her body, those soft, womanly areas where no man had trespassed before, where she was as virgin as the day she was born. He traced each curve, each hollow, every line of her hips and thighs, and then his concentration narrowed and his hand softened its touch.

"Don't fight me, Jen. I don't want to hurt you."

She stifled a sob, for she feared the pain of his invasion would go beyond the physical. She felt violated already, subdued by this man who took her without her choice, who made of her body a thing to be used without care.

Except that he did care. Even in her despair, she recognized that fact. He could have been cruel, for his strength was more than sufficient to overwhelm her. He could have already pierced her maidenhead, for there was no doubt in her mind but that he was capable of doing just that with little effort.

And then, as if he knew her thoughts, those same hands softened in their explorations, his fingers careful as they touched tender flesh, and she knew a moment when pleasure rippled through her. Her body stilled as if waiting for the next move of that hand, the next rotation of his fingers, there where she was vulnerable and exposed to his touch.

He did not disappoint her, for his whispers coaxed her even as his movements tempted her, and she was drawn into a whirlwind of sensation that seemed inescapable. Indeed, she had no thought of escape, but reveled in the ecstasy of giving him what he asked of her.

And then he was over her, between her thighs, and she felt a stab of fear as he looked down at her. The candle had burned low, but he was more than visible, his expression fierce, his cheekbones prominent, his mouth drawn back, exposing his teeth.

She felt the pressure of his arousal against her, knew a moment of terror that forced from her a soft cry. "Don't hurt me, Lucas. Please."

He shook his head and she hoped that he was agreeing to her plea, that his touch would not be piercing, his invasion of her body would not bring her a pain she could not tolerate. "Relax, Jen. Let me…"

The request was lost in a sensation of being torn asunder, and yet it was less than the pain she had feared, for it was more a filling of her very self by the man who held her, who possessed her body with the proof of his manhood. The man who had claimed her as his wife.

CHAPTER TEN

LUCAS OPENED HIS EYES slowly, not wanting to interrupt the dream he'd been involved in, and found, to his surprise, that the major part of that dream was in his arms. She slept cradled against him, and his lips curved in remembrance as he recognized his dream as reality.

She'd been all he'd ever imagined, even as unwilling as she had been to begin with. He'd been afraid for a few minutes that his methods had been too primitive, his treatment of her too harsh. But her response had tossed both of those theories to the wind and he'd basked in her response, recognizing her surrender as she found completion in his embrace.

She was his. Finally and thoroughly. No more dithering around like a lusty youth. He'd had enough of that to last him a lifetime. Being a husband was what suited him best, and given Jennifer's final sigh of exhaustion last night, it seemed to be what lay in his future.

She was his wife, the marriage consummated and well on track. And if he played his cards right, he might even find her willing to surrender once more before they arose from this bed to face the day. Even as his thoughts touched on that idea, he felt her stir beside him, her sigh signaling an imminent awakening.

She slid one hand across his chest and her fingers twined

in the hair she encountered there. A sound much like a soft growl came from her lips and she bent forward, eyes still closed and placed a soft kiss at the base of his throat.

Lucas stilled, unwilling to disturb her exploration, yet hardly able to control the enthusiastic response of his arousal as she opened her lips against his cheek. He turned his head, just a little, enabling her to press her mouth against his, and she did just that. With a degree of enthusiasm he hadn't expected, her lips grew soft and then opened beneath his, suckling at his lower lip and then seeking out the whiskered skin of his cheek once more.

"You need to shave." The words were rasping, her early morning voice husky and inviting.

"Later." He wasn't about to disturb the mood, not when Jennifer seemed so ready to fall in with his hastily made plans. His hands ran the length of her back and she squirmed against him, wiggling closer as if she welcomed the firm proof of his arousal against her belly.

"You're all whiskery." She sounded as if a pout were forming and he looked down at lush lips that were indeed pooched out in blatant invitation. Not one to ignore such a thing, he kissed her, this time making it more of a seduction, losing himself in her soft embrace as she pressed closer, lifting her leg across his thigh and allowing him the access he needed.

He slid his hand down to creep between their bodies, his hand cupping her warmth, his long fingers pressing for entrance, there where she was hot and damp.

"Lucas?" Her voice spoke his name and her eyes opened, wide and startled, as she awoke. "What are you doing?"

"Loving you." He thought it an appropriate answer, given their new status. But Jennifer seemed dubious.

"It's morning Lucas. The sun is shining and Mrs. Bronson

will be up. If fact, I'm surprised that Susan hasn't woken yet She'll be hungry."

"Ida can look after her for a few minutes," he murmured against her ear. "We can just cuddle a bit before we get up."

"Cuddle? Is that what you call this?" As if she had only become aware of the caressing hand that had possessed her feminine parts, she moved her leg, but he pressed more firmly, keeping her captive where she lay.

"Hush, Jen. Just let me do this. Please."

It seemed she would not resist, for the moan that was muffled against his throat was not one of pain or distress. Rather, it sounded to him like that of a woman well on her way to pleasure. She wiggled against his touch, breathing deeply, her arm moving to grip his shoulder, then her fingers found purchase at the nape of his neck and she moaned again.

"You're my wife, Jen. You've made me a happy man, sweetheart." His voice was hoarse as he felt the urge to press deep within her. Rolling to his back, he brought her atop him, and as her legs fell to either side of his hips, he lifted just a bit and his manhood sought and found the entrance that seemed made for his possession.

She winced just a bit and he halted, halfway home, but unwilling to hurt her.

"You okay, sweetheart?"

"Um…yes. I think so. Just a little sore." She shifted a bit as if she would ease his way and her face dropped to rest against his shoulder. "Can you do it this way?"

His answer was designed to set her mind at ease. "You'd be surprised at how many ways we can do this, Jen. I'll show you all of them one day. Or night."

"But not now, Lucas. Right now, I'm hurting just a little."

"Let me help," he whispered, lifting her a bit, insinuating his hand against her, touching the places he knew would bring her pleasure. She allowed it in fact, much to his surprise, she accommodated him without hesitation—and in less than a minute, her cry of completion sounded in his ear.

He pushed deeper and she did not cringe or resist. "All right?" he asked, hoping against hope she would not deny him this.

"All right." It was a whisper, but it was all the encouragement he needed. Satisfaction such as he'd never known sizzled through his veins, plunging him into an abyss of pure joy, and he clasped her closer, as if he would blend their bodies in such a way that nothing could ever change the happiness he'd found in this bed.

SURELY THIS WAS about as unladylike a position as anyone had ever been subjected to, Jennifer thought. She was at once embarrassed and just a bit feeling put upon. Lucas had made of her a hussy, pure and simple. And she didn't like the feeling of shame that swept over her.

She'd expected one day to submit to him and his lusty nature. Never had she imagined herself participating in this act of marriage to the extent of allowing him the freedom to caress her body as he had. And now she had to get up and face him in the light of day, look in his eyes, see the knowing gaze he would turn on her. No doubt he'd be reliving her moments of surrender to him, gloating over the easy capitulation of her body at his urging.

She slid from her position onto the sheet and rolled to the side of the bed. Her feet were on the floor her gown pulled down to cover her body, a body that still tingled in all the inappropriate places he'd managed to bring pleasure to during the last few minutes.

She was angry and determined to remain in control of her own life. Rather, she thought a bit sheepishly, she'd have to gain that control once more, for Lucas had swept it from her grasp during the night, had made of her a clinging female, bowing to his will.

"You all right?" His words stiffened her spine and she reached for her robe, pulling it on and tying it at her waist before she turned to face him where he lay against his pillow. His smile was soft, inviting and she forced herself to ignore the dimple that dented one cheek. She'd never noticed it before. It gave him a boyish look, and she'd had proof positive that Lucas was not a callow youth. Not by a long shot.

"I'm fine."

He seemed to understand her reticence, for he rose slowly, careful to pull his drawers on before he turned to face her. "Don't be angry with me, Jen. I did my best not to hurt you last night. But I knew you'd feel some degree of pain, and it couldn't be helped."

"I'm not angry with you," she said tightly. "Only myself, that I fell into your plan so quickly."

"My plan?"

"Don't try to tell me you didn't have this whole scene set up in your mind, Lucas. I'm not a total dolt. You were determined to consummate this marriage, even though you knew I wasn't ready for this."

His mouth firmed and his eyes darkened as he lifted his arms, crossing them over his chest. "You were ready, Jen. Trust me."

"But that's the problem. I don't trust you. I thought I could and I was wrong. You tossed me on this bed like a sack of potatoes and used me like one of those girls who stood on the balcony over the saloon the day I arrived in town."

"Ah, that's where you're wrong. I treated you like my wife, not a whore. There's a subtle difference, Jen, and I'd be happy to demonstrate if you like."

"You won't be touching me again." Her vow was harsh, her shiver apparent and he was silent for just a moment. And then he uttered words that sealed his fate as far as Jennifer was concerned.

"I'll touch you any time I please. I'm your husband and I have the right."

Her fear and anger must have been apparent in the look she cast him, as he seemed to regret his foolishness immediately.

"Jennifer, I'm sorry. I shouldn't have said that."

"You're right," she told him. "You shouldn't have." With a swirl of her long robe, she turned to the door and opened it. Lucas strode toward her, but she was gone before he was halfway across the room.

"Damn." It was a muffled curse, uttered as he picked up his trousers and plunged his legs into them. His shirt was next and he ignored the buttons, leaving the garment to hang open. Barefoot, he followed her.

Ida gave him a look of inquiry as he burst across the threshold into the kitchen.

"Where is she?" He left no room for questions.

"If you're talking about Jennifer, she just went out onto the porch." Ida cleared her throat. "What did you do to her, Lucas? She looks like she's caught between a rock and a hard place. I've never seen her like this."

"I made a damn fool of myself." He couldn't explain it any other way, and since Ida was as smart as any woman he'd ever met, there was no point in trying to whitewash his behavior.

"Hmm…well I suppose you'd better try to make amends,

but I wouldn't hold out a lot of hope this morning. You might want to give her some time to pull herself together."

He went to the kitchen door and opened it. On the porch, Jennifer stood looking out across the meadow beyond the barn, her arms hugging her waist, her shoulders shaking as if she sobbed.

He could not bear it. That he had made this proud woman cry, that he had demeaned their coming together in the marriage bed in such a way by his harsh words, piled guilt on his head.

I'll touch you any time I please. I'm your husband and I have the right.

"Stupid. You're a stupid man, Lucas O'Reilly." He muttered the words beneath his breath, cringing as he recalled the things he'd said in the heat of anger. No apology would erase them from her mind. Or his, for that matter.

The spring in the screen door announced his coming and Jennifer lifted a hand to wipe her eyes. She would not cry in front of him. Would not let him know how badly his words had pierced her. No man had the right to do as he pleased. Husband or not, he was bound by the privacy entitled his wife.

What privacy? She almost laughed as she considered the total invasion of her body he'd instigated. She'd lost her entitlement to privacy last night, and no court in the land would hear her, should she seek a bill of divorcement. And that was exactly what she wanted. She would not expose herself again to the seduction of his mouth and hands, the control he'd wielded over her.

She'd been like putty, soft and pliable, had moved as he directed. She'd kissed him, held him in her arms, and almost begged for the consummation he'd staged. She'd been a spineless woman in his hands—and never again would she put herself in such a position.

His palms settled on her shoulders carefully, as if he expected her rebuff. "Jennifer, please turn around and look at me."

"I can't."

"Why not?" His words held a touch of amusement and anger bade her face him, lest he think her a coward. She might have lost the battle he'd waged last night, but never would she back down from him.

With a quick movement, she shifted, turning into his arms. "Let go of me, Lucas."

"I don't think so."

"You'll either let go of me or we'll both be falling off this porch," she said. Her feet moved backward and he gripped her, pulling her from the edge.

"Don't be foolish," he warned her. "You're the one who'd be landing on the bottom, and I guarantee you'd be hurt. I won't have that, Jennifer. You've been hurt enough at my hand." He stepped back, leaning against the house and hauling her with him.

"Now, come on in the house with me and we'll have breakfast. We can talk about this later on when we don't have an audience."

She bowed her head, unwilling to look at him. "I'm not hungry."

"Mrs. Bronson will be disappointed if you don't eat. She's made pancakes for you."

"You can have my share."

From the doorway, a soft voice spoke. "Come on in, Jen. Have some coffee." Ida smiled and held the door open. "This baby is hungry," she said. "I'll bet she'd eat a pancake with a little help."

"All right." Unable to deny her responsibility toward Susan,

Jennifer crossed the threshold and picked up the child from the chair she'd been sitting on, working on a bit of bread. It was mush now, between her fingers and on her face, and she apparently thought it still edible, for she lifted one hand to her mouth and sucked her index finger.

"Let me help you," Jennifer said, smiling at the triumphant look Susan wore. The baby chewed on her mouthful, then lifted her hand to seek out another bit of damp bread. "How about a pancake instead?"

Sitting in her chair, Jennifer watched as Ida placed two hot-cakes on her plate, then pushed the butter across the table.

"I'll get you some syrup from the pantry," Ida said.

"Jam might work better." And would definitely be easier to clean up.

Jennifer buttered the brown, steaming pancakes and added the jam Ida brought. Then she held Susan's hands between her own palms, fingers pointed upward. "Thank you for this food," she prayed, slowly and quietly in the baby's ear. And then opened her eyes to find Lucas across the table, his gaze on her, smiling as he shifted his attention to Susan.

"Is she old enough to eat pancakes?"

Jennifer shrugged and picked up her fork. "We'll soon find out, won't we?" She cut a bite and offered it, and with a quick move, Susan pulled it from the fork and popped it into her mouth.

"You little dickens." Jennifer could not help the laughter that escaped as she cut another piece. Again the baby seized the bite, but this time looked over her shoulder and aimed it at Jennifer's mouth instead. Automatically she took it from the tiny fingers and tasted strawberry jam.

"One for you and one for me." An old game she'd played with a neighbor's child came back to her, and Susan seemed to be acquainted with it, for she squealed and pointed at the plate. Jennifer did as she'd been instructed by the little tyrant and they ate their breakfast in short order.

Lucas rose, his plate cleaned, six pancakes in his stomach and picked up his coffee cup, draining it. "I'm going to the mine. I'll be back for supper."

"All right." Unwilling to make a gesture of reconciliation, Jennifer lifted her gaze to his and nodded.

He circled the table and bent to her, lifting her chin, when she would not have offered her face for his kiss, and leaning over farther to press his lips against hers. She tasted the syrup he'd eaten, caught the scent of his coffee, and closed her eyes, feeling the tears gathering behind her eyelids.

She *would not* cry. No matter the urge, she wouldn't be weak in front of him, would not allow him the sight of her tears as he left.

"Keep an eye on things, Mrs. Bronson," Lucas said, as if he knew the battle between himself and his wife was far from over and he feared that Jennifer might flee the arena before he returned.

His housekeeper nodded. "I surely will, Luc. I surely will."

And then as the door closed behind him and he headed to the barn and his horse, Jennifer stood and held the baby in her arms, crossing to the window to watch his progress. He walked from the wide doors in a moment, leading his gelding, his saddle gripped in his right hand. The horse stood with his reins touching the ground as Lucas tossed a bit of blanket across the animal's back and then put on the saddle, with a few quick movements pulling the cinch taut, then dropping the stirrup into place.

He mounted and, with a quick look at the house and an uplifted hand, rode from the yard. Traveling across the fence line and beyond the pasture, he followed a trail leading through the woods to the mine field up the canyon.

"Are you coming with me?" Jennifer asked, still looking from the window.

"I won't turn you out on your own, girl. And I just told Luc I'd keep an eye on you, didn't I?"

"You'll have to do that in town then. And if it's still available, I'd like to take up residence in your house, Ida."

"What did he do to you? You look like a dyin' duck in a thunderstorm."

"Well, that sounds unpleasant." Jennifer laughed and turned around. Susan's hand touched her aunt's cheek, as if she enjoyed the smile that dwelt there.

"You know what I mean, Jen. But I just now decided I don't want to know what he did. Some things are none of my business. And you're not limping and you don't have any bruises to be seen, so I figure he didn't hurt you much."

"Oh, he hurt me, all right. Not where it shows maybe, but his words cut deep."

"That'll happen. Men don't realize how ignorant they sound sometimes. But Luc is usually pretty much on target, Jen. Maybe you ought to rethink what happened between the two of you. I doubt the man would purposely hurt you, either by word or deed."

"I don't want to talk about it. I just want to pack up and leave. We'll use the wagon and he can come pick it up when he wants it back."

"He'll probably want to stick you in it before he heads for home with it."

"Maybe so, but I'm not coming back."

Ida shrugged and shook her head. "I'll go along with you, and I've already told you that my house is at your disposal. Give me that baby and you can put your things together and get hers gathered up, too."

"All right." Resisting the urge to look from the window to see if Lucas was still in sight, Jennifer transferred Susan to the woman's arms and left the room.

LUCAS WAS HOT and weary, his clothes dirty and disheveled, and he was in dire need of a bath and a shave. Recalling his beard rubbing against Jennifer's tender skin early in the morning made him vow to shave every evening, come what may. There'd be no more reddened skin from his whiskers if he could help it.

He rubbed down his horse, propped the saddle against the wall and hung the bridle in the tack room, then put the animal in his stall. Scooping a can of grain into the horse's feed bucket before he left the barn he sighed wearily. The walk to the house seemed longer than usual and he moved a bit faster, suddenly anxious to see Jennifer, to gain an impression of her mood, to plan his strategy for the evening.

He'd be more gentlemanly tonight, give her a chance to— His thoughts broke off as he climbed the steps to the porch and noted the dark kitchen in front of him. There should have been a light glowing from the window. It wasn't quite dark outside, but nevertheless, Ida would have lit the lamp by now.

His heart pounded in his chest as he turned the doorknob and shoved his way into the house. No sounds of voices met his ear, no scents of supper met his nose and not a trace did he see of the woman he'd thought of all day.

"Jennifer? Where are you?" Even as he called her name, he sensed her absence from his house. She was gone.

He sat on a chair and took a deep breath. She was *gone,* and little wonder. He'd treated her harshly, taken her with the force of a man set on seduction, pitted his strength against hers and won the battle. She was small, soft and fragile and he'd treated her like a woman without feelings. And if ever there was a female with emotions aplenty, it was his wife.

He rose and looked from the back door. Through the dusk, he looked toward the lean-to on the side of the barn, where his farm wagon should have been sitting. And then beyond it to the pasture where there was no sign of the two horses he used to plow and pull his wagon and other equipment.

He should have noticed when he'd rode up that they weren't there, but as weary as he was, as ready for the comfort of a warm bath and a hot meal, he'd looked neither right nor left, only headed for the barn and given his gelding the comfort of his stall.

"She's in town. I'll bet she took Mrs. Bronson and Susan and hightailed it into town." He spoke loudly, as if someone might hear his pronouncement, and then sagged a bit, thinking ahead to what he must do tonight before he found any rest in his bed. He'd have to make tracks to Thunder Canyon, seek out his wayward wife and haul her home.

If necessary, he'd leave Mrs. Bronson there with Susan till morning, and just cart Jennifer with him on his horse. She'd have a royal fit, but she could just holler all she wanted to. There was no way he was leaving her in town and sit here cooling his heels while she gloated over her escape.

For that described exactly what she'd done. Made an escape from him, from the home he'd given her and the love— He examined his thoughts. *What love?* What on earth was he thinking? He'd never told her he loved her, never even considered the idea. And now an overwhelming sadness swept through him. He might never have a chance to say the words, he realized. For if Jennifer had truly decided to leave him permanently, it might be that she'd left for New York City already.

But if she was still in Thunder Canyon, he'd find her. Tonight.

CHAPTER ELEVEN

SLEEPING IN A STRANGE BED was not Susan's first choice, obviously, for she protested when Jennifer took her upstairs and coaxed her into lying on the big double bed she'd chosen for her own use. It took almost an hour of singing and cuddling before the child finally settled down for a late nap and Jennifer began to unpack their belongings.

Beside the bed, Buster lay in a heap, his nondescript brown coat shedding over both the rug he occupied and the side of the bed quilt. Nonetheless, he seemed determined to keep watch over the tiny child on the bed, and Jennifer could not fault his presence in the room.

Now she placed her clothing in the room's huge dresser. Mrs. Bronson had kept all of her furniture and each of the seven bedrooms on the second floor combined a bed and dresser or chest of drawers. Since Ida had one room and Jennifer another, that left five to rent, plus the third floor. It held six smaller rooms, plus a huge attic crammed with a veritable gold mine of furniture, surely enough to round out the bedrooms with anything a man might need. It was obvious why Ida had felt the house much too big to live in by herself.

The dresser near the door was filled readily with her own clothing, and Susan's new things were put into a chest of drawers across the room, a lovely piece of furniture that had come directly from Chicago, according to its proud owner. Ida had, early on, urged Jennifer to take this room, telling her that it had the best view from the windows and the morning sun would not awaken her if she pulled the curtains at night.

Planning on rising early, Jennifer decided to leave the draperies open on a regular basis, knowing that she might as well get in practice for the day when their boardinghouse began to serve as home to an assortment of miners, and rising early would be the order of the day.

Upon their arrival during the afternoon she'd spent an hour at the general store, stocking up on foodstuffs while Ida kept the baby at home. She set up a new account, and being the wife of the mayor seemed to give her an unlimited amount to spend. Her list was long, reflecting both Ida's and Sally Jo's input, and the storekeeper was delighted with the total of her bill. Offering to have the boxes delivered to Ida's home, he ushered a grateful Jennifer from his store.

She stood on the sidewalk and looked at the storefronts lining Main Street. Sally Jo was in front of her barber shop and her hand lifted in a welcoming wave.

"Would you like to come and see what we're planning?" Jennifer asked when she reached Sally Jo.

An enthusiastic nod met her invitation. "Sure would. In fact, I'll bring along some things I put together for you. I found a nice piece of wood, not too heavy, something we can handle, and painted it all white. I thought you and Ida could decide on prices and so on, and I'd finish it for you later tonight. I'll bring a can of black paint and a small brush. We'll get you all set up in business right away."

"How long before you close for the day?" Jennifer asked. "I thought we might make a late supper and you could join us."

Sally Jo's eyes lit with appreciation. "I'd like that. See you in a couple of hours, as soon as I get all my gentlemen taken care of."

It was only a short distance back to the house and the store-keeper's son was already unloading Jennifer's purchases at the back door.

"You've done well," Ida said, putting away cans and boxes in the pantry. "I couldn't see anything you missed."

"Only eggs. And they'll have some coming in tomorrow morning. I think we'd better find some chickens so we won't have to depend on someone else's to keep us in eggs."

Ida laughed. "I'm not real fond of chickens, Jen. That'll be your department, feeding them and gathering eggs."

"I'll hire someone else to clean the chicken coop." Jennifer made a face. "I can't stand the smell."

"First we'll have to have a coop."

"I thought I'd go to the lumberyard and find out who could build one for us." She'd paid special mind to the establishments in town on her way home, and noted that the lumber-yard seemed to be a thriving concern.

Home. That word stuck in her mind as she looked around the kitchen. This wouldn't really be home to her, she feared. On the other hand, the big farmhouse where she'd lived with Lucas for those few weeks seemed, upon reflection, to be a haven such as she'd always yearned for. She stood straighter, her shoulders back, her eyes burning as she thought of not seeing Lucas again.

If only he weren't such a...such a *man*. The thought made her smile and she ducked her head, lest Ida think her daft. The memory of Lucas's arms holding her, his kisses against her skin tempting her beyond reason, the hours of darkness they'd spent together, all ran together in her mind. She was besotted with the man, and felt miserable admitting it to herself.

No matter. She'd get over that soon enough, she determined. With enough hard work to her credit on a daily basis, she'd sleep dreamlessly and forget she'd ever known Lucas O'Reilly.

Fat chance. The words traveled through her mind, taunting her, and she busied herself with Susan. Ida had tied the baby in a chair and given her kitchen utensils to play with, and now the child was more than willing to eat her supper, banging on the chair seat with a wooden spoon. The dog once more played guardian, lying beside the chair, looking up at her charge.

"That baby's still tired. Her nap was too short," Ida said. "Just less than an hour. I'll bet she goes to bed without a peep after you feed her."

And so it was, Susan responding to Jennifer's songs and whispered phrases, her eyes closing in slumber within minutes. Jen rose from the bed and went back down the stairs, ready for supper herself, leaving Buster in residence in the bedroom.

"I think that dog has adopted Susan," she told Ida. "He's lying by the bed again. I doubt Susan could get into much trouble with Buster keeping an eye on her."

"He's a good mutt," Ida agreed. Jennifer felt at ease, what with Ida putting the finishing touches on their late supper and things in reasonable order. And now, unless she was mistaken, Sally Jo was knocking on the front door.

Jennifer sped the length of the long hallway, from the kitchen to the foyer, where Ida had already swept an accumulation of dust and dirt from sight. Admiring the fine lines of a small table in the parlor, Jennifer swung open the big front door without hesitation.

"Hello, Jennifer." Lucas stood just two feet from her, but he might as well have been treading on her toes, so imposing was his presence.

She stepped back and swung the door closed, her intentions obvious. But, Lucas proved to be quicker than she, for his big foot halted the progress of the door and he pushed it open and walked inside.

"You weren't invited in," Jennifer told him.

"I'm not waiting for an invite." Hands propped on his hips, he looked down at her. "I came to take you home, Jen. I don't know what you think you're doing, running out on me, taking Mrs. Bronson and Susan with you, and setting up housekeeping here, but you'd might as well call it quits right now."

"I'm going to be running a legitimate business. We're opening a boardinghouse, and in fact, Sally Jo is coming by to make us a sign. I thought she was—"

"I'm not Sally Jo, and it isn't going to do a whole lot of good to make a sign and hang it when you're not even going to be here."

"I beg your pardon." Her back was up now. Just who did he think he was, telling her what she could and couldn't do? And then he answered that query in short order.

"I'm your husband, Jennifer, and the mayor of this town. If the council decides we don't need a boardinghouse, we can shut you down in short order. You'd do well to come with me and avoid a lot of problems."

She opened the door and swept her arm wide. "Go home,

Lucas. You proved last night what a wonderful husband you are. I don't need any more reminders. Leave me be." She felt a flush coat her cheeks as she spoke, and the sight of Lucas's grin didn't help matters any.

"I'm glad you thought I was wonderful, Jen. I can't begin to tell you how much I enjoyed turning you into my wife. As to reminders, I'd be happy to give you another demonstration of what goes on in the marriage bed."

She looked up at him with an appeal he could not miss. "Please, Lucas. I already hate myself for the way I acted last night. Don't make it any worse."

THE FOOL WOMAN was having regrets. Big regrets, if he was any judge. And he knew she'd been happy last night, knew that he'd given her pleasure, that her response had been genuine. There was no faking the satisfaction of a woman fulfilled and she'd expressed it without a doubt. Jennifer was truly his wife, and some way he'd clear this whole thing up and put his marriage on the right track.

"All right, I'll leave," he said agreeably. "Get your boardinghouse in order and work your fingers to the bone, if that's what you want. You'll be ready to come home before long. Cleaning up after one man won't seem so bad, once you have a houseful of dirty miners to cope with."

He turned and made his way out the door. At least he'd know where to find her. And he'd guarantee his words would stick in her mind. She'd had it pretty good, he decided, and she was in for a big surprise.

Sally Jo walked through the gate, carrying a large piece of wood. She smiled and nodded. "Hello, Lucas. Been visiting?"

"Sally Jo." He tipped his hat and stepped aside, leaving the path free for her to walk to the porch. "I see you have Jennifer's sign for her."

"I haven't put any prices on it yet. I wasn't sure what she and Mrs. Bronson wanted to use as a set of fees."

"Whatever they charge, they'll earn every cent, that's for sure. Feeding and providing for a whole houseful of men won't seem nearly such a good idea in a couple of weeks."

Sally Jo smiled. "You may be right, Lucas. But then again, Jennifer seems pretty determined to make a go of this. I wouldn't count on her failing quite yet. In fact, I'm happy to see another woman going into business for herself. I have fond hopes that she'll find success."

"We'll see." He grinned and tipped his hat again. "Good night, ma'am. I'll be seeing you again."

"I'm sure," she murmured, climbing the steps and walking across the porch. The door was opened before she could knock and Jennifer ushered her into the hallway, her smile grim, her eyes shooting fire.

"What did Lucas say to you?"

"Not much. Just gave me dire predictions about your business. It seems he doesn't give you much of a chance to succeed."

"He's in for a big surprise." Jennifer led the way back to the kitchen and Sally Jo propped her board against the wall.

"We'll work on that later," Jennifer said. "First we're going to eat."

THE SIGN was hung against the wall, all three women holding it in place, deciding on the proper level, and then nailing it up next to the stairway. The price list they'd agreed on was impressive and Jennifer had dreams of a long line of men awaited entry to the house, each of them carrying a valise and a handful of money.

She told Ida of her dreams in the morning. "I thought we could put an ad in the newspaper, Ida, and a list of the prices for just renting a room and for boarding with us. What do you think?"

"Why don't you walk on down to the newspaper office and take care of it, and I'll stay here and start sorting out sheets and bedrooms? With any luck, we may have a couple of boarders by nightfall, once the men hear about this place."

Ida was right, for three bedrooms held their first gentlemen that night. Supper had been a jovial occasion, with all three men giving Ida sincere compliments on her cooking, and all three of them eyeing Jennifer, as if they wondered what she was doing there. One of them, Toby Martin, asked her about her presence, a bold man who showed an inordinate interest in her.

"Ain't you married to Luc O'Reilly?" At Jennifer's reluctant nod, Toby grinned. "I'll bet you he ain't happy with you runnin' this place. I heard he sent for you from back East to keep his house and take care of things out there. And instead here you are in town, running a business. You get tired of him already?"

"You better watch your mouth, Toby Martin." Ida shot the man a look guaranteed to peel wallpaper and he ducked his head.

"Didn't mean no disrespect. I was just wonderin'—"

"Well, keep your thoughts to yourself. What Mrs. O'Reilly does is her own business and she doesn't need you pokin' into her affairs."

It was obvious that Mrs. Bronson would rule this house with an iron hand, and Jennifer was pleased at her speaking up. The men made her just a bit uncomfortable and she sensed that they all had questions they'd like to ask, but Ida's words seemed to silence the lot of them.

They sought out their rooms right after supper. As one of

them, a man named Cole Weston, said, they were looking forward to comfortable beds. He halted by the staircase and nodded at Jennifer.

"I sure was pleased to hear that y'all were opening up a boardinghouse, ma'am. I was sure enough sick and tired of eatin' my own cookin' and sleepin' on the ground."

"You come from the South, Mr. Weston?" Jennifer asked.

"Yes, ma'am. From Texas. Heard there was gold to be found here, and I staked my claim."

"I hope you'll be satisfied with your accommodations, sir. Breakfast is at six. I don't know if Mrs. Bronson told you or not."

"Yes, ma'am, she surely did. We need to get out to our claims early on."

Jennifer nodded. "Then I'll wish you a good night, Mr. Weston."

"I THOUGHT it went well." Jennifer picked up the last piece of silverware and dried it, then put the plates and cups in the cupboard. "They sure liked your fried chicken. You know, I watched you real close while you were cooking, and I think I've finally got the idea in my head, you know, about the grease being hot enough, so the chicken doesn't just lie there and soak up the lard."

"You've caught on to more than you realize, girl. Tomorrow you're going to make biscuits for breakfast and fry up the bacon. I'll set things up in the dining room and take care of Susan and such."

"You think I can?" Jennifer asked. "I mean, what if I make a mess of it?"

"You won't. And if you do, it'll be the last time. You'll learn real quick." Ida grinned. "I take that back. You've already picked up on everything in a dadblamed hurry. I'll warrant you could put on supper, too, if you set your mind to it."

"Not yet. Give me a few days."

"Well, you'd better get into bed yourself, girl. Morning is gonna come real early, you mark my word. We'll need to be up at five. I'll knock on your door."

"Five?" Jennifer's brow lifted. That did sound pretty early to her ears, but if that was what it would take to make a go of this thing, she'd have an early bedtime and be ready to climb out of bed at five.

BY THE THIRD DAY she was ready for bed at dusk, and had no trouble sleeping. In the mornings, she left Buster guarding Susan by the bed when she went downstairs. The cooking was going well, both women sharing the kitchen. Jennifer made beds daily, a chore she had down to a science by the third morning. Ida got out the scrub board that day and began heating water on the big cookstove right after breakfast.

"Bring your dirty clothes down if you want to pay for laundry, gentlemen," she announced as they left the table. All three men brightened up at that statement.

"Didn't know that was included," Toby Martin said. "And I'll sure be grateful if I don't have to scrub them out myself."

"You'll pay an extra dollar," Ida said cheerfully.

"It's worth it." Cole Weston was halfway out the dining room door when he tossed the words back over his shoulder. He turned back and faced Ida. "By the way, I heard there's several more men planning on coming by to rent rooms, ladies. They've been askin' us about the food, and this place is the talk of the mine fields."

He shot a look at Jennifer. "Some of them are taking bets

on whether or not you ladies can handle this." He grinned, his hands in his pockets. "My money's on you, Miss Jennifer. And you, too, Miss Ida," he added.

"We'll make it." Jennifer's words were firm. "Don't forget, if you want a dinner pail to carry with you, there'll be an extra charge. Just let Mrs. Bronson know and we'll start tomorrow packing food for you if you each provide the pail to carry it in."

"They got some small buckets down at the general store," Ida said. "Just the right size. All the schoolkids carry them."

"I'll pay you double the price, if one of you ladies can pick me up a pail today," Cole said, pulling money from his pocket. The other men followed suit and all three pressed coins into Jennifer's palm with words of thanks.

"Come on. It's time to get to the livery stable and pick up our horses," Toby said, leading the way out of the dining room and leaving the house by the kitchen door. "Sure wish you had a barn here, ladies." His tone was wistful as if he dreaded the walk to the corral where the miners's horses were kept at night.

"No barn yet," Ida said. "We'll have to make a bundle of money first."

WITHIN TWO WEEKS, all the bedrooms were full and inside a month, the ladies were making up a list of gentlemen waiting for a vacancy. Their bank accounts were thriving, Jennifer's little book showing a fine growth weekly, and Ida's half of their profit being added to her already healthy account.

The only fly in the ointment was the news that Kyle was out of jail and had been seen around town. Jennifer hadn't laid eyes on him, though, and felt sure that being at Ida's house was security enough. Given the fact that they were surrounded by able-bodied men for the nighttime hours, she slept soundly. Perhaps the man had realized his defeat.

One thing was for sure. They needed more help to run this house as it should be, Ida announced early one morning. Saving them the trouble of going out looking for an ambitious soul, a widow lady named Helen Pelfry, who lved near the edge of town, stopped by seeking work. They gladly hired her on to keep house and help with the ever-increasing stacks of laundry the men carted down the stairs twice a week.

Jennifer stretched clotheslines across the yard, between four trees, where they hung countless sheets and shirts and stockings, until they had to increase their supply of clothespins from the general store.

She was proud. Their reputation was growing by leaps and bounds and even though some of the men were not as well mannered as she'd have liked and tended to leave their rooms in complete disarray, she soon solved that problem.

One day at the supper table she read from a list she and Ida had composed, designating several forms of behavior as unsuitable for their establishment. The rule regarding using silverware instead of their fingers brought grumbles from two men, but Jennifer's raised brow, and a subtle reminder that the waiting list for rooms was long, soon solved that problem.

Keeping their room in decent order met with groans from three others, and Jennifer held up a hand for silence. "I expect to be able to get in your rooms in order to make the bed in the mornings without tripping over your clothing," she said. "You each have a basket to keep your soiled things in. Use it."

There was no more said on that matter, except for Cole Weston, who spoke up without hesitation. "I'm not takin' a chance of bein' booted outta here on my ear, ma'am. I'll do better."

Since he was not one of the culprits Jennifer and Ida had had in mind when they'd composed the rules, he was granted a smile of conspiracy as Jennifer recognized his subtle support of her edicts. "Thank you, Mr. Weston."

Her nod and smile were received with a quirk of his lips and he settled down to eat with gusto.

It was that evening that another miner came to the door, just as the supper dishes were being put away. "Ma'am?" He stood politely on the back stoop, looking in at Ida, who'd answered his knock. "I understand y'all are renting rooms and providing meals for some of the miners. Is there room for one more? I'm willing to pay more than the going rate for a clean bed and good food."

"We're out of space, sir," Ida told him. "The only way you can get accommodations here is if we start putting two in a room, and that'll fill our dining room to overflowing."

"Do you suppose you could ask a couple of your boarders if they'd bunk together. Maybe you could give them a cut rate to share a room."

"Are you willing to share?" Ida was trying her best to be obliging, not willing to turn away a man with money to spend, especially one as clean and well-spoken as this specimen of manhood.

"I'd rather not, ma'am." His voice softened and he leaned forward a bit. "I snore pretty bad, and I'm afraid most all the fellas know it already. I'd probably have a hard time finding a roommate."

"What's going on, Ida?" Jennifer approached and the miner smiled and looked at her with interest.

"Gentleman wants to rent a room, if we can get a couple of the other men to share and make room for him." Ida turned and grinned. "He's willing to pay more than the going rate if we can fit him in."

"What's your name, sir?" Jennifer asked, in her thoughts already counting his cash.

"Alexander Stone."

"You're a miner?" Somehow he was too clean to have been grubbing in the dirt all day, she thought.

"Yes, ma'am. I sure am. My partner let me leave early when he found out I was coming to town to find better accommodations than a leaky tent. I stopped at Sally Jo's place and got a bath and shave before I stopped by here."

No wonder he looked clean. Jennifer thought for a moment. "Let us ask at the breakfast table and see if a couple of the men are willing to share if they can get a break on their fees. Come back tomorrow and we'll let you know. But just don't say anything about it to any of the other men. We already have a long list of those waiting for a vacancy."

Alexander Stone nodded and stepped down off the stoop, and Jennifer closed the door, then leaned against it. "Wouldn't you think other folks in town would be willing to rent rooms? There's more men with money here than I've ever seen in one place in my life."

Ida shrugged. "There's a lot of work involved and some women aren't interested in doing any more than they're already obliged to, taking care of their own families."

"Well, we'll see how it goes." And somehow, she hoped it would go well, that there would be at least two men willing to share a room. Mr. Stone seemed to be a gentleman, and heaven above knew they could use a couple more men with the sort of qualities the man appeared to display.

HIS PARTNER RODE UP to the claim two days later and Lucas stood, his hat brim pulled down to shade his eyes as he caught sight of him. "Any luck?"

Sandy smiled and Lucas thought once more that it had been somewhat like sending a fox into the henhouse, pulling this bit of subterfuge.

"I always do what I set out to," the man said. "You've got a room on the second floor, number three is painted on the door, and here's how you get into it." Sandy held out a large key and as Lucas would have snatched it from his hand, Sandy slipped it into his pocket.

"First you pay me the rent for your room for the first month, the money for your laundry being done, and an extra dollar for your dinner being provided every day."

"You didn't tell her—"

"Hell, no, I didn't tell her I was renting it for you, Luc. You think I'm daft? I'm just wondering what's going to happen when they find out they've been tricked. I'll bet that girl will throw a *hissy fit.*"

"Won't be the first time," Lucas said dryly. "She's real good at speaking her mind." He grinned, thinking of Jennifer and the look of surprise she'd wear when he showed up, key in hand, and then moved in, bag and baggage.

"Well, if you change your mind, I'll be glad to move in there myself. Sure did smell good in that kitchen, and that woman of yours is a pretty little thing, isn't she?"

"Don't bother even looking, Sandy. She belongs to me."

"Funny way to run a marriage if you ask me, Luc. Her in town and you at the farm."

"Don't worry about it. Things will be back on an even keel before you know it. I've got some plans in the works."

THE RIDE from his mine into town would be wearisome on a daily basis, but the comfortable bed at the end of the trail and the thought of Jennifer's face when she realized who her newest boarder would be made it worthwhile in his sight. Lucas grinned as he rode to the livery stable and made arrangements for his gelding to be fed and kept in a stall overnight each day for the foreseeable future.

"Not a problem," he was told. His pack was heavy, but he barely noticed the weight as he walked down the street to the big house next to the parsonage. The house where Jennifer and Ida Bronson had set up their business.

The idea of his inept bride cooking for a multitude of men and keeping a three-story house clean was almost funny, he decided. And yet she'd proved to be a ready pupil, according to Ida. Maybe Jen had a knack for cooking and cleaning that had been buried beneath that incapable but impeccable aura she'd exuded from the beginning.

He'd soon find out. Scorning the two steps, he grasped the porch rail and his long legs made short work of the long porch, the swing catching his eye as he scanned the length of the comfortable-looking area. He knocked on the back door, having been told by several of the men that the miners were to use the back door and that leaving their boots in the entryway was a hard and fast rule, one they took to heart. It seemed that hot meals made a man willing to capitulate to the decrees of the ladies in charge of this house.

The door swung open as he was about to repeat his knock and Ida stared into his eyes, her mouth opening and closing like a fish out of water.

"It's only me, Ida. I'm your new boarder."

"How? When? Oh, my, Lucas. You're in for a heap of trouble when Jennifer gets a look at you here."

"I have my room key," he said, flashing it in front of her. "Also a receipt, signed by Jennifer, for the first month's rent."

Ida looked at the paper he flourished and shook her head. "This is made out to a fella named Alexander Stone. Last I heard, your name wasn't Stone."

"He rented it on my behalf, but I've paid him what cash he used for my benefit and the room is mine for a month. I'm sure the sheriff would agree, if he were to be asked his opinion."

"You may be right there, but I know a young woman who's going to make your life miserable if you move in here. Or else you'll give her such a hard time she'll leave me holding the bag while she makes tracks for New York City. Either way, I'm not going to be happy with the outcome."

"Don't worry, ma'am. I only want to put my marriage back on an even keel. I want Jen in my life, as my wife."

"In your life? Or in your bed?" Ida's cheeks burned as she spoke the words without forethought. "Sorry," she murmured, "I shouldn't have said that."

Lucas grinned. "I think you've got the whole thing all figured out. Having Jen in my life sorta puts her back in my bed, don't you think?"

"Well, I wouldn't count on that happening right off. She's not real happy with you, Luc."

He sobered. "I know, but I'm going to fix that."

Behind Ida, the kitchen door leading to the hallway burst open and Jennifer made her way across the kitchen floor. "I'll talk to him," she told Mrs. Bronson. "You go ahead with whatever you were doing."

"Just frying the last pan of chicken. And then you need to be mashing the potatoes and getting the biscuits out of the oven while I make the gravy." She looked at Luc. "Your wife has become quite a hand at cooking lately."

"So I've heard." He dropped his heavy pack on the floor and crossed his arms across his chest. "I came to judge for myself." And wasn't that a stupid thing to say? Almost guaranteed to rile her out of her composure.

It did. "You're not welcome here, Lucas."

"I have a key to room three and a signed receipt."

"Where'd you get them from? The last room I rented was to Alexander Stone."

"That's my partner, Sandy. He came here representing me, and took the room for me. I was pretty tied up at the mine."

"Well, you can just go back to the mine," Jennifer told him. "You don't have a room in our house."

"Ah, but I do," he said. "And if I have to, I'll go get the sheriff to prove the point."

Jennifer looked him with blue eyes that shimmered. Not with tears, he hoped, for he didn't think he could deal with her in a crying mood. "Jen, I want to live where you do, eat at the table with you and if I can't do it back at the farmhouse, I'll do it here."

"That's all you want?" She looked doubtful, he thought, and he didn't blame her.

"For now," he said, modifying his aim a bit.

"I don't want any trouble, Lucas. You can stay here, but

only because I'm afraid the sheriff would side with you, and I don't want my other boarders to be wondering about our ethics. I'll admit I rented the room to Alexander Stone in good faith. But the man didn't tell me he was representing someone else."

"It's a common way to do business here," Ida said from where she stood at the stove. "Lots of the miners have a legal representative, and if two men are partners, they're each allowed to speak for the other."

"Come on in, then." Jennifer looked like a cloud about to drop its contents over his head, but she spoke nicely. "Your room is at the top of the stairs, right across—" She broke off and he watched as a look of fear touched her eyes.

"I'm not here to demand anything of you, Jen." He picked up his pack and chanced another glance in her direction. "I just want to be where you are."

Her jaw tightened and her cheeks were pale, bloodless it seemed. "Supper will be on the table in fifteen minutes. Don't be late or you might not find much left over."

CHAPTER TWELVE

LUCAS MOVED IN. Toting his pack up the stairs, he glanced toward the top of the long flight to see Jennifer watching him. She stood in a doorway just across from the room designated as number three, and he could not resist giving birth to the smile that curved his lips upward.

"Right across the hall, Jen?"

Again she looked like a thundercloud just awaiting the right moment to dump her load of rain on his head, and he reached the top of the stairs before she spoke.

"Not my choice, Lucas. That I'll guarantee you."

"I believe you." He nudged open his door with his shoulder and walked inside. He'd felt safe in leaving it ajar after his first scant inspection of the premises, and had gone to get his belongings in anticipation of a good night's sleep. Now he wondered just how much sleep he'd get, his own bed just twelve feet or so from Jen's, with but two walls between them.

As if she read his mind, she tilted her chin upward and followed him to the doorway of his room. "My room is locked at night, and Susan is a light sleeper. Not to mention that the dog sleeps in there with us. Don't be thinking about visiting me."

"Wouldn't even suggest such a thing," he said, grinning, even as he spoke the lie. For it was exactly what he'd thought, right off.

"You've managed to insinuate yourself into this place, Lucas, but that's as far as it goes. Our marriage is over. I won't go home with you, and I won't allow you any of the rights and privileges of a husband while you're living here in *my* house. I hope we have an understanding about that."

He laughed. "You may have an understanding, Jen. But my plans are somewhat different. I'm your husband, no matter where we're living. And you can be certain that every other man in this house will know how things stand by the time breakfast is over in the morning."

"Don't cause trouble for me, Lucas."

He thought it sounded somewhat like a warning, and at the same time he heard it as a plea for his understanding. He preferred the warning.

"I'd like to cause a lot of things to happen where you're concerned, Jen, but none of them add up to trouble."

She stepped back from his doorway. "I hope you'll find your room to be comfortable. Sleep well." Giving him a final view of her backside, she opened the door opposite his and then closed it behind her. The urge to follow gripped him and he gritted his teeth against the compulsion he felt to snatch her up and keep her in his own bed until morning. The thought of a nightlong exploration of that lush set of curves and hollows made his mouth water, and he sat on the edge of his bed, fighting the arousal that would not be conquered.

"Soon, Jen. Soon." The words were low, a whispered promise he had every intention of fulfilling.

LUCAS WAS RIGHT, she found. By the time the line of miners left the kitchen, lunch pails in hand, they were properly subdued, their eyes lowered as they thanked Jennifer for their lunches, complimented Ida on the breakfast she'd served, and then made their way out the back door.

Somehow, Lucas had let them know that Jennifer was *his* property, and as such was totally off limits to them. Since none of the men had ever been other than polite and appreciative of her efforts, she would not have realized Lucas's effect on them, had they not failed to meet her eyes as they bid her a good day upon their departure.

At least two or three of the men were prone to ask about supper before they left in the morning, as if they relished the thought of good food during the drudgery of their days. Today was different. Lucas had instilled the fear of God in them. Except for Cole Weston, who seemed to be enjoying the sight of Lucas defending his territory.

"Don't work too hard, Miss Jennifer," he said nicely, accepting his lunch pail from her hand. "Looks like you've got a load of washing to do."

"Nothing more than we can handle, Mr. Weston." She smiled up at him, aware that the man had eyes for her, that his interest was obvious to Lucas. And if a smile in Cole's direction was enough to make Lucas squirm, she'd aim it at the handsome man daily.

Lucas appeared in front of her, his own hand outstretched. "Thank you for packing my sandwiches, ma'am," he said. "I'll be thinking of you when I eat them."

"I'm sure you will." The thought of layers of newspaper between slices of cold roast beef made her smile. She'd given him something to chew on, and his thoughts would not be kindly, she'd warrant.

The laundry went well, with Helen doing her share of scrubbing on the board. Jennifer hung countless pairs of trousers on the line, filled another with towels and pillowcases, and then placed the clothing in the parlor, spread over the furniture where the men could sort and find their own items of apparel. Had they marked their clothing in some way, she could have sorted them herself. As it was, the task was theirs and she knew from past weeks that they would not grumble.

And then she picked up a shirt she recognized, held it in front of her and imagined the body it would mold itself against sometime in the next few days. Lucas looked well in this shirt, she thought. The blue stripes matched his eyes. And with that thought, she dropped it to the sofa, as if the very fabric had burned her fingers.

"Something wrong?" Helen asked from across the room.

"No. Just got a case of the dropsy," Jennifer answered, picking up the shirt and shaking it out before she folded it and placed it atop a pair of Lucas's trousers. It seemed his clothing gravitated toward her hands, for she found that she recognized his things among the rest of the men's without hesitation.

Stockings and smallclothes were stacked beside his trousers. Shirts were folded and placed on top and she stood back to view the results. None of the other clothing they'd sorted and folded resembled the neat piles she'd made of Lucas O'Reilly's belongings.

Helen pointed at the results of Jennifer's work. "Those belong to Lucas?"

Jen felt her cheeks turn rosy. "Yes. I recognized them and put them together."

"Too bad you can't just carry them up to your room and let them share space in your chest of drawers, Jen. Lucas is a good man. You're lucky to have married him."

"If he's so wonderful, I can't imagine that he'd have had to send away for a bride."

Helen laughed. "He wouldn't have, given the number of women here who'd have given an arm and leg to have him. But there was something about Lucas that yearned for a woman who was different. He probably thought he'd find someone very special when he applied to that agency."

"And was disappointed when I showed up on his doorstep, so to speak."

Helen shook her head. "I've seen the way he looks at you, Jen. He's not disappointed. Not one little bit. The man is smitten with you. Maybe he doesn't even know it himself, but I can tell."

"Well, I'm not *smitten* with him," Jennifer said. "I'm just waiting till I have enough money on hand to get on a stage and head East again."

"Somehow, I don't think that's gonna happen. I suspect Lucas will win you back long before you have enough in your account to get past St. Louis." Helen laughed at the thought. "You'd be a fool to pass him up. And you don't look like any fool I've ever seen."

Jennifer set her lips in a thin line. She picked up a shirt and folded it quickly, well used to the chore after weeks of doing laundry for a houseful of men. "He can just go whistle for a wife, as far as I'm concerned," she said. And then wondered at the sting of tears as she turned toward the doorway, gathering up Lucas's clothing from the sofa as she went.

It fit into his dresser drawers with space to spare, and she wondered about the scarcity of his belongings. His bedroom at the farm held two drawers of small clothes and stockings, another of shirts and a fourth of trousers. He'd apparently left a good share of them behind.

The memory of that room, the wide bed it held, the night she'd spent there in his arms, filled her with a warmth she could not deny. She bowed her head, lifting one hand to wipe at the tears she'd not been aware of until this moment. The face in the mirror in front of her was filled with sadness, loss and remorse. She'd found she needed more than Lucas would—or could—supply.

She would not be a mere bedmate to Lucas O'Reilly. Nor would she be his maid or mistress, content to pick up behind him and lavish him with affection.

She'd never wanted to play those roles, but now things were different. She had confidence. And Lucas had better recognize that fact. She was capable, and thus far, a success at what she'd chosen to do. If he wanted to pay good money for the right to be fed, the privilege of wearing clean drawers, so be it. She would take his money gladly, provide for him as she did the other eleven men who lived in this house, and at the same time, pretend she'd never lived in his home, had not slept in his bed, was not aching to feel his arms around her again.

With a final look at his bedroom, a last glance at the bed he'd slept in last night, she left his room, unaware that he would find her presence there upon his arrival home.

JENNIFER HAD BEEN in his room. Not only could he catch the scent of her, that floral aura of soap and powder she wore, but as he opened his dresser drawers he saw her fine hand in the folding of his clothing, the placement, just so, of his stockings and drawers, the neatly turned-down collars of his shirts.

Even without benefit of a flat iron, they were smoothed and pressed by her hands and he smiled as he lifted one in search of the aroma of the woman he'd followed to this place.

A basin of warm water assured him of cleanliness and he dropped his soiled clothing where he stood, reaching for the laundry she'd placed in neat piles in the dresser drawers. Rinsing the soap from his body, he dried with a towel and welcomed the luxury of cleanliness, the towel still smelling of outdoors, its fragrance that of wind and summer flowers, caught in the very fibers of the fabric.

Supper was waiting, he knew, for the footsteps of a half-dozen men had gone past his door in the past few minutes, and he hastened to follow them down the stairs to the big dining room. His place was at one end of the table, Ida having decided it to be appropriate, apparently, given his relationship to her business partner.

Supper consisted of a huge meat loaf, topped with a blend of tomatoes and brown sugar, forming a tasty crust that sweetened each mouthful of meat. Baked potatoes were piled high in a bowl and green beans fresh from someone's garden had been cooked with onion and bacon before being served in a large crockery dish. A platter of fresh bread, thickly sliced and ready for butter and jam to be spread on each piece, awaited the men. As one, they eyed the table with admiring eyes.

"Y'all surely know how to cook," Cole Weston said, his fork spearing a large potato. The meat loaf was passed around the table and when it had become but a memory on the platter, Ida rose and replaced it with another identical to it, from the kitchen.

"Lots more where that came from," she sang. "Eat up, gentlemen."

They did. With gusto and hearty appreciation, their compliments flying the length and breadth of the dining room. Lucas ate his share, seconds on the meat loaf and a third helping of green beans. Pickled beets and a salad of fresh lettuce were carried in, the lettuce coated with a milk-and-vinegar dressing sweetened with sugar.

"Never had salad like this before, ma'am," Toby Martin said. "Sure is tasty."

"My mama used to make it thataway," Ida told him. "Makes a dish of lettuce more tolerable."

"Did you pickle these beets?" another man asked, reaching for the bowl.

"Surely did," Ida told him. "Planted, pulled and pickled just last summer."

I have a lot to learn yet. The thought sped through Jennifer's mind quickly, aware that Ida had years of experience on her, that it might take a long time to equal the woman's talents in the kitchen. And it had seemed so simple when they'd first talked of this house.

"I'd say you ladies are on the right track," Lucas said from the end of the table. "You surely won't have any trouble keeping the rooms in this place full."

An assortment of voices agreed with his opinion, and Ida preened. "Well," she said, "it takes more than one woman to pull this load. Don't know what Jennifer and I would do without Helen to lend a hand."

All eyes moved to that lady, who strove to be invisible on one side of Lucas. She bowed her head, her cheeks flushed at the compliment and Lucas lifted his glass of milk high. "A toast to the woman who takes such good care of us, gentlemen."

Without hesitation, all glasses were raised, several of them in dire danger of being cracked or chipped by the vigorous clunking together some of the men employed, and their drinks were downed as Helen blushed even more furiously.

Toby seemed quite smitten with the widow lady, Jennifer thought, and her woman's heart traveled in that direction for a few moments. Maybe Helen would be open to courtship, and if so, Toby would be a good one to offer his hand in marriage. Women being in short supply made every eligible female a target for at least a dozen men to aim for. And Helen was attractive—a bit plump, but pretty, with brown hair and big eyes that reminded Jennifer of purple pansies.

Her own desirability to these men was obvious, but Lucas had managed to keep them ever aware of his possessive nature, and they minded well their behavior around her.

Dishes were done quickly, three women making light work of the chore, and then it was time for bed. Lucas had taken on the task of bouncing Susan on his knee at the kitchen table, leaving Jennifer free for her own work, and as she took off her apron and hung it in the pantry, she heard him singing a foolish ditty to the baby.

"I'll take her now." She stretched out her arms for Susan, but in the way of all flirtatious women, the baby shook her head and wrapped her arms around Lucas's neck. A born seductress, Jennifer thought, and smiled.

"Why don't I carry her upstairs for you?" Lucas rose and awaited Jennifer's answer, watching as she dithered with the idea.

"All right." The words were soft, barely reaching his ears and he simply hoisted Susan higher on his right arm, reaching for Jennifer with the left.

His shoulder hugged hers, his arm lifting to encircle her, and she was caught in a vise she stood no chance of breaking free of. On top of that, she apparently would not cause a fuss that might disturb Susan, who reached to touch Jen's cheek with a chubby hand, as if she welcomed her with a baby's innocence into the magic circle Lucas had created of the three of them.

He left the kitchen, Ida looking bemused as she followed their progress, and they went up the steps, slowly so as not to cause Jennifer to trip on the wide stair treads. She kept pace with him, though he thought she stiffened in his grasp as they neared her bedroom. Her words added to his theory as she stopped at the closed door.

"Let me go, Lucas. I'll put Susan down for the night."

He shook his head. "I'll help you, Jen. She belongs with both of us."

As if she could not deny the child's arms clutching Lucas's neck, and the look of adoration Susan bent on the man she loved with a baby's trust, Jennifer nodded. "All right. Come on in."

Opening the door, she led the way into her room. Lucas dropped his arm from her, freeing her to light the candle by the bed. Buster followed, as if it were his right to claim Susan and Jennifer as his responsibility. Darkness was falling and the house was growing quiet. He heard the sounds of men's voices murmuring from the parlor below, and the unmistakable rasping of a man's snores from a room down the hall.

Lucas closed the door and sat on the chair next to the door, settling Susan on his lap. His fingers were deft as he took off her shoes—small, black, patent slippers that the baby obviously was fond of. She grabbed them from his hand and held them against her chest, chortling. Lucas reached higher to pull off the baby's stockings and then he undid her dress, opening the buttons with care, easing the material over her head.

"You look like an old hand at that," Jennifer said.

"I've undone a few buttons in my lifetime."

"I'll just bet you have." Bending, she picked up the baby and placed her on the bed, locating diapers and a long gown in which to ready her for the night.

"You look pretty competent, yourself," Lucas told her.

"I am. I've just been worrying about the chances of Kyle getting her back, or maybe dreading the day when we have to send her back to her grandparents or whoever the law says will have the privilege of raising her."

"Kyle doesn't know where she is, Jen. And don't you think there's any chance we might be given the privilege anyway?"

"She'll need an established family, with a mother and father in a stable marriage."

"We can have that, Jen." He awaited her reply, holding his breath, lest she deny him outright.

"Not the way things are right now," she said sadly. "We aren't even a couple anymore, Lucas."

"We'll always be a couple. We'll always be married, if I have anything to say about it. And the law gives me that right, Jen. I haven't abused you or denied you a home of your own. I've supported you and provided for you. I don't know what more you want of me."

"What do you expect of *me?*" He thought he caught a glimpse of dampness on her cheek as she glanced his way, and then she bent once more over the bed, changing the diaper Susan wore.

"I don't expect much, Jen. Just that you'll come home with me and be my wife. I'd sorta like you to use all this newfound knowledge for my benefit."

"That's exactly what I'm doing." Her chin had that stubborn set again and as he watched, she wiped quickly at her cheek.

"Me and a dozen other men." His voice was harsh and he rued it, but too late. There was no taking back the bitterness of his tone.

"Eleven." She uttered the word calmly, then stood, Susan in her arms. The baby wore a long nightgown, her eyes were droopy and her head dropped to Jennifer's shoulder as if she could no longer hold it erect.

"All right. Eleven other men." He felt a moment of anger and banished it. Anger would only make things worse. "Put her in bed, Jen."

She looked at him, as if she waited for his departure. "I'll have to lie down with her. She's used to me singing a song before she goes to sleep."

"That's easily solved." Lucas rose and walked to the other side of the bed. "Where will you put her? In the middle?"

Jennifer nodded slowly, as if she wondered at his actions. Pulling down the quilt and top sheet, she placed the baby on the bed, lay beside her and pulled the quilt over them both.

Lucas followed her actions, first removing his boots, then lowering his weight to the bed, stretching out against Susan's back and meeting Jennifer's hand as she enclosed the baby in a loose embrace. "All right?" He asked the question without hope of an answer, but she surprised him.

"Yes. All right." Her eyes were focused on Susan and he held fast to her hand as she began to sing, a soft lullaby he was familiar with, in a gentle voice he was not used to hearing.

In ten minutes time the song had been sung repeatedly, the baby was asleep and the woman who'd coaxed her into slumber had joined her. Lucas gazed at her. Jennifer was tired, of that there was no doubt. She'd been spending long days working at a variety of tasks here in this enormous house—cooking, scrubbing on a washboard, hanging and folding clothing for a dozen men, not to mention the everyday work of dishes and sweeping and dusting the furniture.

He knew that Helen was capable, and was no doubt doing her share, but his wife was working herself to a frazzle, and it didn't sit well with him. If she wanted to wear herself out doing the work of a housewife, she could just as well do it in his home, in his kitchen and for *him* exclusively.

Absorbed in his reflections, he did not hear the faint knock at the door. Only when it opened a bit and Ida stood just outside peering in did he rouse enough to lift a hand in warning, waving it at Jennifer and the sleeping child who lay between them.

Ida nodded, smiled in understanding and closed the door. It was the last thing Lucas remembered until he heard the rooster crowing in the chicken coop down the road at a neighbor's home.

Jennifer's eyes were open, startled and reflecting her confusion. Susan squirmed between them and he automatically patted her back, hoping she would return to the dreams that had kept her dozing till now.

"It's morning. And you're in my room." As announcements went, it was redundant, he thought, but then Jen had barely awakened and could not be expected to sound coherent.

"Yeah, I am," he drawled. "I spent the night here."

"That's sneaky." She cast him a dour look and he laughed.

"I'll let you return the favor whenever you like. My door won't be locked."

"I don't think so." Her pout was prominent as she rolled over and rose from the bed, brushing at her dress and then sighing deeply. "If you'll leave now, I'll change my clothes and get the baby ready for the day."

He supposed there was no sense in irritating the woman any more than he had to, so he followed her request and got up. Picking up his boots, he went toward the door, opening it just in time to walk into Cole Weston, who was obviously heading for the breakfast table.

"Morning, Miss Jennifer," he said. "Howdy there, Lucas." He strolled on and Jennifer's face reddened as if the man had accused her of some terrible deed, Lucas thought. Buster sidled past and followed Cole down the stairway, evidently needing to find the back door.

Lucas frowned, brushing back his unruly hair. "You're my wife, Jen. We're married, we're both fully dressed and I have a right to be here. Don't get upset over this."

"I left you, Lucas. I moved out of your house and your life. If you hadn't followed me here, I'd still be putting money aside to go back East."

"And now what are you saving for?" He halted in the doorway, boots held in front of him, his voice harsh.

"I'm not. I'm not saving for anthing, I suppose. Just trying to get my life in order and do what's right for Susan. And for me. Maybe I'm just waiting for you to get tired of me, tired of hanging around."

Yet, he thought, there was a sense of loneliness about the woman. No matter how irate she sounded, no matter how her eyes flashed with anger, there was a sadness he could not help but see, a sorrowful cast to her features that tore at his heart. How a man could love a woman who cared so little for him was a puzzle he'd yet to solve.

But it was true, he admitted to himself with a sense of wonder. He loved her. He wanted her, and most of all he needed her. Needed the smile she'd offered him as she'd solved the problem of making edible biscuits one day back at the farmhouse. The quick flash of pleasure when he'd touched her, her eyes seeking his with a hidden message he'd cherished, returned to his mind as quickly as it had numerous times before.

Now he stood little chance of keeping her as his own, of taking her home with him, unless he outright kidnapped her and dragged her off. And that he could not bring himself to do.

"I'll see you at the breakfast table." Closing the door, he crossed the hall and entered his room. The clean clothing in his dresser drawers reminded him again of Jennifer, and he could not chase her memory from his thoughts as he dressed and readied himself for the day.

She was in the dining room when he arrived, carrying bowls of food from the kitchen. Susan babbled from behind the swinging door and he caught a glimpse of the baby, sitting on a chair, banging a small kettle with a wooden spoon.

The men made short work of the bowls of sausage gravy and platters of biscuits and sausage patties, only pausing to offer their thanks when Helen entered the room with bowls of scrambled eggs. The biscuits were replenished with another panful dumped from a flat sheet and the tableful of men devoured them, barely leaving enough for the women.

"We'll make more when y'all have gone upstream to your claims," Ida told them. "Don't you worry. We always get enough to eat around here."

Lunch pails were passed out as the men left, goodbyes were called back and forth, and Lucas halted in front of Jennifer as she stood by the back door. "See you at the supper table. Do I have any more newspaper in my sandwiches?"

She blushed and shook her head. "That was mean of me, wasn't it?"

"No. I laughed out loud. It was something only you would think of, sweetheart."

"Did it ruin the roast beef?"

"Nothing could ruin the food you women feed us." He looked down at his pail. "What do we have today?"

"Surprise. You'll find out." She smiled as she added a handful of cookies to the assortment the pail held. "Extra dessert, sir. Just for being nice."

"Nice? Me?" He bent low and brushed a kiss across her cheek. "Now, *that* was nice. The nicest thing I've been privileged to do in days."

She stepped back and Ida laughed. "You're a scamp, Luc. But don't think that kind of kissin' is gonna win your bride back. You'll have to do better than that."

"Not this morning." Jennifer seemed firm as she responded to that idea.

"No, not this morning," Lucas agreed. And then he bent low again, whispering words only she could hear. "I'll talk to you about it after supper tonight."

CHAPTER THIRTEEN

A LETTER from her parents was a cause for rejoicing, Jennifer thought as she stood in the post office and tore open the envelope. Perhaps…but no, the news was not what she had hoped for. And now that she considered the idea, she had no real idea what she had thought to find inside the envelope.

Only Kyle could have told them where she was, and she could only imagine what his devious mind had concocted when he'd decided to reveal her whereabouts. That she'd become a mail-oorder bride was news to her folks, that was certain, for they'd only known that she had left—bereft over the loss of not only her sister, Alma, but also of the babywho had been left to a man who had no notion of how to care for an infant. But they'd cared enough to write a letter, and she read it voraciously.

It was not what she'd expected, this letter announcing their imminent arrival. They planned to bring their grandchild, Susan, back to New York City where they would raise her in their own home. A nanny would be hired, her father said, and his lawyer had already assured him that no court in the land would keep Susan from a home such as her grandparents were willing to provide.

Too bad they hadn't thought of this solution a few months ago when the baby was born, when there had been a chance to rescue her from her father's hands. Jennifer swallowed the bitternes she felt, standing in middle of a flurry of townsfolk, reading her letter for the second time. Surely she'd misunderstood. Her parents could not be planning on taking Susan from her.

And yet, that seemed to be exactly what the letter stated. According to her father's schedule, they would arrive in two days' time and would be staying for a week. They planned to stay at the hotel, so that Jennifer's *little* home would not be invaded by two more adults to tend to. She winced as she read the description her father had chosen to tack onto the big farmhouse. *Little.* The urge to take them there, to show them the home Lucas had brought her to, burned within her. It was clear they chose not to believe she married well.

But it was of no use and her shoulders slumped at the knowledge. The farmhouse was no longer her home, and if her parents saw her in the boardinghouse with twelve men in residence, they would be dead certain that Susan did not belong there. No matter that the twelve men in question had become attached to the baby over the past weeks and even now vied for her attention at the supper table.

"What's wrong?" Sally Jo stood in front of her and Jennifer looked up into a face filled with concern, a tenderness apparent she'd not thought to find in the woman.

"My parents want to come and take the baby back East with them. In fact, they'll be here day after tomorrow." Her voice was trembling, her hands shaking, as she held the letter, and she thought she might sit right down on the floor and cry if Sally Jo offered one word of sympathy.

It was not to be. "Then move yourself and the baby back out to Lucas's place and set up residence there. Susan will have a ready-made family and your folks won't have a leg to stand on." Sally Jo planted herself firmly, hands on her hips and chin elevated, as if she would take on the world should Jennifer need her help in that regard.

"I've already told Lucas I won't go home with him."

"Then un-tell him. Just say you've changed your mind. He'll have you out of there quicker than you can blink."

"I can't do that. It would be like deceiving him, moving back just so my folks won't take the baby."

"And you think he'll care?" Sally Jo laughed. "He'll be tickled pink, woman."

A glimmer of hope was born in Jennifer's breast as she considered the idea. "Maybe I could..." She shook her head. "No, I wouldn't dare."

"I'll bet you could," Sally Jo told her, smiling. "And I suspect you'd dare do most anything to keep things on an even keel for Susan."

"You've got that right." Her tears were dry, her hands had ceased trembling and Jennifer folded the letter and placed it back in the envelope. "I'll see you later."

As she left the post office, she glanced back to see an encouraging smile lighting the other woman's face.

Her feet flew as she traveled back to the big house and her plans were already half formed as she pitched in to help with supper preparations. Helen had the baby tucked in for a nap in the parlor.

"You're cookin' something up, girl. I can tell by the look on your face." Ida stood at the stove and turned pork chops in a pan of bubbling lard. Breaded with eggs and then dipped into bread crumbs, they were brown and sizzling as she placed them in a pan, ready for the oven. A whole pork loin had been cut up for the meal, with over thirty chops nestled side by side.

"They get two apiece," Ida said. "What with vegetables and potatoes and all the rest, I think they'll survive on that."

"I'd hope so." Helen was rolling out pie crusts for the four big pans in front of her. "I think pumpkin will be the easiest to make, don't you, Ida?"

"Whatever you want." And with that, Helen nodded and turned to open jars of pumpkin, canned late last autumn. Adding milk and eggs and seasonings, she dipped into the sugar bin and then began to stir. "I make kind of a custard filling, lots of eggs and milk in it."

"Must be sorta like mine." Ida tossed the other woman a glance. "We work at this from the same direction, Helen. I noticed that right off."

"Only one way I know of to keep menfolk well fed and happy." The crusts were rolled and placed in the pans, the edges crimped to her satisfaction and then Helen poured the filling into the waiting crusts. Jennifer opened the oven door and watched as the bottom shelf was filled with the dessert.

"Leave me enough room for the pork chops." Ida staked her claim and Helen grinned.

"You've got the whole top shelf. If that isn't enough you'll have to wait till the pies are done."

"That's plenty of room. We'll have mashed potatoes and gravy. No need to use the oven for vegetables, either. I've got jars of corn and some succotash we can mix with it. Those men like corn better than limas anyway. Jennifer made applesauce this morning. So I think we're all set."

They made it sound so simple. Jennifer was almost overwhelmed by the quick repartee the two older women conducted, feeling young and ignorant. And yet she knew she was "coming along right well," as Ida had said on several occasions.

Bathing and dressing Susan took up Jennifer's time before supper, and she scooted up to the table as the other two women put on the final platters of food. A chair sat empty beside Lucas and Jennifer looked up to find Helen motioning at the seat.

"I think she wants you to sit by me." Lucas had bent close to whisper the words and Jennifer nodded her agreement. It went along nicely with her own plans, she decided, and smiled as she thought how nicely Helen had helped to fit things together.

Susan ate with gusto, devouring potatoes and pointing at the applesauce bowl each time it passed by, until Jennifer thought the baby would surely burst. Drinking her milk from a glass was a fairly new accomplishment and Susan made bubbles to her heart's content, happy with the laughter of the men who watched her performance.

"Makes me think of my little sister," Toby said wistfully. "Sure miss having my family around." He looked the length of the long table. "This is almost as good as being back home." His blush made him seem young and innocent, Jennifer thought, but the look the man cast in Helen's direction smacked of a male creature on the prowl.

"We'll tend to the dishes," Ida said once the meal was over. "Why don't you men carry your plates to the kitchen for us?"

They joined in willingly, two of them offering to dry the plates and silverware. Helen accepted that offer, shooting a shy smile in Toby's direction, his having been the first voice heard.

Susan's afternoon nap had lasted longer than usual, so now she seemed ready to play. Jennifer took her to their room and sat on the floor with her, building stacks as high as possible with the empty spools Ida had contributed for the baby's pleasure. Four or five were quite enough, Susan decided, knocking the pile over, then squealing with delight as Jennifer feigned disapproval and scooped the spools toward herself. Then they started all over again.

After a few minutes Lucas came upstairs and watched the game from the doorway. Then he walked across the floor to where Jennifer sat with the baby, then sat in front of her, so Susan could crawl back and forth between her favorite people.

For almost an hour they played, singing songs when the spools became tiresome. Then Jennifer formed her fingers, and Susan's, too, into shapes that went along with short poems and songs she'd learned as a child. She gave her complete attention to the baby, reveling in the giggles, the laughter and the kisses she stole from the soft little mouth.

"You're a good mother." Lucas looked at her with a tender expression that touched her deep inside. His hands were gentle as he held the baby, his fingers teasing as he tickled the bottom of her foot, her shoes and stockings having long since been removed.

"I'm not her mother, though. I wish I were. Perhaps some day I'll—"

"If I have anything to do with it, you'll have babies of your own, Jen. We'll have a big family. And the best part of it is that we can easily afford it. My claim is showing good results. Even with Sandy as a partner, I'm adding to my bank account every week."

"I never wanted your money, Lucas." Her voice was solemn.

"I know that. But I want you to know that I'm planning on giving you a good life, Jen. Maybe not now, since you're so dead set on staying here, but one day."

She glanced out the window to where the sun had set, leaving only a pale pink cast in the western sky. "It's time to get Susan ready for bed."

"Changing the subject?" He grinned at her and got to his feet. "I can take a hint, sweetheart. I'm leaving."

SHE WAITED until the parade of men had passed her door, until it was fully dark outside and Susan was sound asleep in the middle of the big bed. Her nightgown was all-concealing, her feet bare, her hair hanging down to her waist, brushed and wavy. And her hands were trembling.

She opened her bedroom door and closed it behind herself. Should Susan awake, which was very unlikely, she couldn't escape the room, given the presence of the large watchdog who never strayed far from the baby's side. And besides, Jennifer would hear her should the baby fall from the bed and head for the door.

The hallway seemed wider than before as she crossed the runner Ida kept to muffle footsteps there. And Lucas's door was closed. But not locked, he'd said.

She turned the handle and pushed the door open a bit, looking in to find him lying in bed, turned from her, facing the window. She thought he stirred and she hesitated, then went into the room and closed the door.

In less than a second, Lucas was facing her, a gun in his hand. Jennifer stifled a cry, lifting a hand to her mouth, lest she be heard. At that Lucas dropped the pistol beside him.

"Don't ever sneak up on me," he said harshly.

"I didn't know you slept with a gun." She approached him, watching as he took the weapon and deposited it on the floor by the bed.

"Most men do," he said. "And for good reason. You never know who'll be after your claim, especially when it's as rich as mine." The moonlight through the window illuminated him a bit, enough to tell that he was unclothed above the waist. And she'd be willing to bet that he wore nothing beneath the sheet, either.

Perhaps this had been a bad idea. And at that thought, she moved to the door.

"Where are you going, Jen? Lost your nerve?"

She thought amusement touched his tone and she turned to him. "No. I never had much nerve to begin with, Lucas. I wanted to talk to you."

"Talk? Then come on over and sit down." He patted the bed beside himself and waited.

She complied, because she didn't know what else to do. She'd been caught in a lie and made to look a fool in front of him.

But his next words belied that idea. "I've been hoping you'd come to see me. I didn't want to waken Susan, or I'd have crossed the hall myself." He touched her arm, then reached for her hand, tugging her closer. "Come on, sweetheart. Lie down with me. I promise not to—"

His words halted as if he would not speak an untruth to her and she almost laughed. "You promise not to what? Make love to me? Keep me here all night?" She bent closer to him, touching his forehead with her lips for a moment. "What, Lucas? What will you do with me?"

"You know what I'd like to do, Jen. But I won't. I won't give you the chance to point a finger at me in the morning and accuse me of forcing you into something against your will."

"What will you do, then?" She kissed him again and felt the control he exerted over his body, his hand tightening on hers, his body rigid beside her hip.

"Lie down here and I'll show you." He waited then and she lifted her feet to the bed, lying beside him, her head on the pillow. He pulled her closer, his arm around her waist, his hand tucked against her ribs, and she thought she might cease breathing.

He was so careful as he gentled her, his hand turning her toward him, his mouth touching hers with soft kisses that seduced her even as he held her apart from his body.

She shifted and he held her. "Lie still." It was a command, and she followed it, uncertain now what she should do. "I'm not going to make love to you," he said. "I only want to hold you." And then he laughed, a rough, growling sound that seemed to come from his depths. "No, that's a lie," he said.

His tone deepened and his voice softened. "I want to do much more than that. But first I want to prove to you that there's more to marriage than making love. I want you to know that I need more from you than the joining of our bodies, though that appeals to me in a mighty way, sweetheart. I want you to know that my need for you will last through out the days of your child-bearing, including your lying-in time, when I have to leave you in peace no matter how great my desire for you.

"I'll still want you when your hair is white and your face is wrinkled. When you have aches and pains and perhaps illness we can't foresee now. Even then, I'll want you, Jen. Even then."

She curled against him, uncaring that he had turned her away in her quest to seduce him. Uncaring that he would not make love with her tonight. Only able to hold him close, spend her kisses against his face, her arms circling his neck, her body warming against his. For the words he had just spoken were those of a man to the woman he loved, and the thought of Lucas feeling such an emotion for her was almost more than she could take in. She only knew that he'd made it possible for her to want to seduce him.

"When?"

He knew what she asked, and his answer was quick. "When the time is right. Then we'll make love, Jen. And not until then. I rushed you into it the last time. I didn't give you a choice and I was wrong. I came pretty close to forcing you and I'll never do that again."

He released her and turned on to his back. "Now go back to Susan. You need to be there for her, and I don't think I can keep you here any longer without breaking my promise to myself."

She rolled from him and stood beside the bed. "I wouldn't have turned you down, Lucas. I came in here ready to... Well, you know why I came in here, don't you?"

"Yeah, I know. But I know it's not the right time for us, Jen. I want you to still like me in the morning."

She was silent for a moment and then she touched his bare shoulder with her fingertips. "I'll always like you, Lucas. Much more than I should, I'm afraid."

She crossed to the door and then found her bed.

JENNIFER SMILED AT HIM as he entered the dining room and once more he congratulated himself on the self-control he'd wielded last night. It had been the right move, of that he was certain. Had he taken her offer last night, she'd be feeling embarrassed today, maybe resentful of him. As it was she smiled and handed him the baby before she carried the last of the food to the table, then sat next to him.

"I'll take her." She held out her hands, but Lucas shook his head.

"I'll feed her." A spoonful of oatmeal found its way to Susan's mouth and she smacked her lips.

"Mmm…" she cooed, grinning, showing off the new teeth that glistened like white pearls. Again he offered the spoon and once more she accepted the offering as if it were her due.

"Why don't y'all put her between you and take turns?" Ida brought an extra chair, settling it at the corner of the table, in easy reach for both Jennifer and Lucas to reach the child with little effort. The plan was a good one, Jennifer realized, for the avid little mouth seemed fashioned after that of a baby robin in the nest, opening regularly toward one, then the other, of the two people who gave her sustenance.

Finally she closed her lips and shook her head. Finishing her own meal took Jennifer but a few moments, and then she rose and lifted Susan to her shoulder.

Lucas tugged at the baby's bare foot. "Time for Lucas to leave," he said in a singsong voice. He was rewarded by the lunging of a child determined to be in his arms.

"I'll get the lunch pails," Jennifer said, heading to the kitchen. The men all carried their plates and bowls out without nudging and Ida thanked them.

"Makes it easier on us with the dirty dishes out here right handy to the sink." She beamed at the miners and they nodded their appreciation. Within ten minutes, they were gone, Lucas the last one out the door, as usual.

He leaned close to Jennifer as she held the baby in one hand, his lunch pail in the other. "See you at suppertime. Miss me, will you?"

She nodded, releasing the handle of his pail into his hand and then accepting the kiss he offered with good grace.

"What's going on with you two?" Ida was bursting with curiosity as they watched the men trail off toward the livery stable.

"Not much."

"You sleep with him?" Softer and lower, the words nevertheless reached Helen's ears. She perked up and raced over, a smile announcing her approval should such a thing have happened.

"No. Not really. We talked a little."

Ida laughed. "In his bed?"

Jennifer felt like a squirming worm on a hook. "Well, kind of." And then she backtracked. "But it's not what you're thinking. It truly isn't. We just talked and then I went and crawled back in bed with the baby."

"Well, he's makin' progress, anyway," Ida said. "Won't be long till he has you back home where you belong."

Jennifer felt wounded by Ida's words. "You don't think I belong here?"

"For now. But in the long run, you need to be with Lucas in his own place, not wearin' yourself out runnin' after a bunch of miners."

"Maybe." And that was all she'd say on the subject, Jennifer decided.

HE CAME IN late for supper, dirty and disheveled, more so than usual. Jennifer left the stack of plates on the dining room table to follow him up the stairs to his room. It was time, she'd decided, to let him know about her parents' arrival, scheduled for tomorrow, according to their letter. Lucas turned to face her just inside his bedroom door.

"Did you come to help me wash up?" His grin made her heart jolt in her chest.

"Not really, but I did make sure you had warm water in your pitcher, and I know you have clean clothes in your drawers." She closed the door and watched him, her mind racing as she considered her words. The chair next to the door beckoned and she sat on the edge of its seat, her hands clasped in her lap.

"What is it, Jen? You're upset about something." He squatted in front of her and picked up her fingers in his, looking into her eyes with an intensity that bid her to speak.

"I got a letter yesterday from my parents."

"You didn't say anything." And then he waited, watching her.

"I know. I had other things on my mind, but I need to tell you that they'll be arriving tomorrow. They're coming to get Susan."

"And what do you want me to do?"

"I don't know." It was a bold-faced lie. She wanted him to hold her close and to promise that nothing could tear the baby from her arms. But that seemed to be a solution impossible for now. Lucas could not make such a vow. And she had less right to Susan than did her parents.

"You want to go home? Back to the farm?" It was an offer she had hoped for, a plea she would have made had he not suggested it himself, and she nodded. "After supper?" he asked.

"I'll go in the morning, after you've gone to your claim. Ida will help me load up what I need and I'll take the wagon."

"I'd rather be here to help you." He frowned, deep in thought, it seemed, for in a few moments his face cleared and he spoke quickly, as if he'd reached a decision. "I'll get word to Sandy that I won't be at the claim tomorrow. Once you're settled back at the farm, I'll go out there for an overnight stay and catch up with my share."

"I don't want to cause trouble for you." And yet her very soul seemed to yearn for the man and his easy acceptance of her need. "Will you stay with me till my parents arrive?"

"You know I will." He rose to his feet, pulling her from the chair and gathering her to himself. It was exactly where she'd longed to be and she leaned against his strength. He kissed her, a soft, undemanding kiss of promise, one she welcomed and returned with her whole heart.

"Now, you'd better get downstairs and do something with that stack of plates you left on the table," he murmured. "I'm gonna get washed and dressed in clean clothes and I'll be down in ten minutes."

"All right." Leaving Ida and Helen with the bulk of supper preparation had been a sudden decision, one she knew they would understand. But Lucas was right. She needed to lend a hand.

The women had things pretty much under control, and only cast her inquiring glances as she joined them in the kitchen. "I'm sorry to have run out when I did," she told them. "It was—"

Ida waved a hand in dismissal. "Don't stew over it. We handled things. The table's set and the food's about ready to carry in." She aimed a long look at Jennifer. "I hope you got things ironed out between you."

"Lucas is staying here tomorrow to take me back to the farm. My folks are coming in and they plan on taking Susan back to New York with them."

Ida paused halfway across the kitchen to shoot a startled look at Jennifer. "And what did Luc say about that?"

Jennifer halted in the midst of tying her apron strings. "He didn't. Just said he'd take me home in the morning. I suspect he thinks if we're a family, they won't have the heart to ask for Susan."

Ida's grin was wide, her eyes twinkling as her voice lowered to a near whisper. "I'll warrant if you go to his room tonight, you'll do more than talk, girl."

A blush climbed Jennifer's cheeks as she picked up twin bowls of potatoes and headed for the dining room door, almost stumbling as she heard the laughter of the two women behind her.

IDA WAS RIGHT. For when Jennifer opened Lucas's door shortly before midnight, he sat up in bed, limned by the moonlight from his window. One hand was extended to her as the other tossed back the sheet to make an inviting spot available to her. "Come here, Jen." It was all he needed to say. She crossed the room slowly, as if this were a decision she must be very certain of before she took the final steps.

He clasped her fingers in his palm and pulled her down to the sheet where he lay. "Come. Let me hold you, sweetheart." It was an invitation she could not resist, nor did she have any desire to deny him this triumph. He was her husband and she yearned to know his caresses, ached to feel his strength again, needed the assurance that he would be there to protect her no matter what the circumstance.

It was simple to lie with him, his arm tugging her against his length, his mouth finding hers to blend their lips in a warmth that gave sustenance to the feelings of desire that had begun to run rampant within her. He did not rush her along the path, allowed her to set the pace she chose, and only responded as she pressed against him with an urgency she didn't fully understand.

She only knew that she must be here, with him, in his arms, and her body ached to contain him, as if she could pull him through her pores, into her very flesh. "I want you, Lucas. I'm not even sure what it is I need from you, but I ache for you to cover me and make me your wife again."

"I know what you need, Jen," he whispered. "Shall I show you?"

She nodded, embarrassed at her own ignorance. She was a married woman, and yet, except for one lone experience, she'd savored none of the joys Lucas had spoken of, that long ago night. *I'll have known, just once, what you might have been to me.*

And now she'd come to him gladly, willingly, aching for his touch, knowing what his hands and mouth could make her feel, and she reveled in the knowledge that he welcomed her with open arms. For Lucas's elation at her surrender to him could not be mistaken.

"Jen? Let me do this." He whispered the words in her ear and she nodded, willing to do as he wanted, needing to be anything he desired. For he did desire her, and unless she was mistaken, his words the night before had been those of a man who loved deeply.

If Lucas could spell out the secrets of his heart, could she do no less? "I want you to love me." It was a whisper he could not help but hear, spoken into his ear with a warm breath that seemed to make him shiver. "Please, Lucas, love me tonight."

And he did. His arms held her against him for a moment and then he released her, long enough to drag the lengthy folds of her gown from her, tossing it to the floor with a murmur of satisfaction. She lay in front of him, a willing woman, a wife aching to belong to him, and he bent to her, taking the gift of her body.

It was not as it had been that other time, for she was amenable to his touch, her arms reaching for him, her legs clasping him to herself, her mouth seeking his with kisses rich with passion.

"Tell me, Jen. Tell me." The words seemed torn from his chest, rough and tormented, as if he could not believe the good fortune she had delivered into his arms.

And she knew what he needed to hear. Knew the words that would fill the aching void within him. "I love you, Lucas. I love you— I need you. Please love me."

He took the words from her mouth into his, with a kiss that robbed her of her breath, with a muttered repetition of her pledge. They were words he need not have spoken out loud, for she'd known, deep in her heart, that his feelings for her ran deep, that his allegiance to her was permanent, that he had meant every promise he'd made to her the day they were wed.

He filled her, not with only his masculine being, but with the joy of his love, and she basked in the pleasure of his caresses, the delight he offered her, his hands gentle yet strong as he brought her with him to a completion she ached to achieve.

"Lucas...Lucas, I love you." The words were intense, so filled with an emotion she savored even as she felt a moment of fright, that this man could so possess her, body and soul.

They lay in the middle of the big bed, Lucas holding her fast, her arms around him, in a grip that showed no signs of lessening. "Do you want to stay here tonight?" he asked as she sighed and shifted beneath him.

"I shouldn't leave Susan alone. She might awaken."

"Then we'll both go back and sleep with her." It seemed Lucas had made up his mind, for he released her and rolled from the bed. Her nightgown was a pale shadow in the moonlight as he held it in front of her. "Put this back on. We don't want to surprise anyone who might be wandering around the house."

She stood in front of him and he lowered the gown over her head, then reached for his trousers. Sliding into them, he steered her toward the door, but she paused as his hand touched the knob.

"Lucas, I've tricked you tonight. I planned this. Sally Jo said if I wanted you, I should go after you. So I did. Will you forgive me for being so sneaky, so…underhanded?"

His laugh was without rancor. "Bless Sally Jo," he murmured. "She's a smart lady. I'm happy you took her advice, Jen. It seems I owe her."

CHAPTER FOURTEEN

THE WAGON was loaded quickly. Jennifer carried bundles and boxes out to the lumbering conveyance Lucas had brought around to the backyard. A supply of milk and eggs were in one box, along with two loaves of fresh bread Ida had pressed into Jennifer's willing hands.

"You'll have enough to do, what with unpacking and putting things to rights, without having to mix up a batch of bread, girl." A good-size chunk of butter joined the provisions and then Ida stood in the middle of the kitchen contemplating the shelves of food visible from her viewpoint. "Maybe you ought to take along a kettle of soup for your dinner," she said, her forehead wrinkling as she considered the worth of that idea.

"I'll take it," Jennifer said. "You needn't ask twice, Ida. Lucas will be hungry by the time he hauls all this clutter into the house."

Ida grinned. "He won't mind. Not one little bit. I've never seen a man any more delighted with a turn of events than he is this morning. He's been whistling since he got out of bed, pret'near."

"How do you know?" Jennifer was shocked by the idea that Ida had heard Lucas's early morning teasing.

"I know where you slept last night, and I'd be willing to bet he wasn't two feet from you all night."

"You'd win." Hands down, Jennifer thought, smiling as she

recalled the night they'd spent curled around Susan, only their hands touching. Lucas had muttered his displeasure, warning her that, "Tomorrow night will be different."

"I'm glad, Jen." Ida's eyes filled with tears and they rolled down her plump cheeks. "You belong together, the three of you."

"I think so, too. But my parents may take Susan back to New York and raise her there."

"Can they really do that?"

"Lucas says not, but I'm not too sure of the ground they're standing on. They're the grandparents and their claim is stronger than mine. She's all they have left."

"They've got you, girl. And there's a lot to be said for that." Ida's voice was rough, her demeanor indignant as she spoke.

Jennifer waved her hand as if to dismiss the woman's opinion. "It can't be helped, and if I can't persuade them otherwise, they'll take her with them. But I'm willing to try to change their minds. You know that Lucas will make a good impression on them."

"You think so, huh?" From the doorway behind her, the familiar tones teased her. She spun to face him and barely resisted running into his arms. "You about ready, sweetheart?" he asked, picking up the last lot of belongings. Her valise and a huge box of baby things remained, and Jennifer cast a long look around the kitchen, as if imprinting it on her memory.

"I'm ready," she said, sad at the leave-taking and yet pleased to be setting up her life with Lucas again. This time on better footing, she reminded herself. And for that she owed Ida more than she could say. Perhaps a hug would solve that problem, she decided, and approached her friend with outstretched arms.

"I love you, Ida. I'll miss you so much."

"Well, you always got a place to come to if Luc doesn't

treat you right, you know." Ida's eyes twinkled as she spoke and then her arms encircled Jennifer in a tight hug. "I'll take care of things here, Jen. Sally Jo has agreed to take over the financial part of the business and I think we can trust her to do the right thing by us."

"I know we can." Jennifer's words were confident. "And with Helen here, things will run well. You may have to find someone else to lend a hand though. This is a lot of work for two women."

"I've already thought of someone I might get hold of," Ida said. "Had her in mind when I realized you probably wouldn't be here forever."

"And when was that?" Jennifer was truly puzzled by the statement.

"About the time I saw the determined look in Lucas's eye and I figured out that he planned to take you home."

"I won't argue that one." With a happy smile, Jennifer picked up the baby from the chair she'd occupied at the table and tucked her tightly into her right arm. "I'm ready," she said, nodding at Lucas. He lifted the last of his load and opened the door, one big foot holding it until Jennifer could pass him and step onto the porch. Buster watched them, resignation on his face, as if he recognized the departure of his favorite human would bring about changes in his life, not to mention his place in this house at bedtime.

"I'll be out one day soon," Ida said, brushing a last kiss on Jennifer's cheek and then aiming another at Susan, catching her unaware and causing her to giggle and squirm.

Lucas lifted both woman and child high in the air and settled them on the wagon seat, where he joined them in moments.

"'Bye, Ida," he said with a happy smile. "Take good care

of yourself. You'll have two more rooms to rent now. Shall I send some men by?"

"Heavens, no," she retorted. "I've got a waiting list a yard long. All I'll have to do is wait a couple of hours or so and the next two men on my list will be showing up, champing at the bit, anxious to move in."

She waved as the wagon moved ahead, through the side yard and then out onto the road. Jennifer turned in the seat, keeping her friend in sight as long as she could, lifting one hand in a final flourish as they gained the road and the horses broke into a quick trot.

"Are you content with being on your way home, Jen?" Lucas's look was solemn as he sought her gaze. "I didn't rush you too fast, did I?"

She smiled at him, adjusting Susan on her lap. "I think I'm the one who did the rushing, Mr. O'Reilly. If my memory serves me, it was *my* doing that got us to this point."

"If you hadn't come calling last night, I'd planned on dragging you out of bed and carrying you across the hall anyway. I'd about had enough of sleeping alone and reaching for you in the night."

"You haven't slept with me for that many nights," she told him. "At least, not many nights that seemed to please you like the one just past."

"I was pleased." His admission was quick, his voice low, as if he might find an audience listening. "It was a dream come true, Jen. I'd been so lonesome without you."

"You saw me every day."

"That's not what I mean. There's seeing you and then there's having you close to me. I'd gone about as long as I could without something giving way between us."

"And are you happy now?" She looked down at Susan, holding the baby's fingers, bending to kiss the soft, rosy cheek she could not resist.

"What do you think?" He held the reins in one hand and slid the other arm around her, scooting her across the wide seat to nestle next to his side. "I've never been so happy, Jen. My claim is producing well. My partner is cooperating with me, filling his shoes and mine, too, while I sort things out. Our house is waiting for us. And best of all, my wife is here with me, and she loves me." As if that were the epitome of success, he tossed his head back and laughed. "What more could any man want?"

She leaned her head against his shoulder, willing to be a submissive wife today. And then a stray thought zipped through her mind. "You didn't leave the house a mess, did you?" She tilted her head to one side and looked up at him, meeting his amused gaze.

"You know better. If I had any hope of bringing you home with me, I knew I'd better clean up behind myself and not leave anything to chance."

HE'D DONE QUITE WELL, Jennifer thought, standing in the middle of the big kitchen, sorting out boxes of supplies as Lucas carried them in. Susan was sleeping in the middle of the big bed upstairs, pillows surrounding her.

The kitchen showed the evidence of Lucas's attempts at housekeeping and not for the world would she criticize the pile of dust and dirt he'd swept into one corner or the mess he'd made of the big iron skillet, washing it and ruining the surface with soap and water. It might take her a week to season it properly again, but she'd never let on for a minute that he'd erred in his care of anything in this house.

The floor needed a good scrubbing, and bits and pieces of dried egg yolk and crumbs of bread on the table were mute evidence that he'd managed to put together a few meals on his own before he'd moved into the boardinghouse.

And into her heart.

And where that thought had come from, she didn't know. Only that it was so.

LUCAS SPENT the rest of the day helping her set things to rights, toting obediently when she pointed a finger at a box or bundle, placing everything where it belonged. They ate Ida's soup at noontime, and Jennifer worked hard to put together a meal he would enjoy after his long day's work was done.

He brought the cow home from a neighbor's house and gathered the chickens from the yard where they'd run wild while the house was empty, eating the chicken feed he'd scattered hither and yon for their sustenance. Late in the day he carried a bucket of milk into the springhouse and reappeared moments later, his long strides bringing him to the back porch, where he took off his boots in deference to the freshly scrubbed floor.

"Come wash up. Supper's ready." With a flourish, Jennifer lifted the lid from her big Dutch oven and exposed the contents to his view. A beef stew simmered beneath a covering of big, fluffy dumplings and Lucas lifted an eyebrow as he gazed at it with appreciation.

"You've learned well, Mrs. O'Reilly. I never would have thought the bride I brought home would have caught on so quickly."

"I was hopeless," she said, laughing at the memory. "You put up with an awful lot, Lucas."

"You'll have to make it up to me." He pouted nicely, moving across the kitchen toward her. "It looks like you have enough food there for a small army. That's a good beginning, ma'am."

A horse's neigh outside brought Lucas's head up quickly and he turned back to the door, his stance that of a man ready for whatever might come. "We have callers." His voice was harsh and Jennifer didn't need to look past him to know who the visitors might be.

"My parents." She walked to the door and his hand was on her shoulder.

"Are you all right?" Warm and comforting, the heat of his body sheltered her and she turned her head, the better to meet his gaze.

"I'll be fine." But her heart jolted within her chest as she recognized that she might never be the same again. If she lost Susan, she would have a huge, empty gap where once a baby had filled her heart.

She stepped outdoors and greeted her parents. "Lucas said I'd cooked enough for a small army," she told them with a smile. "We've plenty to eat. Come on in."

Both her mother and father looked surprised by the greeting. "We found out in town how to get here," her father said. "Rented a buggy and headed this way."

"Well, you must be hungry," Jennifer told them, hugging her mother and then planting a quick kiss on her father's cheek. "Come on in. Lucas will go up and get the baby. She must be about awake by now. She's slept the whole afternoon away."

Jennifer's mother pressed her lips together. "I've been so anxious to see her. Kyle took her away without any notice at all, and we've been frantic, worrying about her."

"How did you—"

Her father waved his hand. "Kyle told us he'd been set upon and beaten terribly by your husband, and the baby had vanished."

"He lied." It was all she could say, so great was her anger at the untruthfulness of Kyle's statements. "He knew where Susan was. He knew I had her."

"Well, we're here now," her mother said. "Come on in, Joseph. I'm curious to see the house where our daughter lives. Not to mention to meet the man she married."

The supper was approved of by all, Lucas playing down his surprise at the tastiness of Jennifer's offering. "She's a good cook," he told her mother. "Had a good teacher. I brought out a widow lady from town and she had an apt pupil. Jennifer catches on to everything quickly." His look in her direction made Jennifer blush, and she stored up her aggravation with him for a later time. *Jennifer catches on to everything quickly.*

The man might just as well have bragged about her prowess in his bed. Although the double meaning in his words seemed to have gone over her mother's head, her father exchanged a look with Lucas that seemed to please them both.

Susan held her audience in the palm of her hand, eating well, smiling at the table full of beaming adults and reaching for Lucas after she had eaten her fill.

"How long will it be before she calls me 'Grandpa'?" Joseph asked Jennifer.

Jennifer felt quick tears as she bent her head. "She's a smart little thing," she said, her voice choking on the words. "She's just beginning to make sounds that mimic words."

"Well, I hope she likes the room we've prepared for her,

and the nanny we've hired," Joseph said. "She's an Irish girl. Together with her mother, they make quite a pair, one of them keeping the house, the other just waiting to get her hands on the baby."

"They'll love her." Jennifer stood and began clearing the table. The pan of stew and dumplings was almost empty, and her father spoke from behind her.

"Don't be throwing that out now, Jen. I'll have it for breakfast."

"Breakfast?" She turned to him in surprise. "I thought maybe bacon or sausage gravy would be good."

"You can eat all the bacon you like. I'll settle for this," he said, peering into the contents of the kettle she held. "In fact, I'd finish it up now, but I haven't any more room."

"Not even enough for custard pie?" Jennifer went to the pantry and brought out the pie she'd baked earlier while Lucas was rounding up his livestock.

Joseph patted his stomach. "I'll manage to find room, somehow."

And he did. As did Lucas and Jennifer's mother. Susan ate the custard from Jennifer's slice, but with the thought of the child leaving her on the morrow, Jennifer found her own appetite to have forsaken her.

"I'll get Susan's things ready tonight," she said, "and you can get an early start in the morning." She fought tears, bending her head to kiss the baby's head. It seemed almost more than she could bear, giving up this child, but if it was the best thing for Susan right now, she'd bend with the wind and allow it to happen without a fuss.

"We'll be on the noon coach," Joseph said. "Then catch a train down the road a ways." He rose from the table and Lucas joined him as they went out the back door, leaving the two women alone.

"You're welcome any time you want to come visit, Jennifer." Her mother's voice was soft and inviting and the look on her face told Jennifer that she understood how difficult this was for her daughter. "I'm so glad you had the baby with you. I was worried to death that Kyle wouldn't take care of her or that he might give her away just to spite us."

"Well, so long as you and daddy have Susan, I won't have to lie awake at night and worry, Mother. She's been a darling to take care of. I almost envy your little Irish nanny. I know she'll love her. It will break my heart to lose her, though."

"I meant it when I offered to have you come for a visit," her mother said. "You and your husband both for that matter." She bent closer and her voice dropped to a whisper, even though the two men were standing near the barn, far out of earshot.

"Lucas is a handsome man, isn't he? I think you did well for yourself, Jennifer—better than I'd thought. It might have been the best thing you've ever done, coming here on the promise of a man's proposal. I'll admit I thought you were daft at the time, but I think you've landed on your feet. The man seems to be well thought of in town, according to the people we spoke with, and he certainly has provided you with a nice home. Mining must be a lucrative way of making a living."

"He's doing well," Jennifer said, unwilling to elaborate on Lucas's assets. "He's very good to me, Mother."

"I could tell he's smitten with you, just the way he watches you." An arch look lit her mother's face. "I suspect he'll take good care of you. And I wouldn't be surprised if you have a baby of your own before long, Jennifer. It would be the best thing in the world for you."

A baby of your own. The words stunned her and Jennifer felt her mouth drop open in surprise. And then she recovered. "Probably not for a while. We'd certainly like to have a family, but I'm in no hurry. I've really enjoyed Susan, but I don't how good I'd be at taking care of a newborn."

"It's something you catch on to in a hurry," her mother told her. "I think you're a natural born mother, the way you've taken over with your sister's child." She looked pensive as she considered her daughter. "I fear you'll miss Susan more than you know."

A sound of complaint came from the chair where Susan sat, and Jennifer took her up and wiped her hands and face at the sink. "I'll put the dishes to soak and we can go in to the parlor and play with her for a while, if you want to, Mother. She loves to crawl across the carpet and play with her toys."

"ARE YOU ALL RIGHT?" Lucas spoke in a low voice, holding Jennifer in his arms much later that same night. They'd gone to bed well after dark, the parlor becoming a room filled with laughter with all four adults on the floor as Susan experimented with a game that consisted of one baby keeping her audience in thrall to her smiles and jabbering.

"She'll run us a merry chase, Mother," Joseph said as Jennifer finally picked Susan up to prepare her for bed.

Susan's grandmother smiled and nodded. "That's why we have a nanny."

Jennifer thought that it would be better for Susan to have a mother or grandmother handling her care than a hired helper, but she kept her ideas to herself.

Now she relaxed in Lucas's embrace and responded to his

query. "I'm fine. Just tired and thinking about tomorrow. I'll have lots of time for myself now, won't I?"

"Maybe we'll have a baby of our own by this time next year," Lucas said casually, as if it were something he'd been considering.

"Funny. That's the same thing my mother said. She didn't mention next year, but she sounded like she thought we should begin a family right away."

"And what do you think?" He bent his head and kissed her. "We could practice a little right now, maybe get started on the project."

"My folks are in the next room." Her words were stilted, her tone frosty. Having the Alstons in the same house probably didn't matter to Lucas the way it did to her.

"I'll be real quiet," he said, his hands roaming over her back and then skating over her breasts and hips. "You don't even have to wiggle, honey. I'll just kiss you a little, in all the places that smell so good. And then I'll—"

"You will not." Her tone was emphatic now, her position clear, even to a man as set on making love to his wife as Lucas seemed to be.

"How about after they leave in the morning?" He sounded disappointed, but Jennifer thought he smiled, his mouth against her forehead forming into a grin if she wasn't mistaken.

"I'll talk to you after breakfast, when they've gone," she told him. And that would be no great sacrifice on her part, she decided. Making love with Lucas had become a part of marriage she'd found to be more than inviting. He gave her a delight she could barely contain, with each touch of his hands, with every movement of his body against hers. The warmth of his mouth, the gentle contact of his skin against hers, his fingers exploring the hollows of her body—all were pleasures she could not resist.

He turned her now, curling against her back, his hand forming to the shape of her breast as he prepared to sleep. His breath was warm against her nape and she shivered.

"I love you, Jen."

They were words she thought she would never tire of hearing, and as her eyes closed, she murmured beneath her breath, "I'm glad, Lucas. I love you, too."

JENNIFER WEPT BUCKETS, more than Lucas would have thought possible. He'd never known that one small woman could contain so much water in the form of tears, yet his shirt was damp and his handkerchief bore the results of her sorrow. Susan had not been happy with her departure from the farm, but Jennifer's mother had shown a grandmother's prowess at calming her by the time the buggy reached the side of the house, heading for town.

Now the house was silent, and Lucas recalled his words from the night before and Jennifer's answer.

How about after they leave in the morning? He held her close now and smiled against the top of her head.

I'll talk to you after breakfast. As if she, too, remembered her words, she lifted her head from his chest and looked at him with eyes that begged his compassion. "I need you, Lucas," she whispered, the words an open invitation so far as he was concerned.

He picked her up without haste, yet his body was already prepared for the loving that was to come. It would be a time for Jennifer, he decided, a time in which she would know his love for her, feel his need of her, and resolve any lingering doubts she might have.

He climbed the stairs, her body light in his arms. She lifted her face to his as they reached the upper hallway. "Love me," she said, her whispered request bringing him to a state of arousal that made him fear his own impatience. Not for the world would he hurt her, not in any case would he bring her to his bed without first knowing she was ready for him, was yearning for this joining as he was.

The bed was unmade, the coverlet tossed to the foot, the sheet crumpled where it had been left when they arose. Now he placed her in the middle of the bed, careful as he removed her clothing, his fingers gentle as he took the pins from her hair and released it from its long braid.

It lay on her pillow, looking to Lucas like a cloud of darkness, tempting his hands to bury themselves in its depths.

He slid from his own clothing and joined her, curling around her, his hands touching her with care, caressing her in a way he knew would bring pleasure to her aching heart. Even as he loved her, as his mouth tasted the sweet flavor of her flesh, he whispered soft words of his desire, reassured her of his love.

And in all of that, he brought her to a culmination of her own passion that caused her to utter soft cries of completion against his skin. She clung to him, her body seeming to form itself to his like a favorite shirt. Beneath him, she lay replete, her body soft and lissome, her smile one he recognized.

He lifted himself over her, arranging her for his own pleasure. Finding the haven his aching body yearned for, he sought out the heat of her, slid with an easy movement into her depths and then was still. This was almost enough, he thought. This womanly warmth that surrounded him, the arms she slid around his waist, her legs holding him fast, lest he leave her empty.

And yet it was not enough, for when she shifted against him, he shivered. When she lifted her hips, the better to contain him, he shuddered, his body responding to the pull and drag of her own, holding him fast, yet releasing him by increments. He moaned his pleasure and spoke against her forehead, telling her of his love, asking for assurance of hers. Finally, when he could no longer contain himself, he emptied his seed into her.

"I love you, Lucas." Her declaration resounded in his ear, even though she whispered. It echoed through his mind, although each syllable was soft. And he stored up this moment in his memory as a panacea for all ills in the days to come. For now, at this moment, he loved and was loved. A man could ask for no more.

CHAPTER FIFTEEN

THE DAYS turned into weeks and life assumed a rhythm that pleased them both. Mining, as always, was the focus point of Lucas's days, the piece of land he'd claimed in Thunder Canyon proving to be a rich vein of gold, one that was making him and his partner, Sandy, more prosperous than they could have imagined.

Being the mayor of Thunder Canyon was not time consuming, Jennifer decided, the town council only meeting once a month, the townspeople a law-abiding group of citizens. Pleased to profit by the men who spent their days panning gold and digging into the hillsides of their claims, the owners of the shops and stores of the small town prospered.

Women were still in short supply, but the newspaper editor had hit upon a lucrative scheme: bringing young women from the eastern United States to Thunder Canyon for the express purpose of marriage to the male contingent of the community. Most of the men planned to settle down in the area and raise families, and in order to do that, they needed wives.

Much the same as had Lucas, Jennifer thought, reading the ads the editor had come up with. They spoke of men with good prospects, a country rich in gold with flowing rivers and mountain peaks in the distance. Of a town ripe and ready for the influx of women who would surely come to make their homes there.

But none of them would be as happy as she. Jennifer preened as she prepared for the day, braiding her hair, then donning her best housedress in preparation for a visit from Ida. Word from Thunder Canyon had it that the boardinghouse was thriving, and Jennifer was certain that Ida's visit would support that claim.

She had much to show her friend: the new curtains she'd made, the pantry shelves filled with cans and jars of vegetables put there by her own hard work, and the sparkling floors and windows of the big farmhouse that had become Jennifer's pride and joy.

On top of that was the possibility of a new life in her future. The cessation of Jennifer's monthly cycle and a tendency to lean over the slop jar every morning seemed to proclaim an event she had hoped for, had even prayed for. Now, if her instincts were on track, and unless she was possessed of a dread disease that made its presence known by frequent trips to the outhouse, not to mention a desperate need for an afternoon nap most days, she was well on her way to motherhood.

Ida would know, she told herself. Ida would recognize the signs and validate her own suspicions. And then she could tell Lucas, would see the smile of anticipation on his face, the pride in his eyes as he heard the news.

The kitchen was cleaned, dinner set to cook on the back of the stove and the floor wiped up before Ida's arrival. She pulled her buggy to the back of the house with a flourish and tied her mare to the hitching rail.

"You home, girl?" she called, heading for the porch, her hat askew, her smile wide, her skirts flying.

Jennifer came from the kitchen and met her friend with outstretched arms. Ida stopped short at the edge of the porch and her eyes narrowed as she gazed into the younger woman's face.

"You all right? Not sickly, are you?"

Jennifer shook her head, her lips pressed together, so badly did she want to blurt out the news of the child she was certain grew within her even now. Ida ushered her into the kitchen and pushed her down onto a chair.

"You certain you're all right?" she asked, removing her hat and placing it on the table. "You'd better let me get you some tea and a piece of bread. You're lookin' kinda puny this morning."

"You should have seen me yesterday," Jennifer told her, remembering with a shudder the weakness and nausea she'd suffered upon arising. Thankful that Lucas had risen early and already gone to the claim, she'd sat on the edge of the bed and finally put her head back on the pillow. Some days just weren't worth getting up for, she'd decided.

"You're in the family way, ain't you?" With unerring accuracy, Ida got right to the point. She hauled Jennifer from the chair to embrace her. "I'm tickled pink," Ida said, holding Jennifer from her and examining her face and the newer, lusher lines of her bosom.

"Your dress is gettin' tight, too. I'd say you're about two months gone, girl. Am I right?"

"Here I thought I was about to tell you something exciting, and you've stolen a march on me," Jennifer said, pouting just a bit. "I don't know how far along I am, but you can probably figure that out, too, if I know anything about it."

They sat together, Ida's tea hastily made, their cups steaming as they spoke of babies and the problems of pregnancy. Ida's eyes twinkled as she told Jennifer of her own lying-in times, of the happiness her newborn babies had brought and the joys inherent in raising children who were loved and wanted by both mother and father.

"Lucas will be tickled pink," Ida said. "He's a family man if I ever saw one. Just you wait and see." She looked Jennifer over from one end to the other. "He been treating you right? Is everything okay?" She looked around the kitchen. "He's not letting you work too hard now, is he?" She looked out the back door. "You been putting up your garden? It looks like you've been picking green beans."

"Got almost a half bushel yesterday," Jennifer told her. "They're in the pantry now. I'm sure glad you told me how to do it. And my tomatoes are doing well. Almost ready to pick. I'll have more than I know what to do with."

"I'll come and help you with them," Ida told her. "Are you sure you're not doin' more than you should? Lucas better be lookin' after you."

"I can't begin to match him for hard work." Jennifer's voice was firm as she told of Lucas's long days at the claim, and the gold he'd taken to town. "He's home every night," she said. "And when he can't come home, when it's his turn to guard the claim, sometimes he takes me up there and we stay in the tent together."

"You like that, don't you?" Ida grinned. "It's an exciting place out there in the canyon, what with all those men stirrin' around and tellin' tall tales every night by the campfires. Have you learned to cook over a fire yet?"

Jennifer nodded, feeling a sense of pride in her accomplishments. "Lucas says I'm the best cook in the canyon. Of course, that isn't too difficult a title to gain, since most of the cooking is done by men and their idea of a meal is a potful of meat and vegetables all cooked to a frazzle. Kind of like pig slop, I think. But it seems to be nourishing, though several of them come by when I'm there and sit around waiting for an invite to our meal."

Ida smiled at her. "I knew you'd be just what Lucas needs, Jen. You're a good wife."

"I'm trying hard. And Lucas is happy. That's the main thing."

"Well, I'm gonna stay the night tonight," Ida said, rising and heading for the back door. "I'll put my rig in the barn and turn my mare loose in the pasture, if that's all right with you. Thought I'd take advantage of Helen and the new girl being there today to run out here and spend some time with you. My valise is in the buggy." She opened the screen door and stepped onto the porch. "I'll be right back."

Clearing the table took but a few minutes and Jennifer heard footsteps on the porch sooner than she'd expected. But it wasn't Ida who pulled the door open and stepped inside. Whiskered and seedy-looking, his clothing apparently worn for days on end, Kyle watched her with unconcealed hatred.

"Where's the kid?" he asked. "I want you to go get her and give her to me, right now."

"I don't have her," Jennifer told him, her heart thumping.

Kyle laughed, an ugly sound that shot terror through her, and Jennifer felt a wave of dizziness. "I'm takin' her back East to her grandparents. Go get her and all her things, too. I'm leavin' for New York today."

"Then you'll go alone," Jennifer said. "I don't have Susan here. Her grandparents came and got her weeks ago. She's in New York already."

"How much did you get for her?" Kyle's meaning was clear and Jennifer was incensed.

"How could you think I'd *sell* the child? What's wrong with you, Kyle? Don't you have any human decency at all?" She was appalled at his words, yet realized that the man was far down on the totem pole of civil behavior.

"I know a good thing when I see it," he said, laughing as Jennifer gripped the back of a chair, holding herself upright.

"And what's that supposed to mean?" She looked past him, fearing that Ida would come upon the scene unaware, and face the gun that Kyle wore on his thigh. Yet her only hope right now seemed to be the presence of the other woman. Surely, Kyle would not make threats in front of a witness. But that seemed to be an idle thought as he turned his head to see what had drawn Jennifer's attention.

"Someone out there?" he asked. "You got company? I didn't see a horse."

Ida hurried through the yard and across the porch, and Jennifer's heart fell. "Just a friend," she said. "No need for any fuss, Kyle. Just take yourself out the door and leave. There's nothing for you here."

"Two women? My, my. This is my lucky day," he said. Turning to the door, he pulled his gun, and Ida's eyes opened wide as she crossed the threshold.

"What's goin' on? What's this rascal doing here, Jen?" The woman who dwelt behind the housedress and apron was a stalwart female, unafraid of anyone.

"Looking for Susan," she said. "He thinks the baby is here and won't believe me that her grandparents came to get her."

"Well, the fool oughta be smart enough to realize that if Susan *was* here, she'd be out in plain sight. Seems pretty obvious to me he's not the brightest star in the sky."

"You can get yourself shot thataway, lady." It seemed that

having his intelligence belittled by a woman in an apron did not sit well with Kyle.

Jennifer stepped closer to the pantry and Kyle's sharp gaze touched her. "Where you think you're goin'? Just stay right there where I can keep a good eye on you, Jennifer."

"I need…" She paused, unable to think of an excuse to enter the long, narrow room, wherein two long guns were placed for easy access. Shooting a man was not her first choice, but keeping herself and Ida from harm was essential.

"You don't need nothin' in there," Kyle told her. Ignoring the threat presented by his gun, she stepped into the pantry, out of his sight, and heard the sound of a chair hitting the floor as he neared. The shotgun stood in one corner beside the door, and it was heavy in her hands as she lifted it, then aimed it point-blank at the man who stood in front of her. His own weapon pointed downward as he saw the double-barreled gun lifted to within a foot of his belly.

"I'll kill you, Kyle." Her voice was firm, her mind made up. Pulling the double trigger was well within her capabilities, and she would not allow this man to bully her any further.

"You wanta be careful there," Kyle sputtered, backing away from the weapon she held. "That thing could go off real easy."

"Not unless I pull the trigger," Jennifer told him. "But I'm warning you, I'm not afraid to do just that."

"It won't be necessary." From beside the back door, Lucas's rough tones brought Jennifer's gaze to rest on him, his own gun held in front of him, his hat pulled down to shade his eyes. "Drop that pistol, Kyle, and get over against the wall." He looked then at Jennifer and she felt the cold sweat of reaction break out on her forehead.

Her hands trembled, her legs felt weak and she stumbled from the pantry, the shotgun pointed at the floor beside her.

"Sit down, Jen." Lucas left no room for quibbling, and she did as he said, placing the shotgun on the floor beside her chair. *Lucas is here. All will be well.*

Kyle stood by the outside wall of the kitchen, his gaze twitching from Lucas to Jennifer, then back again as the barrel of the rifle seemed to zero in on his body. "No sense in gettin' all upset here," he muttered, his hands trembling. "I never intended to shoot her. Or her friend there, either."

"Well, you put on a pretty good show of it." Lucas's cheeks were stained crimson, his mouth drawn into a harsh line. "Step out here onto the porch," he told Kyle, backing from the doorway and leaning his own gun against the kitchen wall.

The man did as directed and Lucas closed the back door, leaving Jennifer and Ida in the kitchen, away from the scene being played out on the narrow porch.

"What's going on?" Jennifer's voice was but a whisper and she laid her head on the table, as if she could no longer hold it erect.

"Better we don't know," Ida surmised. "I think that fella is about to learn a lesson, and then, unless I miss my guess, he'll be on his way outta here."

The sounds of a battle could be heard through the kitchen window, and Lucas could be seen amid glimpses of Kyle being knocked to the floor and then picked up again, only to meet the same fate several times.

"He'll kill him." Jennifer said. "Don't let him kill him, Ida."

"Lucas is too smart for that. He's just teachin' the man a lesson. And I'll warrant it's one he won't forget in a hurry."

With that, they heard Lucas's voice raised in anger and saw

him tote Kyle's battered body to his horse. Lucas's limp was pronounced but he ignored it, continuing to berate the victim of his punishment. Lifting Kyle astride the horse, Lucas handed him the reins and turned the animal in the direction of town, slapping him on the rear flank as he broke into a trot.

"I'd suggest you get your tail out of here. Leave Thunder Canyon behind," Lucas called. "If I find you here tomorrow, as mayor of this place, I'll have you thrown in jail."

Jennifer collapsed again in her chair, her head resting on the table. Ida brought a glass of water to her.

"Here, drink this," she said. "You look kinda green, Jen. You don't want Lucas to see you thisaway, do you?"

Jennifer shook her head, sat upright and drank from the glass. "He's angry." As if the words were a surprise to her, she muttered them beneath her breath.

"Yeah, but I don't think he's mad at you." Ida opened the back door and watched as Lucas came in to the house. "You get everything settled?"

"You oughta know," he said gruffly. "I saw you lookin' out the window, Ida." He turned to Jennifer and his gaze softened. "Are you all right? Did he hurt you?"

She shook her head. "Not a chance. Just startled me a little." She looked down at the table. "What about you? Is your leg all right? You're limping badly."

"My leg is fine, except for a twinge when I walk. It'll go away…always does."

Jennifer nodded as if placated by his words and then she sighed. "I didn't want to shoot him, Lucas, but I would have."

"I kinda thought so." He knelt beside her and took her hands in his. "I'd have killed him in a heartbeat if he'd made another move toward you. You know that, don't you?"

She nodded and lifted her eyes to his. "I love you." It was a whisper, but the words resounded in the room, as if she'd spoken in a shout. Lucas bent his head and kissed her hands, then leaned upward to touch his lips to hers.

"And I love you, Jen. More than you can ever know. I'll love our child as much, and protect you both with my life."

"Our child?" She opened her eyes wide, looking into his in surprise. "How did you know?"

His eyes glittered, a darker blue than was their normal color. His grin was wide. "I'm aware of everything that goes on with you, sweetheart. I knew when things didn't come about in a regular way." He looked up at Ida then and his mouth twitched as if he might laugh out loud.

"Don't be smirking at me," he told her. "I'm not just a dumb miner. I've got some notion of what will happen when a man takes his woman to bed on a regular basis. I know how babies are made, Ida."

She looked at him, then at Jennifer, her smile broad. "Yeah, I suspect you do, Luc. And I'm not surprised that you figured out how to make one all on your own. With a little help from your wife."

He rested back on his heels. "Is she really all right?" he asked Ida, frowning. "None of this hurt the baby, did it?"

"That baby is as well protected right now as it'll ever be," Ida told him. "And your wife is strong. Tough as old boots."

"She doesn't look tough to me." Lucas cast a measuring glance at Jennifer and then lifted her from her chair and held her close. She leaned against him, aware of the blood that spattered his shirt, but uncaring. Lucas was here, his arms were strong, and he loved her.

BEING THE MAYOR gave a man some standing in the community. And when the judge came to town, reporting on Kyle's escapade at the hearing made Lucas a hero of sorts. "It's my aim to keep Thunder Canyon clean and well rid of scalawags like that man," Lucas said.

"I'd say that between you and the sheriff, you're doin' a good job of it." The judge sat behind his table, in lieu of a proper courtroom, and made his judgment. "The mayor is cleared of all blame in this matter. He was defending his wife and household and cannot be held responsible for any injuries suffered by the man who threatened Mrs. O'Reilly. Especially since that man is not even present to press charges."

He looked up. "Where'd he go, Luc? You send him back to the city?"

"If he knows what's good for himself, that's where he is, sir. Although I doubt that Mrs. O'Reilly's parents will be happy to see him, should he come calling there."

"Well, good riddance," the judge announced. "We don't need that sort in Montana. Got enough trouble with the ordinary, everyday miners." He shot a look of undiluted humor at Lucas as he spoke and was given a cocky smile in return. "Now, young man, I'd say you need to take your wife home and look after her. And that claim you've got up in the canyon."

"Thank you, Your Honor." Lucas took Jennifer's arm and led her from the makeshift courtroom. Various men greeted them as they headed for the doorway.

"You're a popular lady in town, Jen," he murmured against her ear. "Folks are right proud of your success in the boardinghouse business, and Sally Jo has been making money hand over fist for you. Raising the rent was a good stroke of business, and Ida's about as well set as any widow I've ever seen."

Helen waited for them outside, Toby close by. "Why aren't you working your claim today?" Lucas asked him, then chuckled. "As if I didn't know."

"You see too much," Helen said. "Toby and I have things to do, Lucas. We thought we'd ask if you and Jennifer want to come along with us."

"Gonna take a walk to the parsonage?"

Jennifer heard Lucas's query with surprise. She'd known that Toby'd had eyes for Helen, but hadn't realized that his intentions were bearing fruit so soon.

Helen nodded, blushing, and Toby took her hand, tucking it into the bend of his elbow. "We decided to save money by getting married. Toby will live at the house and do some of the heavy work on the side and we'll share a room. It should work out just fine."

Lucas reached across to shake Toby's hand. "And is saving money all you had in mind?" His grin encompassed Helen and the man she'd chosen to wed. "Seems to me like there's gonna be a few fringe benefits, too."

Helen blushed. "You're a wicked man, Lucas. We need help at the house and couldn't afford to hire a man to help out. This seemed like the perfect solution to all our problems."

Jennifer spoke soothingly. "Well, I for one think it's a fine idea. Helen needs someone to look after her, and Toby certainly needs a wife to keep him in line." She glared at Lucas. "As does my own husband. It seems to me that he's getting pretty sassy these days."

"Well, I just feel like the luckiest man in the world, getting Helen for a bride," Toby said. "I've been thinking this would be a good idea for a long time now, and finally got the courage to ask her just the other day."

"And I jumped at the chance." Helen laughed at Toby, clutching his arm and cuddling close as he wrapped the other arm around her waist. "We wanted you and Lucas to go with us for the big event, maybe stand up with us as witnesses."

"I'd be honored, and so would Lucas," Jennifer said. "And I'll bet if word has gotten around, you'll have a guest list a mile long."

A crowd of at least a dozen miners, plus several of the businessmen and towns folk of Thunder Canyon, were gathered at the gate of the parsonage when they arrived. Their small group blended with the others, calls of congratulation filling the air as the miners took this infrequent opportunity to celebrate.

The marriage of one of their own was a triumph for all, for if one man could find and win a wife in this place, surely there was hope for the rest of the women-hungry population. Toby was the center of a circle of his cronies, most of them residents of the boardinghouse, and no one was surprised when Ida made her appearance.

"You surely didn't think there'd be a party without me joining in, did you?" She wrapped her arm around Helen's waist and winked at her. "See? What did I tell you? You can't be around a bunch of men for hours on end without finding one of them that'll suit you."

"Well, he does just that." Helen looked at Toby with affection and he returned her look with hungry eyes.

"Who's minding the store?" Lucas asked, scanning the crowd as several business owners made their presence known. "And who's out at the claim, Sandy? We'll have someone running off with our earnings if we're not careful."

"Everyone's taken the day off," Sandy said. "Once the word got around that there was gonna be a wedding, we all got slicked up and ready. Gave Sally Jo quite a shock to see almost two dozen miners lined up outside her shop, waiting their turns for a bath and shave. She did a few haircuts, too."

"That's 'cause we couldn't see past the mop of hair you had hangin' down your back," one man called, and Sandy made a mock fist, waving it in the air.

"You're just jealous, with no woman willing to give you a tumble, Rafferty."

The men laughed as one, their spirits high as they watched Toby and Helen open the gate and walk toward the parsonage. The young preacher came to the porch and greeted them, and then turned his attention to those gathered in his front yard.

"Come on a little closer, folks. You can all join in this celebration."

The crowd surged through the gate. Jennifer and Lucas found a place next to the bride and groom on the porch. Within minutes, the short ceremony was over, the bride had been well kissed by her new husband, and the miners were lining up for a shot at the blushing Helen.

"Just one little peck each," Toby told them. "Don't forget, this is *my* bride, and I can tell you right now, I'm a downright possessive man. Haven't had a wife before and I don't plan on lettin' this one get away."

The party spilled over into the parsonage, where the young wife served cookies and a hastily thrown-together punch. A few of the miners grumbled at the lack of hard liquor but were silenced by some who held a certain amount of respect for the church and the man who tried to keep this town in line.

For, more than the sheriff or the mayor, the young minister kept a tight rein on those who attended his church and made it his business to visit those unfortunates who were jailed for one reason or another. Everyone in town knew that the parsonage family was willing to help in a crisis, even though they were poorly paid.

So it was that they were held in high regard, and when two of the newest miners made an attempt to spike the punch, they were dealt with quickly and firmly.

After an hour, Ida called the group to attention and told them there would be food served at the boardinghouse right next door, that the wedding reception would continue there within the hour. As one, the men left the parsonage, carrying the bride and groom with them, teasing and taunting poor Toby to within an inch of his life, telling him of the shivaree they would hold after darkness fell.

"They won't, will they?" Jennifer asked, and was shocked when Lucas only nodded. "You aren't going to be a part of it," she announced, and Lucas gave her a kiss that caused her arms to curl around his neck.

"I've got better things to do after dark," he told her. "I've got a wife who needs pampering and I intend to take care of her…in the best possible way."

"Lucas!" she chastised him for his bold demeanor, but he would not be halted, for he picked her up and carried her the rest of the way to the boardinghouse. Around them, the crowd ebbed and flowed and they were the center of attention for a few minutes.

The big table was set, platters of meat and crocks of pickled beets sitting side by side with bowls of potato salad and a huge pan of baked beans, hot from the oven. "There's more where this came from, folks," Ida called as she led the way to the feast.

It seemed she'd had some prior notice of the festivities, for she was well prepared. Ladies from the church brought in cakes and pies and one delivered four loaves of bread, already cut in sandwich-size pieces. A beef roast, thinly sliced, fit well on the bread, and crocks of butter appeared from the pantry. Fried chicken was contained in a huge basket, wrapped in a towel still steaming and smelling like ambrosia, as one miner said.

He received a ribbing from several who mocked his use of the word, asking him where he'd learned to speak in such a high-falutin' manner. "I sure enough know what it means," he said. "And I could name lots of other things that smell just as good."

Before he could begin to list the objects of his affections, he was shushed by Lucas, who seemed to be the self-appointed doorkeeper of the day, holding the rowdy men down to a low roar when they would have begun a series of lusty remarks.

"We're going to the hotel," Helen confided to Jennifer. "All the men think we'll be here, but Toby said we can sneak out the back door of the house and go in the back way at the hotel without the fellows being any the wiser."

"Lots of luck." Jennifer wished her the best, but she'd found in her days in this house that the men had various ways of procuring knowledge when it was to their benefit. If they wanted to locate the newly married couple, she'd warrant they'd find a way.

On their way home, snugly settled on the buggy seat, she brought up the subject to Lucas. He laughed, assuring her that the subterfuge would not work. The miners were already planning on raiding the hotel at midnight, and Helen and Toby had a long ride ahead of them. They were to be loaded into a wagon and taken outside of town, where they would be left in their nightclothes, with only a single blanket for shelter.

"That's mean and hateful," Jennifer said. "And how did you find out?"

"Who do you think took a tent and a stack of bedding a mile high out there earlier this evening?" Lucas asked.

"When?" Jennifer was still incensed.

"When you and Ida were feedin' that gang. I got a new tent from the general store and a couple of horses from the livery stable, hauled it all out there and tied the horses to a tree at the edge of the woods, about where the fellas are gonna dump Toby and Helen."

"Will they know the horses are there?"

"Toby knows. I told him I couldn't do much about the shivaree, but I could see to it they were warm and isolated for their wedding night. And they'll have transportation for tomorrow morning when they want to go back to the boardinghouse."

"And what did he say?"

"Let me tell you, Mrs. O'Reilly, that man doesn't care where or how he manages to bed his bride, so long as he can pull it off. And trust me, he'll figure out how to put up the tent in no time flat and spread those blankets down on the ground in jig time. They'll be like two bugs in a rug before you know it." He grinned. "Toby owes me, big time. And he knows it."

"So do I." She looked up at him in the moonlight. "You're so good to me, Lucas. I can't tell you how happy you make me."

"Well, that door swings both ways, ma'am. I predict we're gonna have a time of our own tonight, complete with a nice soft bed and a candle lit by that bed, so I can see what I'm doing. I'm tired of searching for you in a dark bedroom."

"You manage all right in the dark any other time," she said. "What do you need a candle for?" And then she sighed. "Never mind. I don't think I want to know, do I?"

He laughed, pulling the buggy up to the back door and jumping down. "Probably not, sweetheart. But I'll be glad to demonstrate to you how much more fun we can have with the room all lit up." He lifted her down and patted her on the fanny. "Go on in the house. I'll be right there."

"One candle," she said with a haughty glare in his direction, and walked up to the porch, missing his answering remark as he led the horse toward the barn.

"At least four, plus the lantern."

CHAPTER SIXTEEN

THE ACHES and discomfort of pregnancy seemed to be a small price to pay for the anticipation she lived with daily, Jennifer decided. For the knowledge that a tiny being was even now moving inside her gave her a joy she could not have explained, had she been required to give an accounting for the foolish smile she wore.

Looking at herself in the mirror in the mornings was an experience she had once dreaded, seeing the locks of disheveled hair, the still-sleepy eyes and the slightly petulant look of a woman who had been called from her bed at five o'clock, surely long before anyone should be forced to rise and shine.

Even that phrase, one Lucas used to little effect, made her cringe. She'd never been one to smile so early after daybreak, requiring a cup of coffee before she felt fit to face the day.

Now, however, she found that her face in the mirror was a reflection of the joy in her heart, and she relished each morning, awaiting the first small flutters, and then later on, the not-so-gentle kicks of a baby making itself known within the depths of her body.

And so she smiled, even Lucas commenting that no one had the right to be so all-fired happy in this world. But, even as he spoke, he held her tightly, careful not to squeeze too hard, lest he bring discomfort to his child. His hoots of laughter when the baby protested his eager hugs and their effect on the child's mother only served to increase his joy. Nudges and wiggles against his back at night were cause for celebration so far as he was concerned.

Barely a night passed without Lucas holding his wife close, his very presence a plea for the love she alone could provide to his hungry heart. Without words, he pled his case, his kisses growing more passionate by the moment, his hands resting on the rounding of her belly, wherein lay his hope for future generations.

Jennifer was generous, he decided, in giving him what he needed. Indeed, some nights he felt guilty when he recognized her weariness, when she slept in his arms almost before the loving was over, and he found himself holding her close, her skin soft and warm against his own, her arms clutching him.

She amazed him with her strength, her stamina and her ability to accomplish so much in the house. Meeting him every evening with open arms and offering him a table heavy laden with food fit for a banquet, she gave him cause to feel the luckiest of men.

And now, she would bear his child, not as a duty, but in a joyous manner, as if she were the most blessed of women.

He watched her as she dished up his supper one evening very late in the autumn. The night air was cool and crisp, the kitchen warm and redolent with the scents of pot roast and apple pie, and his wife was weary. It showed in the shadows beneath her eyes and in the lack of balance as she turned from the stove, two bowls in her hands.

Lucas stood quickly and took them from her grasp. "Come sit down, Jen. I'll get the rest." He noted her lack of argument, the white line around her mouth and the flutter of eyelashes as she obeyed. Her chair seemed to welcome her and she settled there, watching as he served up the pot roast and poured his coffee. Her own cup held milk, cool since it had been kept on the porch in a covered jar.

"I'm glad that winter's almost here," she said, taking a sip of the creamy white yield from her cow. "Makes it easier to keep the food."

"Also means we'll be shoveling snow before long."

"And that the baby will be with us in no time." She sighed. "I'll admit, I can hardly wait. I love knowing she's there, inside of me, but I'll be happier when I can hold her in my arms and see how pretty she is."

"She?" Lucas asked, a single word holding a wealth of meaning.

"She." It was spoken with finally, but softened by a smile.

"What if it's a boy?" Lucas looked worried, she thought, as if having a son instead of a daughter might not be to her liking.

"Then I'll love it even more, knowing I've given birth to a boy who'll be the spittin' image of his daddy."

His smile was tender. "You really feel that way, don't you, Jen?"

"You know I do. This will be the most welcomed baby in Montana if I have anything to say about it. After all, when the mayor of Thunder Canyon has a son, it's cause for celebration. And even if it's only a lowly girl child, the folks will still be ringing bells and carrying food out here to provide for you while I'm abed."

Lucas looked forlorn for a moment. "It'll be ten days, Ida said, before you'll be up and around."

"Ida doesn't know everything there is to know," Jennifer told him. "I'm young and strong, and I can't imagine lying in bed all that time, letting someone else do for me."

"You'll do whatever the doctor says."

"I probably won't even see the doctor. I'll bet Ida and Helen will be here and handle things all by themselves."

"Well, before they're done, you may wish you'd only had one man to cope with, instead of those two women."

"Maybe." He thought she looked smug, as if she knew secrets he had no way of determining. "I just want you to go get Ida as soon as things start to happen, you hear?"

He nodded. "My hearing is very good, ma'am. And on top of that, Ida would kill me if she wasn't the first to know that her chick was about to hatch."

"She'll play the part of grandma well, won't she?" Jennifer seemed pleased with that idea, Lucas thought. With the absence of her own mother, she'd clung even more to Ida Bronson, and he thought that the older woman had given a good amount of much-needed support to the first-time mother.

"She'll be a wonderful grandma to him." He got his last licks in with his subtle reference to the baby's gender.

The meal was delicious and Jennifer was more than acquiescent as Lucas offered to clean up the kitchen and wash the dishes. He left them to dry on the sink board and she did not quibble, even though he suspected her hands itched to dry them and put them away properly.

LUCAS WAS RIGHT, for the first snow came just three weeks later. More than a foot of fluffy white stuff covered the ground when they awoke, and shoveling a path to the barn took Lucas almost a half hour. Jennifer came out, milked the cow and gathered up the eggs on her way back to the house. Lucas followed with the bucket of milk and strained it into the churn for her.

"It'll keep there just fine for the day," he said. "Tonight I'll skim the cream off and by tomorrow you'll have enough to make butter." He looked her up and down. "You don't think that's too hard a job for you, do you?"

She shot a scornful glance his way. "When I'm so puny I can't churn butter, it'll be a cold day in you-know-where."

He laughed. "You wouldn't say a cuss word if it came up and bit you, would you, Jen?"

"Do you remember how long it took me to cure you of the habit?" Her lifted eyebrow was cocky, he thought.

"All you had to do was ban me from our bed, if I recall correctly."

"I never did," she protested.

"No, maybe not, but I got the message loud and clear. I knew I'd better clean up my talk or risk getting tossed out on my ear."

She went to him, her arms sliding around his waist, her cumbersome shape making it difficult for her to stand as close to him as she liked. "Not a chance, Mr. O'Reilly. You're not getting away from me."

"Well, I don't like to argue with you, but I'm planning on leaving you right now, ma'am. I'm due out at the claim, or Sandy will be wondering what happened to me. You'll be all right, won't you? No sign of the baby coming early or anything, is there?"

"I'm fine." Her lips curved into the smile he'd come to seek out daily, and he held her as if she were the pot of gold at the end of his rainbow.

"I love you, Jen. I'll be back early if I can make it, though I fear it'll take a bit longer than usual, what with the snow. But I promise you, I'll be home tonight."

THE KITCHEN lamp was lit, the curtains pushed wide open, lest he not see the glow of the flame from far off, and she'd even done the chores on her own. Now Jennifer sat at the table, doing her best not to worry as she drank a cup of tea. The wind had come up and with it a new storm made itself known.

Snow fell in a steady white curtain and she knew the lamp from the kitchen could not be detected from beyond the barn. And still Lucas did not come. Supper was on the back of the stove, a mess of green beans from those canned just months past simmered fragrantly on the fire, and she thought of the day she had put them into jars, with Ida's help. The kitchen had rung with feminine laughter and she'd thought that all was right with her world.

Except for the fact that Susan was gone, she found little to fret over, and the knowledge that a child of her own would soon fill her arms and heart made Susan's leaving a bit more palatable. Still, the sadness lurked and she wished for more than the occasional letter from her parents, telling of the child's growth and intelligence. They were doting grandparents, but her mother noted that Susan seemed to be looking for Jennifer around every corner.

Now Jennifer felt alone, almost bereft, and she wondered at the depth of emotion that overcame her. Surely Lucas hadn't—no, he was all right, just slowed by the snow. As a man determined to seek out his home and wife, he'd surely appear any minute now.

A horse outside made himself known with a shrill whinny,

soon answered by another and Jennifer went to the door, checking to see that her shotgun stood beside it, lest she have visitors who might be unfriendly. Since Kyle's visit, she remained in the general vicinity of her shotgun at all times while she was alone in the house.

Opening the door a bit, she made out two horses, the first caught in the light of her lamp through the doorway.

"Ma'am? Mrs. O'Reilly? It's Sandy."

She recognized Lucas's partner and swung the door wide. "Come in, Sandy. What are you doing out in this weather?" And then she saw the second horse, noted the rider, slumped in the saddle, and her heart caught in her throat.

"Lucas? Lucas." She stepped onto the porch and would have sought the steps had not Sandy spoken sharply.

"I'll bring him in, ma'am. Go on inside and I'll be right there. You might want to get some warm blankets. He's pretty cold."

She did as he bade her, hurrying to the bedroom where three quilts were piled on the chest. Carrying them back to the kitchen, she watched as Sandy half carried, half dragged Lucas inside. Both men were pale and obviously shaken, Lucas almost unconscious, his eyelids lifting but a fraction as he saw her in front of him.

"Jen." It was all he said, but it was enough. He was alive and her heart beat more strongly. No matter what the problem, she could handle it, so long as Lucas lived and breathed.

"What happened?" she asked Sandy, and received only an abrupt nod in reply.

"Let's get him warm first," the man told her, placing Lucas on the floor in front of the stove. He bent to his partner, stripping Lucas's coat from him and tugging off his boots. They wrapped a quilt around the prone man and

Sandy murmured a soft word of comfort in Jennifer's direction. "He'll be all right, ma'am. Right now he's just chilled to the bone, what with falling in the river when his horse went down. There's a gash in his scalp where he landed on a rock."

"Lucas fell off his horse? What are you talking about? What happened to the horse?"

"A stupid yahoo shot his horse out from under him, and my guess is that he was aiming at Lucas and missed," Sandy said. "But the rascal didn't last long. He made the mistake of getting closer to check out his work and one of the men got him with one shot."

"Who would hurt Lucas? He's a good man," Jennifer said, tears flowing as she bent over her husband's beloved form.

"A fella you might know," Sandy said, his discomfort showing. "One of the men said it was the man who was givin' you a bad time in town, way back. Kyle somebody or another."

"Kyle." She spoke the name, shivering as she did, and lifted blurry eyes to Sandy's face. "Did you say someone shot him? I don't have to worry about him showing up here, do I?"

"He's deader'n a doornail, ma'am. Somebody took him into town already. I reckon you'll have a houseful of folks out here pretty soon, once they hear that Lucas got hurt."

"Help me get him into bed," she said. "I'll need to look at his head."

"We already washed it out and put a bandage on it," Sandy told her. "He'll be fine, just plagued with a dandy headache is my guess. I'm thinking he's just as well off out here by the stove where it's warmer."

"I'll fix a pallet for him then," she said, rising with the help of a chair.

"I'll do whatever needs doin'," Sandy told her, taking her arm and helping her to sit on the chair. "Just tell me where everything is and I'll take care of it. You can wash him up a little if you want to. He's kinda grungy, what with workin' all day, tryin' to get things done so he could come home."

"All right." She needed to do something to help Lucas, even if it was only to clean him up, wash his face and maybe his hair. At least get the dirt out of it. He must have landed on the river bed, for bits of gravel and stone were there in the thick, dark hair on the back of his head. It was a wonder he hadn't drowned. And at that thought she shivered, her body gripped by a chill.

A basin of water and a towel were easy to search out and she placed them beside him on the floor, then lifted his head to her lap. At least what there was left of a lap below the bulge of her baby.

"Lucas." She spoke softly, not really expecting an answer, only wanting to speak his name, needing to let him know she was near. But much to her surprise, his eyelids fluttered and he looked at her, his eyes unfocused, but holding a look of recognition.

"Sweetheart." It was all he said, but it was enough. Lucas would be all right. As surely as she knew there were stars in the sky, beyond the clouds that were dropping their burden of snow, she knew that Lucas was not hovering on the brink of death. He was strong and vibrant, and would be able to conquer even this injury.

A sound outside the back door alerted her. When the door was opened carefully and Ida peeked through the opening, she waved the woman into the room.

"There's a bunch of folks out here," Ida said. "I won't let

them in unless you say so. All but the doctor. I think you need him, from the looks of things."

"Ida." Speaking her friend's name seemed to release the floodgates and Jennifer found herself crying silently. Quickly, she stifled her fears, knowing that Lucas would not have her weeping over him.

I never cry. Those words, spoken so many months ago, would forever rise up to haunt her, she thought, and Lucas would laugh every time at her insistence.

She smiled as Ida came in, followed by the doctor from town, a man Jennifer had only seen once when one of the miners had broken his leg up the valley and had been brought back to the boardinghouse. Now she welcomed the man into her kitchen with an uplifted hand.

"These men will freeze out here, ma'am," the doctor said. "Can they come in and get warm?"

"Of course." Jennifer felt ashamed that she hadn't issued the invitation herself. The men of the town council filed in silently and stood against the far wall as the doctor approached Lucas. He'd closed his eyes once more, his head cushioned on Jennifer's legs, her hand on his forehead, fingering the bandage Sandy had applied.

"Let's take a look-see, ma'am." With a tender touch, the man's big hand patted Jennifer's back as he knelt beside her. "I think you're in about as bad a condition as Lucas here. When's that baby due to arrive?"

"Soon," she said, not caring about herself, so wrapped up in Lucas's wound she could hardly think of the child she carried. "In a few months."

He bent over Lucas and dealt with the bandage. "Looks like he hit pretty hard, but the main thing is to get him out of this wet clothing and wrap him in warm quilts," he said, and Jennifer sighed in relief. "This looks clean to me. I'll just put some good salve on his head and a fresh bandage and then we'll see about getting him into bed."

He looked up at Jennifer. "Do you need someone to stay here with you tonight?"

"I'm staying." Ida's words were expected, but Jennifer was grateful nonetheless when her friend spoke emphatically, leaving no room for questions. "I know this house like my own and this girl needs to sleep, or we'll be having us a baby before we're ready for it."

"I agree," the doctor said. "I've got some pills for him to take for the dandy headache he's gonna have for the next couple of days. Other than that, you'll just need to change the bandage twice a day, Ida, and watch him for fever. If you have a problem, send for me."

"And who am I supposed to send?"

"I'll be here," Sandy piped up. "Lucas is my partner, and I'm not about to leave him alone without a man's protection." At Jennifer's words of protest, he held up one hand. "I know you can shoot, ma'am, but Lucas would never forgive me if I didn't stick around and look after things for him. There's animals to tend and I'll bet I can find a couple of other things to keep me busy."

"You got that right." Gruff tones spoke the words and Jennifer looked down at her husband. "Let him stay, Jen." Lucas might be laid out with a gash on his scalp and a throbbing headache, but that hadn't made him any less arrogant, she decided.

"All right." She could do nothing but agree. When the men carried Lucas to bed, she followed docilely, content to have lost control of the situation. Ida pulled the sheet back and the men stripped Lucas, replacing his drawers with a clean pair Jennifer took from the dresser. Then they placed him in the bed, covering him to the neck.

He moved restlessly and called her name. "Come lie down, Jen." It wasn't a request but an order, given in typical fashion by a man who expected his will to be obeyed.

"Everyone clear out now," Ida said, watching Jennifer, as if she recognized the weariness that seemed to have enveloped the younger woman. "Thanks for putting Lucas to bed, fellas, but I think his wife needs to get off her feet, too."

The men seemed to agree, each of them walking past Lucas to pay their respects as they said their goodbyes to him. "See you in a few days, Luc," said one.

"Don't let 'em keep you down," advised another. A third gave Lucas a succinct reminder that he had work to do and didn't need to be 'layin' around fritterin' away his time.'"

The bedroom emptied and Jennifer found her gown beneath her pillow. "You don't need that," Lucas said, his eyes half open as he watched her.

"Oh, yes I do. You're going to lie still and behave yourself, and I'm calling the shots tonight, mister. You'll listen to me for a change."

"Yes, ma'am." His voice held amusement, but she recognized his capitulation to her edict. Lucas would cooperate.

He was warm, only his feet and hands holding a chill, and she threw another blanket over his feet. Then she crawled into bed beside him and placed his hands against her breasts, holding them with her own, rubbing them so that the blood would circulate more freely. He murmured his approval of her method and she scolded him briefly. Then she touched his mouth with kisses that told him without words that he was loved, that she would be close during the hours until dawn broke in the eastern sky, that she would keep him safe against any danger throughout the night.

"Sandy?" he murmured, and she soothed him.

"He's on your pallet out in the kitchen and Ida is on the couch in the parlor."

"Love you." He mumbled the words and she nodded, understanding the effort it took to utter them out loud.

They slept, Lucas waking once in pain, his head seeming to be pounding. Jennifer rose and found his pills, held him upright as he swallowed two of them with a glass of water, and then touched his forehead with careful fingers lest she disturb his wound.

He slept until dawn then, and when the stove lid clanged, he jerked in the bed. "Damn fool." The words might have been a mystery to another, but Jennifer read his mind well, after months of living with the man.

"Kyle should have been hanged for doing this to you."

His voice slurred the words, but he seemed lucid. "He's dead, Jen. That's good enough."

"I can't believe it. And I can't understand what he came back here for. Surely not just because he was angry with you."

"Probably." And that, it seemed, was all he had to say on the matter for his eyes closed and he reached to touch her, one big hand curling around her breast.

"Your hands aren't cold anymore," she told him, but nevertheless allowed the caress. *Allowed?* She reveled in it, that this strong, brave man should want her, loved her enough to give her his best, and even now was willing to seek her favor.

"I'll be better in a day or so." His voice sounded firmer than it should, she thought, almost as if he were back to normal.

But a long look at his pale features and the bandage on his head made a lie of that notion.

"You'll stay right here till the doctor says different." She was proud of her staunch stand, the solid tones of her vow, and was set back but a little when he smiled, his face assuming the lofty look she'd often scorned.

As if he were the one setting the rules, he murmured one word. "Phooey."

And she was overcome with laughter, so much so that Ida poked her head in the door and scolded her. "You've got a sick man there, girl. Don't be having a party in here now."

"Good idea." His murmur reached Ida and she sniffed as she closed the door.

KEEPING HIM IN BED was a lesson in patience, Jennifer found, for Lucas was not a man to be held captive against his will. Only her presence kept him from rising and dressing and heading off for his claim. After the second day, Sandy left in a huff, weary of Lucas telling him to get back to work in the valley.

"You ought to be ashamed," Jennifer said, scolding him as she helped him into a shirt. "That man has been here for two days, looking after things and keeping us all safe. And you treated him disgracefully."

"He's fine. He was itchin' to get going anyway. I could see the signs."

"Lucas is probably right," Ida agreed. "Sandy isn't one to sit around for long. He needs to be working. He said he figured he could do Lucas more good by working the claim than he could by staying here looking at the walls. Besides," she said, "we haven't anything much to worry about, with Kyle out of your lives."

"He must have been crazy to come back here after Lucas. Do you suppose he really thought he could get away with shooting him?"

"I think the man was demented," Ida told her. "He didn't behave logically in any way, shape or form, so far as I could see. The silly fool brought that child here, taunting you and being hateful, and then tried to come at you with a gun. If Lucas hadn't stopped him that day, he'd have laid you out dead on the kitchen floor, you mark my words. And so, the idiot was madder than a wet hen at Lucas for ruining his revenge against you, even though he really didn't want the baby, just wanted to make some money off of her."

Ida shook her head, stuffing her hands into her apron pockets. "We'll never know what was going around in his head, girl. He was loony, is my guess."

"Evil." With a single word, Lucas spoke Jennifer's mind and again she was reminded that their thoughts seemed to run in the same patterns.

"Lucas is right. Any man who would be willing to sell his own child doesn't deserve to live," Jennifer said. "I never thought I could be so cold-blooded, but there it is. I didn't know how fortunate I was to have Lucas until I took a good look around and saw the men in this world. I hadn't ever spent much time thinking about men before I got out here in Montana. And I'm more thankful than anyone knows that Kyle was such a lousy shot."

"Thank God," Lucas muttered.

She looked at him. "I'm not sure what you meant by that."

"He's talkin' about you lookin' over the men in your life. What he meant was if you'd looked around at the menfolk back home any too good, you'd probably have been snatched up by some Yankee and he wouldn't have had a chance at you."

"Amen." Lucas seemed to be getting somewhat religious today, Jennifer thought.

"Well, anyway, I'm glad Kyle is gone and we don't have to be concerned about him any longer."

"Now, you get yourself finished with dressing that man, and come on out in the kitchen for some dinner," Ida told her. "I think he's well enough to sit up to the table and take a little nourishment."

Getting Lucas's trousers on was not a simple task, Jennifer found, for he put on an act of total helplessness, requiring her to close up the front placket, first tucking in his shirt before she buttoned the buttons and put him together. He enjoyed it far too much for a man with a gash on his head, but there was no accounting for Lucas. And if the truth be known, she wouldn't have him any other way.

CHAPTER SEVENTEEN

LUCAS FRETTED and stewed. The fact that Jennifer was handling chores he deemed to be beyond the strength of a pregnant woman didn't seem to cut any ice with her. She just smiled and did as she pleased, and all of his growling seemed to have little effect on her.

"I need to be taking care of the horses," he told her. "What if one of them crowds you up against the side of the stall? Then what? What if—"

"What if, nothing," she responded. "I'm capable of taking care of horses, or milking a cow and feeding a few chickens. I did it before, and I can do it now."

"You weren't pregnant before." He glared at her, but confined as he was to a chair for the next two days, it seemed he hadn't much choice. The doctor had been explicit. He'd had a concussion and it was nothing to fool around with. He'd do as he was told or Jennifer was to come to town and get him.

The thought of his wife heading off for town alone was enough to make Lucas blanch, and he tried to cease his grumbling. She'd do it. As sure as shootin', she'd get on that damn horse, or else harness the mare and hitch her to the buggy. Either way, she stood to be hurt should either animal make a wrong move. They were gentle horses, but it wouldn't take much to knock Jennifer off her feet, as unwieldy as she was.

"Please, Jen." He thought he sounded contrite and she glanced at him from across the kitchen.

"Please, what?" She didn't sound friendly, he decided. Perhaps more tact would be required.

"I'll worry if you go off to town. Let me take over some of the chores, honey."

"You never call me *honey*," she said. "What's the occasion?"

"Jen, I don't want anything to happen to you. Think what it would do to me if you got hurt out there in the barn. I'd have to come to the rescue and between us we'd be in a fine fix." He paused a moment. "Haven't I ever called you that before?"

She shook her head. "You know you haven't."

"Maybe I was saving it for now. For a time when I needed to get your attention and make you listen to me."

"And you think that's gonna do it? I don't think so, Lucas."

"Jen." All kidding was set aside now. He felt a sense of desperation. "If you'll let me go out and help with the chores, I'll take it real easy, and I won't fuss at you about making love for another two weeks or so."

"Fuss at me? About making love?" She looked thunderstruck. "What on earth are you talking about? That should be the furthest thing from your mind, Lucas. You've been badly hurt and come right close to dying, right here on the kitchen floor. On top of that, you could have died in that river."

Her hand waved at the spot in front of the stove where he'd sprawled just the other night and he caught a glimpse of tears in her eyes. "Don't cry, Jen. Please. I love you, and I don't want to have to worry about you."

She walked to where he stood and looked down at him. "Are you strong enough to hold me on your lap?"

"You betcha, sweetheart." He patted his knee and pulled her closer. She settled there and leaned to kiss him.

"I'll make a deal with you, Lucas. If you promise to behave and not do too much, I'll let you go out to the barn with me and help with the chores."

"And what do I get out of this?" he asked.

"You'll see."

It was late at night when the last light in the bedroom was extinguished and Jennifer was a pale shadow against the wall. She wore her loose gown, since almost nothing else fit her anymore. She spent a lot of time in this gown and a robe that covered it.

She made her way to the bed, stood on the oval, braided rug beside it and stripped her nightgown off, dropping it on the floor. "Lucas?" She spoke his name softly, trying to determine his location in the big bed, and was not disappointed by his quick answer.

"I'm here, Jen." And so he was, within touching distance, in fact. And touch her he did, with warm hands and long fingers that held the weight of her pregnancy in their grasp. He brushed one hand up and over the rounding of her belly, felt the nudge of a small knee or elbow, and laughed.

"He's awake." As if the baby heard her father's words, Jennifer felt the quick jerk of her child as she kicked. There was little room left in there to maneuver, but somehow the baby made space for herself and had even taken to stretching out full length, pushing with tiny feet against Jennifer's ribs.

"I'm not complaining, truly," Jennifer had said just last night.

"Oh, yes, you are," Lucas had told her with a rich chuckle.

"But I don't blame you, baby. I'd do more than complain if I were you."

"Like what? This is a nine-month sentence, Lucas. I can't shorten it in any way, just serve it out."

He'd hugged and kissed her, comforted her as best he could, and gained a certain amount of pleasure for himself from the warmth of her body. Now he wondered just how far he could go along those same lines tonight.

"Do you think it would hurt the baby if we snuggled a little, maybe did some smooching?"

"Smooching? I've never heard it called that before." She laughed. "You can smooch if you want to, Lucas, but don't expect a whole lot from me. I'm rather beyond the point of passion, I fear."

"I can still make you feel good," he promised her. "Don't you believe me?"

"Seeing is believing."

Her cool return made him choke with laughter. "You're a wicked woman, Jennifer. It's a good thing you're my wife already or I'd have to chase you down and marry you."

She lifted her arms to circle his neck and kissed the side of his throat. "I love you, Lucas. If you still want me, big belly and all, you can have me. I'm not much to look at, but I'm available."

"Not much to look at? You're the prettiest thing I've ever seen, love. There's not another woman in this world who can come near you." And the thought that she loved him was enough to bring his tightly reined passion into full bloom. He kissed her eyelids and the crests of her cheeks, and brushed numerous caresses across her forehead, even as his hands gathered handfuls of her hair, releasing the sweet scent of her soap. The perfume rose to tempt him, the aura of the woman he loved. She was lush and inviting, and she'd given him the right to do as he pleased with her.

What he pleased was to give her pleasure, to bring her with him to a culmination of their loving, and in so doing, deliver the ultimate release to himself. For nothing delighted him so much as the response of his wife in this bed.

She clung to him, whispering soft words he could barely hear. It was not the words he cared about but rather what they implied: the joyous giving of her body into his care. She loved him, not as boldly as she might have several months ago, or as she might several months from now, but with a pure delight that transformed her into a temptress he'd never before seen.

She moved to slide beneath him and he rose quickly, unwilling to place undo pressure on the baby. "Can we do this?" she asked softly. "Is there some way?"

"I've got an idea," he told her. "Not guaranteed, but I'll warrant it'll work well enough."

"You told me once you'd show me lots of things," she teased. "Is this one of them?"

"I've never done this before with a pregnant woman, and in fact, it's been longer than you'd believe since I did it with anyone other than my wife."

"I believe you, Lucas. If you tell me it's true, I believe it."

She was but a pale form in the darkness and he leaned over her to where a lone candle stood on the table by the bed. "Can I light this?" he asked.

"If you're really fond of fat ladies, you can," she said with a laugh.

"I'm real fond of you." And as if that were his final word, he found the box of matches and lit one, watching as the candle wick caught fire and burned.

Jennifer blinked. "It's bright."

"Yeah, I know." He felt like a man about to unwrap a precious gift and bent low to kiss her again. "You're so pretty, Jen. So soft and sweet. Have I told you that before?"

"Not lately," she said, pouting a bit. "But you can keep right on with it. Every woman likes to hear such things."

He spread her legs wide and knelt between them, lifting her thighs atop his own. "We've done this before, sweetheart. Remember? It'll keep my weight off of you."

"I can't hug you, though."

"Later on, I'll hug you all night long," he promised, and then began his slow seduction of her fruitful body. She was lush, her breasts full and heavy, and he lifted them, kissing them and touching them with his tongue, careful lest he hurt her, knowing she was sensitive.

In moments she cried out for him, lifting to bring him closer to the place that wept for his presence. His hands loved her gently, his mouth gave her pleasure and she responded with murmurs of desire, reaching for him, luxuriating in his care. His entry was smooth, easy and gentle, and he took short strokes, knowing it would not be enough for her, yet fearing to go too deep, lest he cause harm, either to her or his child. His hand touched her, there where soft folds hid the sensitive place he sought, and trembled as he felt her warmth and the damp sweetness of her desire.

His body rushed toward completion and he tried in vain to hold himself back, but to no avail. Even as his seed rushed forth into the warmth of her body, he heard her cry of delight, felt the clasp of her muscles, and knew that he'd given her the pleasure he'd set out to bring her.

He rolled to his side, bringing her with him. "I didn't hurt you, did I? Was I too rough?" He held her, aware that she was fragile. "I had no right to do that," he whispered. "I should have left you alone, sweetheart."

"No, no. I'm fine, Lucas. More than fine. And you haven't hurt me. Please don't think that."

"What if I've made the baby come too early?" The fear that had beset him made itself known in the question he asked.

"This baby will come when it's ready. Ida told me that. She said there's not much can bring a baby early, not unless I were to have a bad fall or an accident. I've had neither and I'm not worried about it."

He heaved a sigh of relief. "Come here, then. I need you as close as I can get you, baby."

His arms were strong around her, his whispers soft in her ear as he lavished love upon her in those hours.

IT WAS AS Ida had said. Nothing would bring the baby until it was ready to come, and that day did not arrive for a few weeks. It was a morning that promised spring, warm air causing Jennifer to leave the door open, allowing the breeze to flow through the house. She sorted out the eggs, setting aside six dozen in a crock to take to town. The chickens were producing more than the two of them could possibly use and she'd found that the storekeeper was happy to get fresh farm eggs.

They would carry them in later, she thought, after Lucas finished with the chores. He'd told her that he'd worked his last day on the claim until the baby arrived, and she hadn't argued the point. Happy with his company, she looked forward to the next weeks. Surely the baby would wait another few weeks, maybe a month.

It was not to be. She stood from her chair, bending her

back, twisting it to gain relief from the aches that had plagued her today. With a gush of fluid, she found herself soaked from crotch to ankles as her bag of waters broke, making a mess on the kitchen floor.

"Well, I'm glad that didn't happen in bed," she said to herself, setting about to clean up the mess.

It was a bigger task than she'd thought possible, and she had only just located a bucket for hot water and a rag to clean up things when Lucas came in the back door.

"What are you doing?"

"What does it look like? I'm going to clean the floor."

"Oh, no you're not. I'll do it." He was adamant.

"I made the mess. I'll clean it up," she argued.

"What did you spill?" he asked, looking around for an empty pot or container of some sort she might have dumped onto the floor.

"Nothing. I didn't spill anything." Inexplicably she began to tremble and he rushed to her, snatching her into his arms, looking her over from head to toe, as though she might begin bleeding any moment.

"Are you hurt, sweetheart? Tell me what's wrong. I can't fix it if you don't tell me."

She responded by offering him a fresh deluge of tears. "You can't fix it. It's all your fault, anyway. And don't you say one word about me crying. I have a right to cry if I want to."

"What's my fault?" He was stunned, looking down at her now as if she might explode any minute. "What did I do?"

"You got me in this fix, and I haven't got things all put together yet, and the baby's going to come anyway, and I'm not ready for it." Her nose ran and the tears flowed without end. "I'm a mess," she howled, "and it's all your fault."

"Then I'll have to fix it, won't I?" He backed her to a chair and put her in the seat, watching her closely. "First I'm gonna clean up the floor, and then I'll help you get washed and put a nightgown on you."

"My nightgown isn't clean. I put it in the wash basket this morning."

"What were you going to wear to bed tonight?" he asked, puzzled.

"Nothing. I was going to go to bed naked. So there." She cried without ceasing and he watched her even as he wiped up the floor, rinsing his cloth several times and then using clear water to wipe up the final mess.

"Don't you get off that chair, you hear me?" He stalked out the door, the bucket was plopped upside down on the back porch, the rag over the clothes line, and he looked into the sky for a moment before he came back to the kitchen. He was at a loss. A woman in tears didn't generally affect him to this extent, but this was *Jennifer,* a creature without guile, a woman who did not cry, not ever. *Ha! She was the leakiest woman he'd ever set eyes on.* And at that thought, he could not hold back a smile.

She was tender and softhearted. And if she wanted to cry, he knew just the fella to comfort her, even though she was a veritable waterfall right now. His heart ached for her as he recognized her fright. The thought struck him a telling blow and he knelt in front of her.

"Don't be afraid, sweetheart. I won't let anything happen to you."

"There's not a whole lot you can do about it," she wailed. "I want Ida here. You can help, but I need her to take care of me."

Privately he agreed with her, but getting Ida meant riding to town and leaving her alone. And that was not a viable option.

"Hello. You in there, Lucas?" From the yard, a voice called out and Lucas stood and turned toward the door, relief flooding his being.

"That's Sandy," he said, and felt as though his prayers had been answered all at one time. "He can go get Ida, honey. I'll stay here with you. Is that all right?"

She nodded, reaching into his pocket for his big handkerchief. "Please tell Sandy to hurry," she begged, wincing and bending over as though something had twisted her body.

"Are you having pains?" he asked, and then silently cursed his stupidity. Of course she was having pains. In fact, he'd bet she was in the midst of one right now. Her cheeks were bloodless, her lips drawn back, and he thought her eyes had the look of an animal caught in a trap.

He stalked toward the door and jerked it open. "Got a job for you, Sandy. I need you to go to town and get Ida Bronson. Jennifer's about to have the baby, and I don't want to leave her alone."

"Listen to me first, Luc. We've hit it really big. You know that little vein we thought was just a trickle? Well, it's a jimdandy source of more gold than you can shake a stick at. I brought as much with me as my horse could carry and hid the site pretty well. I'll take this much to the assayer's office, and tell Mrs. Bronson to get herself out here right quick. Then I'm goin' back to the canyon to keep an eye on things."

"You can go with him if you need to, Lucas." Jennifer's voice was strong now, the pain obviously having passed.

Anger surged through him. "Are you crazy? You're worth more to me than the largest gold strike in the world, Jennifer. If you think for one minute I'd leave you when you're about to bear my child, you're out of your mind."

She smiled. The fool woman smiled at him, after he'd shouted at her as he'd never done before, as he'd never thought to. And she wasn't making a show of it. This was the smile he loved, the one that told him the song of her heart, that gave him a glimpse into the woman's mind and soul. She loved him, no matter that he'd raged at her, never mind that his words had been harsh.

"I love you, too, Lucas," she said.

He considered the words he'd said. They were true, every last one of them, and he'd just told his wife she meant more to him than all the gold in the world. Again, he knelt at her side, taking her hands in his. "I didn't mean to shout at you, Jen."

"I know," she whispered. "I know what you said and what you meant by it, and I love you for it." She bent to kiss his mouth, her lips opening a bit as if she would savor the taste of him, and then her breath caught and she stiffened.

"What is it, Jen? Another pain?" He gripped her arms, but she reached for his hands, unwrapping his fingers from her flesh and then holding them in an unbreakable grasp. He knew the answer to his question, knew that she lacked the breath to utter the words that might reassure him. For he could not be fooled at this point. Jen was going to have the baby tonight, and he'd do well to haul her up the stairs and put her to bed.

Rising, he patted her hands and went back to the door. Sandy sat atop his horse, unmoving, as if he sensed that Lucas needed him in a new and different way than ever before.

"Make it a quick trip to town. Don't dawdle, Sandy. I need Ida here, right quick. And while you're at it, stop by and tell the doctor I want him to come out too."

Sandy rode off, his horse breaking into an easy lope as he headed toward town.

"I want Ida." It was a wail of anguish and Lucas felt help-less in the face of Jennifer's pain. This was why women did this sort of thing, he thought. Men were no earthly good at babies and the bringing of such little creatures into the world. This had seemed like a really good idea months ago, but now that the time was on him, he felt more helpless than he'd ever planned to be in his whole life.

Action would be the way to go, he decided, picking Jen-nifer up from her chair and walking toward the hallway and the staircase beyond. Without argument, she wrapped her arm around his neck and clung. He made it up the stairs without puffing, a feat he felt quite proud of. Jennifer was no light-weight these days, her body rounding almost to the bursting point, it seemed.

"You shouldn't have done that. I'm too heavy," she said, as he stood her on the rug beside the bed and began stripping off her clothing. He made short work of it, only her robe and undergarments garbing her body. Bending, he pulled her stockings down and off her feet, then went to the laundry bas-ket. Her gown was there, but he could see no signs of use.

That was simple enough. It had been lying on the floor for the past three nights, Jennifer uncomfortable with the folds wrapped around her body. "This isn't dirty," he said. "I want you to put it on."

She didn't argue, just pulled it over her head and then sought the comfort of her bed, only to sit up abruptly. "I for-got," she said. "Ida made some pads out of newspapers, cov-ered with pieces of old sheets, for me to lie on. They're in the bottom drawer of my dresser. She said this is a messy busi-ness and I won't want to get the mattress stained."

Another surprise, Luc thought, crossing the room to retrieve the needed pads. He lifted Jennifer and slid one beneath her, then placed the others on a chair. "Okay?" he asked, watching her, waiting for the next pain to begin.

It was not long in coming, and indeed, by the time Ida and the doctor arrived, Jennifer was well on her way to delivering her child.

"How long you been having pains?" Ida asked, washing her hands in the basin.

"Just a backache early on, but I've been cramping like this for a while now."

"Cramping, my foot. This is labor, Jen. You should have sent Lucas in early on."

"Let's take a look," the doctor said, approaching with a clean towel in hand. He'd scrubbed with a brush for long minutes and Jennifer was convinced his hands were spotless. She lay immobile, Lucas holding her hand as the doctor pressed on her belly with a gentle touch and then waited until the next pain began before he continued his examination.

She cried out then, for the first time losing her sense of control and Lucas knelt beside her, gathering her to himself.

"She told me it was my fault," he muttered. "She's mad at me."

"I don't think so," the doctor said. "If she was, she wouldn't be hugging you so tight, young man." He stood again and shot a glance at Ida. "We got lots of hot water and clean towels, ma'am?"

"Jennifer and I stocked up good on towels the other day, and there's water in the reservoir on the cookstove. Run down and get a bucketful, Luc."

As if he were relieved to have a job to do, Lucas rose and dashed from the room, his boots clattering on the stairs.

"He'll live through it, missy," the doctor told Jennifer. "I haven't lost a father yet." He laughed at his joke and winked at Ida. "Let's get this show on the road," he said. "My missus will be lookin' for me along about dark."

It was just after dark when Jennifer took her final deep breath, pushed mightily and groaned, ushering a squalling baby boy into the world. Dark hair covered his tiny head and long arms and legs gave future promise of a man built like his father.

In minutes the doctor had completed his work. Wrapped in a clean bit of flannel, the baby was placed in Lucas's arms. He went to Jennifer and bent low over the bed.

"We have a boy, sweetheart." His pride was obvious, his love a tangible force in the room as he placed the tiny babe in his mother's arms for the first time.

"Can we name him after you?" Jennifer asked. "I planned on a girl, and I don't think that Rosalie would fit him."

Lucas looked at the tiny face, so like that of a wise old man, and nodded. "Whatever you want to call him is all right with me, sweetheart."

"How about Lucas Alexander? And we can call him Alex, if you like."

"Couldn't have done better myself," Lucas said. "And Sandy will be pleased. He's a good man."

"So are you, Luc," she said softly, waiting for his kiss, a kiss not long in coming.

"Let me have that child," Ida told her, taking the baby and sitting with him next to the pan of warm water. "We need to be washing him up a little. And then you can have him back."

Lucas held Jennifer close, as if he couldn't get close enough to her and needed to feel her very breath against his

EPILOGUE

JENNIFER SAT in the swing, pushing idly with one foot against the floor, holding her son against her breast while he suckled. She'd been out here for many hours over the past months, including last night, when the baby had awakened and decided that his hunger needed appeasing. Either that or he wanted company, she'd told Lucas.

Either way, she knew that these moments alone with the tiny baby boy would soon turn into sessions of scraped knees and bruised shins. But no matter what the future held, these precious hours spent with Alex as a baby would forever bond them into a close fellowship of mother and son.

A few minutes ago, with Lucas in the barn, she'd once more been awakened by the baby's snufflings and the sound of him suckling his own hand, and had risen from her bed to carry him to the porch, where she watched the sun rising above the treetops, wrapped in the knowledge that all was well in her world, that somehow she had managed to put together a life that offered bountiful rewards.

Alex released his grip on her and a soft burp notified her that he had been sated by the food his mother had provided. From the barn, Lucas whistled and Buster ran to meet him. The dog had found a new home with them, and showed every cheek. But when Ida came back with the baby a bit later, he released his wife and opened his arms to contain his son. Bending over Jennifer again, he fit the baby between them and took a deep breath.

"For the first time in my life, Jen, I feel like I have everything I've ever wanted. I have my whole world in my arms, sweetheart."

Her eyes filled with tears and she brushed at them. "I don't know why I'm crying. I'm so happy I just can't hold it all inside. Does that make sense?"

"Yeah, I'd say so. Nothing else could add to our happiness tonight."

sign of being as attached to Alex as he had been to Susan a year earlier.

Susan. The name still sounded as sweet as ever, vibrating within her mind, as memories of the child chased through her thoughts. And then, as if she had somehow brought to life the vision in front of her, she saw a buggy approaching. It was not yet breakfast time, the dew not burned off the grass and it seemed far too early in the day for visitors. Yet two women sat on the seat, one of them holding a small child. A girl, Jennifer discerned. She abandoned her comfortable seat and stood, holding Alex close to her breast.

It was Susan, yawning and stretching, yet chattering as if such early morning excursions were an everyday occurrence in her life. The woman holding her pointed with her index finger in Jennifer's direction and then noticed the large, brown dog who had left Lucas's side to run, barking joyously, toward the buggy.

"He won't bite." Lucas called out the reassurance with a loud voice, and only the little girl replied.

"Dog," she shouted, and the dog bounded higher, as if he would leap into the buggy, given the chance.

"She's talking, with real words," Jennifer said, standing on the top step of the porch, unaware of the tears that rolled down her cheeks. Lucas took two long steps and clutched her to himself.

"Come on down and see her," he whispered, lifting both Jennifer and her precious burden to the ground, then leading them to the buggy, which had halted by the hitching rail.

"Did you know?" And if he had, would she be angry that he hadn't warned her? Not likely, Jennifer thought. The overwhelming sight of Susan, the sound of her voice calling the dog over and over, and, at last, the warmth of her tiny body pressed up against her bosom, were enough to bring Jennifer beyond the brink of tears to a powerful overflow of emotion that caused Susan to frown and rub at the tearstains.

The child bent closer and kissed Jennifer, a warm, damp caress that did much to calm Jennifer and dry up the waterfall she'd turned loose. "She remembers me." It was all she could think to say as her arms became acquainted once more with the solid weight of the girl child she'd missed so desperately.

"'Course she did." As if it were most logical, the younger woman climbed down and approached the porch. "Her grandma told her about you every day, and when they decided she was a little scamp and belonged with younger folk, they sent her back to you." A broad smile accompanied the message, and then the girl looked a bit worried.

"The problem is that we come as a package—me, the baby and my ma. I'm Shanna, and my mother is Bettina, and we'd like to take care of babies and keep house for you."

"Your folks sent them. I'm afraid it isn't all good news, sweetheart. Your mother isn't well. In fact, she's not able to tend to Susan any longer, so she sent her to us. I told them we'd need some help for you before long and they thought with this big house we had plenty of room for three more to sleep."

Jennifer nodded, stunned by the events taking place.

"You're all welcome. Come on in and we'll have breakfast. Lucas is hungry, I suspect, and this young one is ready for a nap." She patted Alex on the back, Susan having gone to Lucas, leaving Jennifer's hands a bit more free. Now she stood to lose possession of her son, for Bettina slid from the buggy and approached with widespread arms.

"Let me take a good look at him," she crooned, lifting him against her plush bosom and bending to kiss the top of his downy head. "What a dear child. He won't be a bit of bother, and we can fix him a cot in the kitchen if we need to. We won't want him very far away, will we?"

"We'll see how you feel about this 'dear child' along about two in the morning," Lucas said glumly. "He tends to be a nighthawk, hungry at the worst possible times."

"Well, I'd dare say we can take care of that, can't we, Miss Jennifer?"

Jennifer nodded, dumbstruck by the woman's easy grasp of things. And then was delighted when her kitchen was filled with the sounds of two children, one of them rolling across the floor with a dusty, brown dog, the other snuffling in his mother's neck, settling himself for sleep.

Breakfast was on the table quickly, Bettina an old hand, it seemed, with cooking and preparing a meal. Lucas brought the cradle from the bedroom for the baby and he nestled down in comfort, leaving his mother free to eat.

It was a dream come true, a slice of heaven she'd not thought to experience, and Jennifer looked around her kitchen with a joy she could barely contain.

"We'll settle all the details of me working for you later on. For now, I'll just take the load off you here in the kitchen and with the washing and such." The older woman announced her plans as if she would accept no argument, and Jennifer nodded still too stunned by the turn of events of protest.

"And I'll take care of the little ones and give Ma a hand when she needs me," Shanna added. And then she looked at Jennifer. "I hope you don't mind us just showing up and makin' ourselves at home."

"You're as welcome as the flowers in May," Jennifer told

her. "If Lucas says we can afford help, then I couldn't ask for more than to have the both of you here."

"Let's just consider us family for now," Bettina said. "If we can live here and find a new life in this big country, we'll be pleased. The city was getting to me, so much hustle-bustle and dirt, I was fed up to my teeth with that sort of life. This is a place where a body can stretch herself a hundred ways and still find room to explore."

Lucas sat back in his chair and grinned. There was no other word for the expression on his face, Jennifer decided. And then he looked at her and his smile became more personal, his mouth softening, his eyes turning darker as he gave her his full attention.

"I'll do whatever it takes to keep you happy, love. We have plenty of money and a house large enough to hold a big family. And if we fill this one to the brim, we'll build another, even bigger. Or we can move to town if you want to."

She stood and rounded the table to where he sat, then bent to kiss him with enthusiasm and hug him with gusto. "I love you, Lucas O'Reilly, more than I'd ever thought to love another person in my life. I love your son, and Susan, and I'll probably drive these two women up the wall, getting in their way and trying to be a help to them, not a hindrance. I'm so happy I could just burst."

Lucas stood and enclosed her in an embrace that was familiar to her. Her head fit in the hollow of his shoulder, her lips not too far from the strong lines of his throat, and she snuggled there, uncaring of those who watched.

"Well," said Bettina, with a sly grin at Shanna, "this is gonna be a fine place to work. I can see that already, girl. I'd say we landed in a soft bed, sure enough."

Lucas bent closer and whispered a message in Jennifer's ear that made her snort inelegantly. "Speaking of soft beds…" he began, only to laugh as his wife glared up at him.

"You'll never change, will you, Lucas?" And then she wrapped her arms around his neck and leaned against his strength, knowing he would never fail her. "And if the truth be known, I hope you never do. I love you just the way you are."

"Well, thank God for that," he said fervently. And then his tone softened as he looked down at her. "And thank God for you, Jennifer O'Reilly. You'll always be worth more than all the gold in the world, as far as I'm concerned."

Harlequin® Historical
Historical Romantic Adventure!

THREE RUGGED WESTERN MEN
THREE COURAGEOUS LADIES
THREE FESTIVE TALES TO WARM
THE HEART THIS CHRISTMAS!

ON SALE OCTOBER 2005

ROCKY MOUNTAIN CHRISTMAS
by Jillian Hart
Summoned on a dangerously snowy night to deal with two stowaways, Sheriff Mac McKaslin discovers they are none other than a homeless young widow— Carrie Montgomery—and her baby. But will the sheriff send them out into the cold...or find a warm place for them in his heart?

THE CHRISTMAS GIFTS
by Kate Bridges
When Sergeant James Fielder arrives with a baby on his sled, he turns to Maggie Greerson for help. This special interlude allows Maggie to fulfill her secret dream of having a child— and explore the attraction that has always drawn her to James....

THE CHRISTMAS CHARM
by Mary Burton
Determined to prevent her younger sister from marrying the wrong man, widow Colleen Garland enlists the help of her onetime love Keith Garrett. Will their rescue mission finally lead them on the road to true love?

HARLEQUIN®

AMERICAN *Romance*®

A three-book series by
Kaitlyn Rice

Heartland Sisters

To the folks in Augusta, Kansas, the three sisters are
the Blume girls—a little pitiable, a bit mysterious and
different enough to be feared.

THE LATE BLOOMER'S BABY
(Callie's story)

Callie's infertility treatments paid off more than a year
after she and her husband split up. Now she's racked
by guilt. She's led her ex-husband to believe the toddler
she's caring for is her nephew, not Ethan's son!

Available October 2005

Also look for:
The Runaway Bridesmaid (Isabel's story)
Available February 2006

The Third Daughter's Wish (Josie's story)
Available June 2006

American Romance
Heart, Home and Happiness

Available wherever Harlequin books are sold.

SAGA

National bestselling author
Debra Webb

A decades-old secret threatens to bring
down Chicago's elite Colby Agency in
this brand-new, longer-length novel.

COLBY
CONSPIRACY

While working to uncover the truth behind
a murder linked to the agency, Daniel Marks
and Emily Hastings find themselves trapped
by the dangers of desire—knowing every
move they make could be their last....

*Available in October,
wherever books
are sold.*

**Bonus Features
include:**

**Author's Journal,
Travel Tale
and
a Bonus Read.**

Where love comes alive™

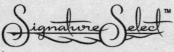

SPOTLIGHT

"Delightful and delicious…Cindi Myers always satisfies!"
—*USA TODAY bestselling author Julie Ortolon*

National bestselling author

Cindi Myers

She's got more than it takes for
the six o'clock news…

Learning Curves

Tired of battling the image problems that her
size-twelve curves cause with her network news
job, Shelly Piper takes a position as co-anchor on
public television with Jack Halloran. But as they
work together on down-and-dirty hard-news
stories, all Shelly can think of is Jack!

Plus, exclusive bonus features inside!

On sale in October.

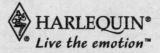

HARLEQUIN®
® *Live the emotion*™